Highland
Hellion

Mary Wine

sourcebooks
casablanca

Published by Sourcebooks Casablanca, an imprint of Sourcebooks,
Inc.
P.O. Box 4410, Naperville, Illinois 60567-4410
(630) 961-3900
Fax: (630) 961-2168
www.sourcebooks.com

Printed and bound in Canada.
MBP 10 9 8 7 6 5 4 3 2 1

One

1578

"YE'RE A FOOL," ROBERT MACPHERSON GRUMBLED. "And likely to get us both lashed."

Katherine Carew didn't offer him even a hint of remorse. She settled herself on top of her horse, confidence shining in her midnight-blue eyes. "I've trained as hard and as long as ye have."

"Yes, but ye're—" Robert clamped his lips shut and took a hasty look around to make sure no one was listening. "Ye're a woman now."

And Robert was a man. Katherine found the new element in their relationship curious, and she didn't care for the change. It threatened to upset the balance of her life—an existence that she liked very much. So she fixed him with a hard look, determined to change his thinking. "You are the one who suggested I start wearing a kilt in the first place."

Robert frowned. "I was young and a damned fool."

His eyes lowered to where she'd bound her breasts. His lips thinned and his jaw tightened, sending an unexpected sensation through her. It was slightly unsettling because Robert was her friend and compatriot. Yet he had taken to spending more time with the older men. She didn't dare venture too close when he was with them for fear they would realize her game. Dressing contrary to her gender was a sin, an argument against what God had decided she would be.

"We're going raiding," Robert insisted in a low voice. "It is no place for a…for ye."

"Ah, let the lad be," Bari spoke up from where he was securing his saddle. The burly MacPherson retainer peered over at them, his face covered by a thick beard. "If he pisses himself, he'll jump in the river before we return home, and he can share his whisky with us so we all don't tell the tale."

There was a round of laughter from the men close enough to listen in, proving that Katherine and Robert's words were very much in danger of being overheard. Robert went still in a way she'd never seen before. Katherine actually felt the bite of fear as she realized he was considering unmasking her.

He was her only friend, and the betrayal cut her deeply.

Well, she was going.

Katherine made sure the straps of her saddle were tight. She took a great deal of pleasure in the fact that she knew as much about preparing a horse for riding as every one of the men surrounding her. That would certainly not be the case if she'd been raised in England.

Her old life was only a memory now, hidden behind her adventures in the Highlands. She smiled as she recalled the many things she'd done at Robert's side while disguised as a boy. She gripped the side of the saddle, making ready to mount.

But a hard hand dug into the back of her jerkin and lifted her into the air.

"What?" Katherine was startled, or she wouldn't have spoken because her English accent persisted. More than one head turned in her direction as she landed and found herself looking up into the eyes of Marcus MacPherson, war chief of Clan MacPherson.

"I told her she should nae go." Robert was quick to assign blame to her.

Marcus had braced himself between her and the horse. The war chief was huge and stood considering her from a position she'd seen too many times to count while she trained under his command in the yard. Of course, he thought she was a boy, which made Robert's choice of words very bad.

Very, very bad.

"You clearly did nae tell her firmly enough." Marcus shifted his full attention to Robert. "There will be a reckoning owed when we return, sure enough."

Robert bristled as more men came to witness his chastisement. "She's the one who will no' listen to good sense."

"Agreed," Marcus said. "Which is why ye should have pulled her off her horse as I just did, since it was you who brought her into me training yard six years ago."

Katherine gasped. She hated the way the sound came across her lips because it was so…well, so feminine. The men were frowning at her, clearly disapproving.

She shook her head and leveled her chin. "I have trained, and I am as good as many a man standing here."

"Ye are a woman," Marcus stated clearly. "And ye do nae belong riding out with us when we are going to needle the Gordons."

"It isn't a real raid," Katherine protested, but she kept her tone civil. She would always respect Marcus for teaching her to defend herself. "Just a bit of fun."

"Aye," Marcus agreed. "And yet, not as simple as that. Men get their blood up when they are testing one another's nerve. It is no place for a woman, even less so for a maiden."

"Ye see?" Robert said. "I told ye."

"But ye did nae make certain she could nae venture into danger. That's the difference between a lad and a man." Marcus spoke softly, which only gave his words more weight. "It's past time for ye"—he pointed at Robert—"to recognize that a little lass like Katherine has more to lose if our luck does nae hold. As a MacPherson retainer, I expect ye to make sure the women are taken care of. That's the real reason they respect us, no' simply for the sake of our gender."

Marcus shifted his attention back to Katherine, and she felt the weight of his disapproval. "Ye could be raped and ruined."

"My reputation is already ruined because I am here," Katherine protested.

"That is no' the same thing at all," Marcus informed her in a steely voice. "And I hope to Christ ye never discover the truth of the matter. For tonight, ye'll take yerself back inside, and I will deal with ye when I return."

Marcus's word was law on MacPherson land. Only his father and his brother, Bhaic, might argue with him, and Katherine wasn't dense enough to think either of them would disagree. So she lowered her chin and bit her lip. It earned her a soft grunt from Marcus before he moved back toward his horse.

Then the muttering started.

"English chit…"

"More trouble than we need…"

"Damned English always think themselves better than Scots…"

Men she'd thought of as friends suddenly turned traitor, calling her "English" as though she had only recently arrived on their land.

She'd truly thought her feelings dead when it came to the subject of her blood. The rush of hurt flooding her proved her wrong.

Well, that was foolish.

And she would have none of it.

Her father's blue, noble blood was a curse, and she'd learned the burden of it by the time she was five. His legitimate wife detested her because of the cost of the tutors needed to educate her and the dowry she'd require. She'd been abducted because of that dowry and nearly wed at fourteen.

Marcus MacPherson had taken her into the Highlands instead. It had seemed to be the perfect solution. So far removed from England and her family, there was no one to tell her what she must be. She had been free.

Even from her gender.

Katherine lifted her chin because even after

mounting, the MacPherson retainers were still considering her. She refused to crumble. Training among them as a lad, she'd learned to keep her tears hidden, and she'd be damned if she'd show them any now. A stable lad suddenly came up and tried to take her horse.

"I'll tend to my own mount," she informed him, making sure her voice carried. "As I always have."

Katherine didn't wait to see what those watching made of her words. She reached up and ran a confident hand along the muzzle of her horse before she turned and started to lead it toward the stable.

Indeed, she took care of herself, and that brought her much-needed relief from the sting of her bruised emotions.

❧

"What do ye mean by that?" Helen Grant demanded.

Marcus eyed his wife, crossing his arms over his chest and facing her down, as was his fashion. Helen's eyes narrowed. "Ye heard me clearly, Wife."

Helen scoffed and settled her newest babe into its cradle before she turned on him while pulling the laces on her dress tight. "What I heard was that ye seem to think what a woman does with her day is easier to learn than a man's lot."

Marcus frowned. "Do nae go twisting me words."

"I should have had charge of her years ago if ye wanted her trained properly in the running of a house," Helen continued. "Ye are the one who allowed her to be a lad."

"And for good reason," Marcus answered back. "She's English. Ye know how often ye have heard curses against her kin, and I assure ye, I have heard three times as much because the men do tend to mind their tongues around the women in the hall."

Helen had finished closing her dress and settled her hands on her hips. "As I said, I do nae know what ye expect me to do with her now that ye've let her run wild for the past six years. She's twenty now."

"I know." Marcus's control slipped, allowing his exasperation to bleed through into his tone. "She's a woman, and yet she was intent on riding out with us last evening."

"It wouldn't be the first time," Helen replied. "Why is it a concern now?"

Marcus's jaw tightened, and his wife read his expression like a book. There was no point in trying to keep the matter to himself. He let out a soft word of Gaelic.

"We went out and lifted some of the Gordons' cattle."

His wife stiffened. The Gordons hated the MacPhersons and would spill blood if they could. Old Laird Colum Gordon wanted vengeance for the death of his son, Lye Rob, and the old man didn't seem to care that Bhaic MacPherson had killed Lye Rob with good reason. Lye Rob had stolen Bhaic's new wife, Ailis, and no Highlander worth his name was going to let a man get away with that. Nothing seemed to matter to the old laird of the Gordons except vengeance.

Marcus knew he was playing with fire by going anywhere near Gordon land. Needling the local clans was one matter; going onto Gordon land was another altogether because it might get him killed. His wife was going to tear a strip off his back for chancing it.

"Damn ye, Marcus," Helen berated him. "So, ye are still acting like a child?" She pointed at their son. "And what will become of the children I bear ye if ye get yer throat slit?"

Marcus only lifted one shoulder in a shrug. "Ye know it will nae come to that. The Grants took some of ours last month. It's just a bit of fun."

Helen made a soft sound. "With the Gordons, it is very different. Which is why ye do nae want Katherine along. Do nae think to pull the wool over me eyes."

Marcus opened his arms in exasperation. "Aye!" He snorted. "There, I've agreed with ye. And ye would have a place if I were to pay for me choices in blood, so do nae insult me by asking such a question. Now tell me ye will take her in hand." He made a motion with his hand. "And teach her…what a woman should be doing with her time."

Helen wasn't pleased, and as she looked at her baby, worry creases appeared at the corners of her eyes.

"I love ye, Helen, but ye know full well what manner of man I am." He pulled her close, wrapping her in his embrace. She settled for just a moment, inhaling the scent of his skin before she pushed against his chest and he released her.

"Aye, well," Helen said softly. "At twenty years of age, Katherine has decided what sort of woman she is as well. Something ye have allowed. Now ye expect me to be the one to destroy her world?"

Marcus's expression tightened as he crossed his arms over his chest. "I'll have words with her."

❧

"The laird is asking to see ye, mistress."

Katherine had been expecting the summons. It was a relief, in a way, to have the matter at hand, and yet she felt her belly twisting as she rose and followed Cam through the passageways toward the laird's private solar. For all that Cam had spoken softly, there were plenty in the great hall who noted what was happening.

From the moment the sun rose, Katherine had felt the weight of everyone's judgment. She'd seen such treatment before and realized it had its uses because it maintained order inside the clan. Those who transgressed learned it would not be tolerated, and being shunned was their fate until they made recompense.

Justice.

They all relied upon the laird for that, and she was expected to comply as well.

At least that idea restored some of her composure. The MacPherson clan still viewed her as their own, or something close. She truly didn't want to think about any alternative, so she followed Cam willingly enough. The laird of the MacPherson clan was waiting for her behind a desk. Shamus had a full head of gray hair and a beard to match. A portrait hung behind him, depicting him several decades before when his hair had been as dark as his son Bhaic's.

"Aye, I was a young man once." Shamus proved that his eyesight wasn't failing by noting her interest.

Katherine lowered herself and straightened back up while the laird contemplated her. He was tapping a finger on the top of his desk. Marcus and Bhaic framed him on either side, proving the gravity of the moment.

"As foolish too," Shamus concluded in a voice crackled with age.

"Hardly foolish to learn to defend myself." In the back of Katherine's mind was the memory of a time when she'd been taught to hold her tongue in the presence of men and her betters. It was too dim to hold back her impulse, though.

Shamus snorted and slapped the tabletop. "From a lad, I'd no' have to take exception to that comment."

"I don't see why it matters that I am a female." Katherine shifted her focus to Marcus. "I can best half the boys with a rapier."

"But ye can nae carry one or risk reprisal from the Church," Shamus said gravely. "A fact ye surely know, lass, or ye're daft."

Katherine closed her mouth and nodded a single time.

"Me son Marcus trained ye because he thought it best, considering yer circumstances," Shamus said.

He made it sound like she was to be pitied, and that stirred her temper. Katherine lifted her chin in defiance. "I find my circumstances very pleasing."

Shamus offered her a grunt of approval. "Aye, that pleases me, and yet ye are, as both me sons have noted, a grown woman now. The Church might overlook a fair number of things when youth is involved. They are not so lenient when it comes to adults."

Katherine didn't care for the feeling that a noose was being slipped over her neck. She recalled that feeling from when she was young and living in England. What she detested was the way tears stung her eyes.

She did not cry.

And hadn't since the day the Earl of Morton had looked at her like a creature to be bartered. She'd realized growing strong was her only way to avoid becoming exactly what he saw her as. She would be more than a thing.

"Well…" Shamus resumed tapping the top of his desk. "I'm glad to see that ye agree with me, lass."

"You have yet to tell me what you wish of me."

"Aye." Shamus made a motion with his hand. "Ye'll need to keep company with the women. Helen will instruct ye on the running of a house."

"And ye will keep a skirt on," Marcus added sternly. "No more kilts."

She knew that voice. Had trained under it and learned to respect it because Marcus was preparing the youths of the clan for the realities of life, where his training would mean the difference between surviving and an early grave.

Arguing with him felt wrong because he'd given her so many years of joy, and yet she felt cut to the bone by his order. So she lowered herself and left.

She hadn't been dismissed, but Shamus didn't call after her. She needed fresh air, feeling like a stone was crushing her chest.

But relief wasn't hers just yet. Robert appeared next to her, clearly having been waiting for her meeting with the laird to be finished.

"It's for the best," Robert began, his soft tone grating against her frayed nerves.

"Don't you dare speak to me in that fashion." She turned on him.

His eyes widened.

"Like you do to a child," Katherine clarified.

Robert stiffened. Somehow, she'd failed to notice his shoulders had widened and his chin was covered in a full growth of hair now.

"I'm no' talking to ye like ye're a child," Robert said, defending himself. "Just—"

"Like a woman?" she demanded. "Go take the hand of Satan and walk yourself to hell."

His cheeks darkened. "Ye have to stop talking like that, too. Women do nae curse."

"Easily accomplished," she informed him. "For I will not be speaking to you anymore."

She turned to leave, but Robert reached out and caught her wrist. The bit of strength was there, one she knew and detested because it proved that time was going to destroy the life she had thought she'd built.

"Kat," he said. "Do nae be cross with me. Ye are a woman, and they are right. The bloody Gordons will no' rape me. Ye need to keep to yer place. Do ye want to be known as a hellion? No man will ever have ye if that happens."

"And so my entire worth should be measured by what a man wants?" She scoffed at him. "My prospects for a good match died when I was abducted by the Earl of Morton."

Robert didn't disagree. He wanted to, opening his mouth but shutting it when he couldn't form an argument.

"Keep yer hands off me," she declared before she twisted and stepped to the side, breaking his grip. "And do not follow me to speak to me alone. It is improper."

She turned her back on him and found Marcus

considering them. She lifted her chin and shot him a hard look.

Wasn't that what they all wanted? Her acting like a woman?

Well, she'd certainly not be apologizing.

Even though she ached to, for Robert was her only true friend.

And now, she was forbidden that comfort.

Why had Fate cursed her with being a female?

❧

"Did Katherine stay with ye today?"

Helen looked up from the baby and sent Marcus a tired look. "Aye."

He placed his sword by their bed and reached down to gently stroke the hair away from the face of their older son, Rae, who was fast asleep in his trundle bed near the wall.

"Ye know why it must be so," he remarked to his wife as he sat down on the edge of the bed and began to work the lace holding his boot closed.

"I also recall very well how it feels to be a stranger here," Helen replied. "I saw that look in Katherine's eyes today."

"She'll settle in."

"Because she's a woman?" Helen scoffed at him, upsetting Roderick. She drew in a deep breath as she soothed the infant and guided him back to her nipple.

"Because there is no other choice," Marcus said once the sound of suckling resumed. "We have both done as much as we can for the lass. I thank God she is no' sitting here as me wife."

"Aye," Helen agreed. "Morton was a fool to try to force that match. Katherine was far too young."

"She is nae any longer, and I am no' the one who stole her from her family. I simply made sure she'd not be wed to another man who valued Morton's opinion more than decency," Marcus said as he lay back in the bed. "Ye know it must be done."

Helen still sent him a look that made it clear she disagreed.

Marcus let out a sigh. "If she was caught with a sword or, worse yet, using one, she might well be accused of being bewitched, if no' an outright witch. For all that we're no' feuding, there is plenty of bad blood between the MacPhersons and Gordons to make them want a little retribution."

"And what better target than an English girl that we call yer sister," Helen finished. "I recall well yer reasoning for training her."

"Aye." Marcus reached for their son now that the baby was fed. "Morton would no' be able to call it feuding if the Gordons claimed it was a matter of witchery. The lass was trying to ride out with us. She does nae understand the evil that is inside some men. Colum Gordon has more than his share. It has been festering since Bhaic killed Lye Rob Gordon, and Colum is too old to see the truth of the matter."

Helen lay back, enjoying the sight of her husband cradling their newest babe. Marcus was huge and hard, but he cupped the baby's head and smiled. Yet it was a happiness that must be earned. Strength meant stability in the Highlands. Clans would do anything to ensure they were not viewed as weak.

It was a truth she didn't care for much, but one she would have to make certain Katherine understood.

❧

She was a woman, and yet vastly different from those around her.

Katherine tried to smile, but discovered her attempts were greeted with uncertainty. The women inside Castle MacPherson knew one another as well as the men in the yard did. But they did not know her, and Katherine discovered herself a stranger among them all over again. It was daunting and, coupled with her lack of friends, sometimes overwhelming.

She walked to the stables one evening because the feeling of flour between her fingers became too much to bear.

At least she'd finished her duties, so no one bothered to follow her.

The sun was a glowing ball on the horizon, the air still warm with the promise of summer. She inhaled deeply, enjoying the scent of the outdoors.

She'd missed it sorely.

There was a snort as her horse caught sight of her. The animal tossed its head, making Katherine smile.

"I missed you too," she whispered as she rubbed its muzzle. The animal was dancing, its hooves kicking up a small cloud of dust.

Yet no one came down the row of stalls to investigate. She realized it was the monthly court, and everyone who wasn't on duty had gone to the great hall to hear the cases being brought before the laird for judgment. It was often a fine evening of amusement.

Men fought for the most ridiculous reasons. Women too, but it would be the laird's daughter-by-marriage who ruled on those cases.

There were two young lads left with the horses, but they were busy enjoying their supper by the fire, far away from the stalls and the straw.

Temptation rose inside her like music building during the market fair. At first, it was only a soft melody, but it quickly became a lively beat as one drew closer. Her heart was accelerating, fed by the way her horse was stamping at the ground.

And the fact that no one was about to judge her.

Did she dare?

Was she foolish to ignore the opportunity? Honestly, she hadn't known the hours of a day could be so long. Today had felt endless, and now, with the last of the light fading, it felt like freedom came on the wings of the night.

Do ye want to be known as a hellion?

Robert's words rose from her memory and gave her resolve a firm kick in the backside.

What she wasn't going to do was squander her unexpected moment of freedom. She turned and looked around again. No one was anywhere near. She smiled as she tugged a shirt off a peg where it had been left by the men who worked in the stable when they changed into their better clothing for the night's court. It was too large, but she was used to making do. She pleated up a kilt and lay down to buckle it around her waist. A jerkin and bonnet completed her look.

Well, she'd like to have a sword, but such an item was expensive and not likely to be left behind. She'd have to make do with the dagger Marcus had gifted her with. It was a good one, and he'd made sure she knew how to use it. She pulled it out of her garter and happily stuck it through her belt before saddling the horse.

The night beckoned to her with warm air and enough clouds to keep the moonlight low. It was just a ride. A few hours to restore her spirit before she had to resume the role Fate had decided was hers.

Hellion?

Perhaps.

❧

"Sure yer sire won't be tanning yer backside for ye?"

Rolfe McTavish turned his head slightly to the side and sent his captain a half grin. "Only because I did no' invite him along."

Adwin chuckled. "Aye, he'd likely do that, sure enough."

Rolfe reached across the space between the horses and playfully punched his captain in the shoulder. "Let's get to it before our chance to have fun at the MacPhersons' expense is wasted."

"Aye," Adwin agreed. "What with the Earl of Morton insisting we no' feud anymore, we get few enough opportunities."

Several of the McTavish retainers listening spat on the ground at the mention of the king's regent, the Earl of Morton. The man wanted peace and unity in Scotland, and while Rolfe didn't disagree with that notion, he wasn't going to embrace the earl's methods of forcing marriages on the Highlanders and trying to insist that all the lairds' sons be raised at court. Morton could go piss himself if he thought Rolfe would let any child of his be taken to that den of serpents.

Not that he even had a wife, but it was the principle of the thing. He grinned as the clouds shifted, darkening the moon. Morton wasn't the first man to try to suppress the Highlanders.

But he would be another one disappointed when he learned the northern Scots would not bend to his will.

They were Highlanders.

❧

Katherine rode farther than she'd intended.

But she was still on MacPherson land when she pulled the horse up. The animal wanted more, but Katherine slipped from its back and rubbed it soothingly. She must not allow it to become lathered. It was still too cold for that to be a wise thing.

Maybe she didn't know how to turn bread well, but she knew how to treat a horse. She pulled the bit from its mouth to give it a few moments of ease while she walked it toward a flowing river and let it lower its head to drink.

The wind rustled the leaves of the trees as the clouds shifted and blackened the night. It wasn't darkness that made her nape tingle; no, it was something else. She started to turn, realizing she'd made a grave error in facing the river while the sound of the water might cover the steps of anyone nearby.

The realization came too late. She felt a hard blow land on her head and pain nearly split her in two. She struggled to hold back unconsciousness as she raised her hands to defend herself, but she was slow and clumsy. Her captors laughed as they pulled her away from her horse and looped a length of rope around her. It bound her arms to her chest, and they gleefully added two more loops before tying it off.

"Now that's a fine prize, to be sure," one of them declared. "Yer sire is going to blister yer arse, lad, once he pays yer ransom."

"Wager Marcus MacPherson will take a turn at that too, since ye're one of his lads."

There was a course round of amusement at her expense, while the man holding the end of the rope tugged on it and pulled her along with him. She ducked her chin and stumbled after him.

"Look what we have here."

Someone kicked her in the backside. It sent her sprawling, and with her arms bound, she tasted the dirt as she went rolling.

"Hold."

Katherine was just sitting up when the order came. Compliance was immediate. Silence fell around her as she felt the weight of a stare.

It was a foolish thing to think, but as the man stepped closer and lowered himself onto his haunches in front of her, she would have sworn she actually felt his gaze on her. The clouds shifted, casting him in yellow moonlight, and she stiffened. The reaction rose from deep inside her, shocking her as much as the sight of the man considering her.

He was huge.

As hulking large as Marcus, but he struck her so much differently. Her belly tightened, and she felt her eyes widen before she tucked her chin, as she'd learned to do to keep her gender hidden.

The man reached right out and cupped her chin to raise it again.

She gasped and recoiled.

The contact of their skin was jarring. She kicked away from him, but her gaze remained locked with his.

"It's just a little MacPherson laddie," one of the men spoke up. "Should be worth a few pieces of silver."

"Got his horse too," someone else said. "I'm thinking it's worth more than the whelp."

There was another round of chuckling.

The clouds shifted again, giving her even more light, and this time she saw the feather standing up on the side of the leader's bonnet. There was a twinkle from the brooch holding it that could only come from gold.

"Ye're blind, Cedric," the man in front of her said. His voice was deep and controlled. A shiver went down her spine as she recognized how completely in his power she was.

"How so?" Cedric asked. He gave the end of the rope a shake. "I caught him sure enough."

The man in front of her looked toward his man. "This is a lass."

He rose, proving just how powerful his body was. The motion was fluid and graceful, like a hawk when it swooped down on its prey.

"Ye should have noticed how that rope is binding her arms and pushing her breasts up against whatever she bound them with."

Katherine felt her cheeks heat. It had been a long time since she'd blushed, and she didn't welcome the return of such reactions. But her distemper didn't change the truth. Her breasts *were* being pushed up, making a little pair of mounds in the front of the jerkin that wouldn't be there if she were male.

Curse her gender.

"I am Rolfe McTavish." He leaned over and hooked her by the coils of rope, lifting her up with one hard pull. "And ye are foolish in the extreme, mistress."

He pulled the rope off her, tossing it toward his man, Cedric, who caught it but glared at his laird's son. "So what if it's a lass? Still worth a ransom, I bet. Likely running away from a match. That means she has a dowry worth fighting over. Who knows? I might just wed her meself."

Katherine took a step back, and then another when she realized they were letting her get closer to the horse. It occurred to her that they didn't think she was very accomplished at mounting. After all, most women would use a mounting block. It had taken her months to build up enough strength to do it, and still more months of strained muscles after that.

Tonight, every bit of pain seemed insignificant compared to the knowledge that she could fend for herself.

"I'm looking for good sport, Cedric," Rolfe admonished his man.

"Can't see much of her in those clothes, but she might be sporting enough."

Rolfe stepped partially in front of his man. There was an odd tension in the air that made her belly want to heave, but she didn't have time to be distracted by her emotions. She drew in a deep breath and let Marcus's voice fill her head. The one he used when instructing.

Fighting is no' just about who is strongest, but about who has better control...

Rolfe's men were chuckling, while the laird's son had his back to her. She took advantage of the moment, turning and jumping off a rock before gripping the sides of the saddle.

The first fifty times she'd tried it, she'd blackened her eye or hit her nose so hard she was sure it was broken.

Persistence had paid off though, and she'd learned to swing up and onto the horse like the other lads in her training class. Now she did so again, gaining the saddle as she clamped her thighs tight and pulled the horse's head around before digging her heels into its sides. The animal reared up, screaming as it came down with a bone-jarring impact. She felt it tense as it used its powerful hindquarters to push off the ground and start bounding up the hill.

❧

"Never seen a female do that before."

Neither had Rolfe. She was in the saddle as securely as any of his men.

"It's not natural."

"Nay, it is no'."

"I'd say it's impressive," Rolfe interjected. "And it comes from training."

His men weren't sure what to make of his comment. They considered him, two of them stroking their beards while Rolfe watched her reach the crest of the embankment and go over it. She kept motion with the horse expertly, her body moving with lithe, fluid grace that spoke of strength and training. It raised his cock and his opinion of her.

Cedric was staring at him. Rolfe shrugged. "No one learns to swing up into the saddle without working at it."

His men agreed, even if a fair number of them were uncomfortable with the topic. Rolfe found his mind lingering on her long after the sound of her horse diminished into the distance.

"Are we lifting cattle or no'?" Cedric asked at last.

Rolfe found himself hesitating to answer his man. He was torn now. Something was prodding him to go up to Castle MacPherson.

"Ye're thinking of going after her." It was Adwin who spoke. His captain knew him too well, it seemed.

Rolfe turned to lock gazes with the man. "Someone should take her in hand."

"Aye, she was in luck that it was us who caught her," Adwin agreed as he locked his hands around his wide belt and rocked back on his heels. It was his favorite position for thinking. "And still, someone has been teaching her, so they bloody well know what she does."

"The MacPhersons must have a priest with a finer sense of humor than we have on McTavish land," Cedric added.

"It just means she's been playing at being a lad, and Marcus MacPherson has let the matter go. Priests do nae venture into the training yards often," Rolfe said.

"Maybe Marcus did nae notice."

"No' a chance," Rolfe answered. "Marcus is no fool."

"Ye took him by surprise sure enough," Adwin stated, to the delight of the men.

Rolfe was used to them recalling the tale. Today, he didn't take as much heart in it. Yes, there had been a time years ago when he'd managed to sneak up on Marcus MacPherson while the man was distracted by his new wife.

"I'd be a fool to think I could do it a second time," he announced. "And double so for thinking Marcus does no' know that is a lass."

"So it's true, then," Adwin announced. "Me cousin said the MacPhersons have an English hellion living among them. I thought it was just a good story."

"English, ye say?" Rolfe asked.

"No' a chance," Cedric argued. "Now, a Highlander lass might"—he held up a thick finger—"just *might* have the strength to keep up with the lads. But English? Nay. Their blood is too thin."

"Who else would be allowed to train like a lad?" Adwin insisted.

Rolfe didn't listen too closely to his men as they began to debate the shortcomings of the English. His mind was full of the girl and the way she'd blinked when he touched her chin. Damned if there hadn't been something strangely hypnotic about it. Like he'd touched a fae creature.

He chuckled at his own whimsy.

She was just a lass, and a foolish one at that. If anything, he should go home and pen a letter to Marcus MacPherson, because Rolfe wasn't going to ride up to MacPherson Castle. Marcus would enjoy slapping him in shackles, no doubt. Rolfe had once held Helen Grant for ransom. It was all in good fun, in a Highland fashion. Helen had never been in any real danger. That was a point of honor.

Colum Gordon was a different matter. The man had lost touch with the world around him, cradling his vengeance for his dead son and blind to the fact that Bhaic had killed Lye Rob for a just reason.

Rolfe was torn. Somehow, he felt protective toward his nameless fae creature. She was playing a dangerous game, riding at night when clansmen were out raiding. More than one man would consider her a fine prize, and if she had no family to notice her missing, her fate might be a grim one.

"Let's get the cattle," he commanded in frustration. Marcus deserved the dig at his pride for allowing any female to train in his yard. Look what sort of recklessness it had bred in the lass! The bloody Gordons would not be so kind to her if they found her.

Hellion?

More like hell-bound. Her behavior was going to land her in her grave.

❧

She'd ridden the horse too fast.

Katherine spent over an hour rubbing the poor creature down and praying that she would go undiscovered while she was tending to the chore. At least the work gave her something to do, because she was pulsing with nervousness and yet, at the same time, a strong sense of victory.

She couldn't stop smiling, and she was muffling her giggles while working on the horse.

She'd really, really done it.

Escaped.

All of the reprimanding looks and lectures melted away as her accomplishment burned bright enough to overshadow them all. She'd been so frightened for a moment when the rope was biting into her and she was being pulled along like a cow on the way to be slaughtered.

And then she'd used her wits to cut through that panic, opening a doorway for her training to come through. Things Marcus had said during training classes suddenly made sense in a bold manner that filled her with a confidence she had never experienced before. It was heady and dark and seductive.

Just what she'd needed after weeks of toiling in the kitchens, where she was clumsy and ignorant and so much less skilled than the rest of the women. She held a new respect for the toil necessary to put a meal on the table, and that was a solid truth.

Yet, she didn't belong there.

The men didn't want her near either. It was a puzzle that seemed to have no solution. At least not one that pleased her. Katherine wound through the passageways toward her chamber, left with the sure knowledge that she was not frightened of the shadows or the night hours or even McTavish clansmen. She would not trade that for any amount of acceptance from the other women. She'd earned it with every blow and knock, all the times she'd fought back her tears and kept training. Her courage was hard-won and, it would seem, her sole possession. For her name was tarnished, and among the Scots, her blood was hated.

So she held the courage she'd cultivated tightly to her chest and felt something that had been missing since the day Robert had told her she couldn't ride out with the men.

Contentment.

A sense of belonging.

She realized that she'd been longing for it, and now she felt at ease again, as if she'd found a part of herself she'd thought was broken away. It wasn't. Even if she was separated from the training yard, everything she had learned was still hers and could never be taken from her because she'd earned it.

The moment she closed her eyes, she saw him again.

Rolfe McTavish.

Out in the darkness, he'd been a brute, to be sure. Not that she doubted he was any less fearsome by the light of day, but the night hours cast things in a way that made them seem more intense. That had to be the reason why she would have sworn she still felt his fingers on her skin.

He'd touched her for a mere moment. Moon madness was the explanation for why it lingered in her thoughts.

She'd heard his name many times. He'd held Helen for ransom when Marcus had first brought Katherine to the Highlands. She had been barely fourteen at the time, and grateful to Marcus for not wedding her as the Earl of Morton had demanded. Katherine had been too young, and Marcus had been outraged. He had stolen her away into the Highlands to ensure she'd have time to grow up.

She was doubly grateful tonight because Marcus had trained her. Rolfe McTavish would have been sending another ransom note if she hadn't known how to escape.

But she had, and she fell asleep with that truth warming her.

✌

"Ye allowed Katherine to leave the kitchens?"

Marcus arrived in their bedchamber, demanding an answer to his question before the door closed. Helen shot him a hard look of reprimand because he'd startled their babe. Roderick opened his eyes and let out a wail. Helen cradled him close as she rocked him, waiting for him to close his eyes once more. Marcus waited while she settled the infant in his cradle, caught in the moment, still finding it hard to believe that he was so fortunate.

His wife turned to him, lifting one eyebrow. "Do ye think I have any more stomach for crushing her spirit than ye do?"

Marcus didn't miss the point of her reply. He'd braced his feet wide and crossed his arms over his chest, but now he ran a hand over his head. He kept his hair cut short so it couldn't be grabbed in a fight.

"Ye're right." He placed his sword by their bed and checked on Rae before sitting down next to her.

"The kitchens are an unkind place to put her now," Helen continued. "She lacks the skill of the other women her age."

"Because I allowed her to train," Marcus finished as he set his boots aside. He turned and considered their second son. "I think it might be a good thing that we have only sons. I seem to have no wisdom when it comes to raising lasses."

"I'll have a daughter," Helen warned him. "Don't be thinking to deny me one."

Marcus slowly grinned at her. It was a wicked one that she enjoyed seeing on his face.

"Well now, Wife," he began in a deep voice that warmed her blood, "ye know I hate to leave ye unsatisfied."

Helen snorted at him as she was drifting off into sleep. "I do nae believe that nonsense."

"That ye only conceive daughters when a man leaves his woman unsatisfied?" Marcus clarified.

Helen opened her eyes and looked at him. "We are going to have to move Rae to a different chamber with the way ye talk."

"Ye mean with the way I pleasure ye."

She made a little sound of agreement under her breath. "As for Katherine, what is yer quarrel with her working with the hawks?"

"It's in the stables, a place where men are often rougher in their words."

Helen scoffed at him. "Katherine has been training in the yard for nearly six years. If ye were concerned with her hearing about lust, ye are far too late, and I don't doubt that she has seen everything there is to see about what is beneath a kilt."

"Aye," Marcus agreed as he pulled her close and inhaled the scent of her hair. "As I already admitted, I do nae seem to have much wisdom about where a lass should and should no' be."

"Ye were thinking of her English blood and the hatred of it here in the Highlands."

Marcus nodded. "I was. Fate has given the lass a hard hand to play. Bastard born to a noble, no less, and with her mother lowborn, her noble stepmother will not be wishing her good health."

"The Earl of Morton would no' have found it simple to steal her away and keep her if that weren't so," Helen agreed. "She's been left to whatever fate Scotland holds for her. She was far too young for that."

"I knew it was nae correct to train her, and still, I could nae argue with the sense of it." Marcus spoke softly. "But now, well, she's a woman grown and can no' hide it."

"Who does nae know how to be a woman," Helen finished. "Nor does any of the clan treat her like one."

Marcus's hand stilled on her hip. "Well, now, that's something I do know a bit about. I'll see to it tomorrow."

"See to what?" Helen asked.

But her husband had lost interest in the conversation, now that he'd come to a conclusion. He was far more interested in stroking her body and bringing it to life as he always did. Helen lost track of anything beyond knowing that they needed to move their children to another chamber soon, because time had not dulled the reaction she had to her husband, and she still could not keep her cries of delight to herself.

❧

"Katherine Carew."

The great hall of MacPherson Castle went quiet as

Shamus MacPherson spoke her name. The laird of the clan was old now, but at times, his voice still rang with authority.

Tonight was one of those nights.

His retainers turned to consider her as she hesitated with one leg over a bench and her supper still in her hands. One of the women who was serving the long tables that filled the hall reached over and took it away from her.

Katherine pulled her leg back and lowered herself.

"Ye'll join me," Shamus informed her.

One of his men went toward the end of the high table and pulled a chair out for her. It was a position of honor, one reserved for members of the laird's family and his captains. Everyone seemed to be watching her, so she started moving toward the head table, though it felt as if each of her boots suddenly weighed as much as a young colt.

She stopped and lowered herself once more before she climbed the steps to where the high table sat. The chair was large and furnished with a pillow, and the retainer pushed her in toward the table once she'd sat down.

"It has been some years since Katherine came to this castle." Shamus spoke clearly, and his men gave him their attention. "So tonight, I want to take a moment to remind everyone that she is considered me son Marcus's sister. The Earl of Morton, the king's regent, wanted an alliance with me family, and we will honor his wishes."

There was a long moment of contemplation from the men and women of the clan. Many of the men stroked their beards while their eyes narrowed in thought. But the laird's word was law, and in the end, his men nodded to him before they turned back to their supper.

"Ye may stay with the hawks, so long as ye keep to wearing a dress," Marcus said softly beside her. "And ye will sit beside me at meals so no one forgets yer place."

She nodded, but Marcus turned and his eyes narrowed.

"So that pleases ye?" he asked.

Marcus was suspicious by nature. A trait that served him well as war chief to the clan. Katherine had been frightened of him for most of her first year in the Highlands, but after that, when it seemed he wouldn't keep her from training, she'd decided it was part of his charm.

"Aye," she answered him. "It pleases me far more than turning bread."

"Ye would no' have been a maid," Marcus explained.

"Helen was clear on that matter." Katherine stiffened as she knocked elbows with a maid who was leaning in from behind her to serve her. Marcus chuckled softly.

"It takes a bit of getting accustomed to," he muttered once the maid was finished. "Being served, that is."

It seemed she'd also have to learn how to eat while being watched. Katherine snapped her mouth shut as she realized there were plenty of people looking directly at her. She lifted a linen napkin from where it was laid over her right shoulder and made sure her lips were clean. After that, she took only small bites to ensure she wasn't chewing with her mouth open.

Marcus made a sound under his breath. "Helen asked me how one managed to eat at the high table when she first wed me." He sent Katherine an amused look. "I told her, very carefully, or ye'll be used as a teaching example by MacPherson mothers."

"No, thank you," Katherine answered. She was strained, so her English accent was more pronounced.

"I knew."

Marcus had spoken so softly that she had to think for a moment to make sure she'd heard him correctly. He cut her a look.

"I knew ye were there, lass. In the yard."

He watched his words land, taking note of the smile that lifted the corners of her lips. He scoffed before reaching for a round of bread. He tore it and placed a piece on her plate.

"Pleases ye, does it?"

"You are not a man who gives out false flattery, so yes." Katherine reached for the bread, forcing herself to handle it more daintily. "I consider it a compliment earned."

"Fair enough," Marcus responded. "Mind me, Katherine. On the matters of yer dress and this table. I would make certain ye are afforded protection."

"From my blood, you mean?"

Marcus looked back at her, and this time she saw the frank, bluntly honest man who had trained her. This was the war chief of the clan. "Ye've heard with your own ears the way the men speak of the English. I allowed ye to train because I can no' be changing the fact that many men will visit the sins of yer countrymen upon ye. Yet Robert is correct: ye are a woman grown now. So, ye'll sit beside me so every man here understands I consider ye me family."

She nodded and went back to her supper. Marcus got caught up in a conversation with his brother, Bhaic, so she was left to contemplate his words.

Being on the outside was something she understood well. It had been her life; Scotland was no different. So she would celebrate her victory in escaping the kitchens.

A wicked little thought moved through her as she contemplated just how much easier it would be to ride out at night now that she didn't serve directly under Helen. The master of the hawks was an old man who had plenty of younger apprentices to do the work for him. He took to drinking before the sun set and slept soundly until after dawn.

Yes, a victory. That's what it was indeed.

❦

"Looking back toward MacPherson land?"

Rolfe jumped and growled at Adwin. His captain only flashed him a grin, which the moonlight illuminated.

"That little lassie will no' be venturing out again."

"I am no' so certain of that," Rolfe declared. "She is brazen by nature."

Adwin made a low sound under his breath. "Learned so much about her in that wee moment ye were together?"

Rolfe answered him with a shrug. "Perhaps I understand females a wee bit better than ye do."

"No' bloody likely," Adwin scoffed. "I'm still a good eight seasons older than ye, lad."

"And still," Rolfe said softly, "ye missed that fine pair of tits."

Adwin humphed and gripped his belt.

❧

It was a moment that seemed frozen.

Katherine had no idea how long she stared at the scene before her. One moment, she was feeling the sting of a blush on her cheeks as she heard Rolfe boldly talking about her breasts, and the next, she blinked, because a conversation was coming up behind her.

"If I catch whoever has been raiding our cattle, I'm going to hang them."

"Feuding is forbidden by the regent," another voice said.

There was a grunt and a brushing of leaves as Katherine crouched in a thicket.

"The Earl of Morton can go fuck himself. Ever since he's been insisting on peace in the Highlands, all I do is watch me inheritance bleed away. One hanging will send a message. MacPhersons, McTavishes, Robertsons... They all need to know the Gordons will nae be trifled with. Now shut yer jaw... Cleo is coming back."

There was a blur of motion. Katherine watched as a bird glided past and perched on a tree near her. It turned, displaying its large, amber eyes.

An owl.

It could see in the dark and had been trained to hunt men. She shivered as one of the shadows shifted behind her and lifted a gloved hand. The owl took flight, gliding over to the gauntlet and eagerly taking the bit of meat offered to it. But the meager amount of food was consumed quickly, and the bird turned to look for the prey its master would reward it for. As it started to lower its head and raise its wings, Katherine started moving.

Rolfe and his men had no idea how close they were to being discovered.

She bumped into the thicket on purpose, making it shake and fill the air with a rustling sound. The owl turned toward her, flying straight at her as she turned away from Rolfe McTavish.

It was a rash action, and yet so satisfying to know she'd protected them. She turned to run back to where she had left her horse. Rolfe had only a few men with him, and the Gordons were more than twenty strong. Many would label her foolish for interfering in the business of men, but she did not regret doing so.

"After him!"

Katherine ran, digging her feet into the earth as she pushed herself up the hill toward the crest. On the other side, her horse was waiting, and the animal's strength would carry her away. Her lungs burned as she heard the men behind her. They were closing the distance, but she knew not to look behind her because it would slow her down.

So she ran, demanding more speed from her straining muscles, insisting her lungs draw in enough breath to keep her moving. She made it to the top of the hill and glimpsed her horse on the other side before she was brutally pushed to the ground.

She felt her skin scraping the dirt as someone slammed their fist into the back of her skull. Pain went smashing through her, making her dizzy, but she fought it, using her feet to push herself up as she pulled the dagger free from her belt.

Whoever was on her jumped back as she slashed at him with the weapon.

"Bloody Christ!" he exclaimed. "Ye'll pay for that!"

He lunged at her, but Katherine had learned to move quickly. She dodged to the side, using the hilt of her dagger to deliver a blow to his temple. There was a dull thud as she struck true, and he fell to the ground in a heap.

"Ye'll no' be fighting all of us off, boy."

Katherine saw that what she had thought were twenty men were in reality more than thirty. They had her surrounded now, their breathing harsh as their leader chuckled at her plight.

❦

"Get off me!" Rolfe snarled.

Adwin and his men refused. "Ye can nae help her," his captain hissed next to his ear. "Let her sacrifice be for something."

"I'll be damned if I'll see a woman protecting me," Rolfe declared.

He strained against his men, but they held him down.

"I'll no' be taking yer body back to yer father," Adwin informed him.

"Ye're me captain first."

"But yer sire is me laird." Adwin refused to budge.

Rolfe growled, and then his world went black as Adwin thumped him on the back of his skull.

❦

"Piss off." Katherine tucked her chin, trying to mumble to disguise how high her voice was. "I wasn't on yer land. Ye're on MacPherson property."

"Yer fucking balls haven't dropped yet" was the response she got. "Ye sound like a bleeding whelp crying for a tit."

"I want his balls." The man she'd downed was staggering to his feet. "He drew my blood."

"You got what you deserved," Katherine answered.

"I told ye…" The leader spoke again. "I'm going to hang him and let the bloody MacPherson see what happens to those who steal Gordon cattle."

"I'm too small to steal a cow by myself." It was a risk to keep talking, but one of the men was already pulling a rope from where it had been draped on his hip and fashioning a noose. "And this is MacPherson land."

"Well, now, it won't take much to drag ye onto Gordon land," the leader commented. "Yer bloody Tanis Bhaic MacPherson killed me laird's son."

"Lye Rob took Bhaic's wife."

The man who seemed to be leading them moved closer. Katherine tightened her grip on the hilt of the dagger. He didn't miss the way her body tensed.

"Thinking to try me, lad?" he asked from just far enough away to make a lunge at him ill advised. "I am Tyree Gordon. Ye should know the name of the man who is going to hang ye."

"Maybe I'll kill ye, and yer men will think better of feuding and earning the wrath of the Earl of Morton."

Tyree threw his head back and laughed. He was close enough that she could smell how rotten his teeth were.

"I hope to Christ Morton is pissed!" Tyree declared,

to the delight of his men. "That bastard is no' fit to call himself a Scot! He wants us all to bathe in perfume like the French and bugger boys!"

There was a rumble of discontentment as many of the Gordons spat on the ground.

"Make yer peace with God, because I'm going to choke the life out of ye for cutting me."

He came for her, and Katherine moved in the way Marcus had taught her. She was smaller, so she'd learned to use her speed and agility against larger boys. Tyree was a powerfully built man, and he misjudged how light she was on her feet, stumbling past her on his first charge. Horror made her want to retch, but it was kill or die.

Tyree let out a curse as she drew blood. He whipped around, but not before she felt the warm slide of his blood across her hand. He roared at her before charging at her again.

"What the fuck are ye doing, Tyree?"

He froze, and it looked as though the man who had spoken had reached out and grabbed him by the nape. She could see his expression, distorted by rage, but he held himself away from her as a new group of men came closer. One of them struck a flint and a torch caught, washing the scene in yellow light.

"He fucking cut me!" Tyree snarled.

"If ye'd told me ye were going to hang me," the newcomer said softly, "I'd have done the same. Ye are on MacPherson land."

Tyree spat at the feet of the newcomer. "Barely. Did ye expect me to wait for the bloody bastards who are thieving from us?"

"I expected ye to follow me orders, and there was no mention of hanging."

The men around her took a step back. The man facing her was a good ten years older than Tyree. He held himself still as he contemplated her. "I am Diocail Gordon."

He reminded her of Marcus, with his silent stance.

"Ye sent me out here to deal with the thieving," Tyree insisted. "Let me get on with cutting this whelp's balls off."

Diocail's lips twitched a tiny bit before he chuckled softly. "Ye'd be a fool if ye did. Colum makes the decisions on Gordon land when it comes to who gets strung up."

Katherine gasped as one of the men caught her from behind. She'd made the fatal mistake of being focused on the deliverance Diocail seemed to offer and had failed to keep her mouth shut.

"Hold," Diocail said as her captor aimed a fist at the side of her head.

"Ye're young," he said as he came closer. "But that sounded a wee bit more than just young."

He wasn't the only man who thought so. Taken by surprise, she'd failed to make her voice gruff, and the horrible truth that had destroyed her life on MacPherson land was being heard.

She was a woman.

And now she was faced with men who had their passion up. Katherine raised her chin. She'd face her fate.

Whatever it was.

Courage was what she'd learned from Marcus, and she would not shame him.

Two

Colum Gordon was old.

One of his retainers kicked Katherine in the back of the knee when she didn't offer the laird deference by lowering herself. She stumbled and ended up on her knees, to the delight of the Gordons.

Colum only regarded her from his throne-like chair set on a raised platform. It was covered in a bearskin, and he wore a necklace of the creature's claws. He snorted when he noticed where her attention was.

"Gordons…" he began in a crusty voice, "prove their worth."

Katherine climbed to her feet. It gained her a grumble from the men behind her and a grunt from the laird of the Gordons. The old man pointed at the man behind her. "Tyree there wants to hang ye."

"He doesn't take being bested well," Katherine replied. For certain, many would have advised her to grovel, but she'd chosen her path when she left MacPherson Castle in a kilt.

"Ye did nae best me…" Tyree sent her sprawling onto the floor again. This time, she went with the motion, rolling and coming up on her feet. The rope was looped around her chest several times, keeping her arms bound tight to her body.

I am not helpless…

Katherine repeated that several times, using it as a shield to defend herself against the fear swelling up inside her.

"I was not on your land," Katherine said smoothly.

"But ye are in a kilt," Colum declared. "And someone has taught ye how to use that dagger like a man."

He stopped and made a low sound in the back of his throat. His men were contemplating her, their foreheads furrowing as they took in her male attire.

"Unnatural…"

"English…"

"So," Colum said. "At last I have an answer to why the MacPhersons seem to always best me men." His eyes suddenly glowed with vicious intent. "For why my son is rotting in his grave and no' here to lead this clan."

His men looked to him while Katherine felt her breath catch. She recalled that tone of voice. It stirred the memory of the way the Earl of Morton had sounded so many years before, when he'd ordered her to be wed at barely fourteen years of age.

"The MacPhersons have an English witch."

"I am not a witch," Katherine insisted. Her rising alarm brought out her English accent and earned her more than one curse.

Colum listened to the rumble of discontentment from his people for a long moment, the gleam in his eye becoming one of enjoyment that sickened her with just how brightly it glowed. Hatred truly was an ugly thing.

"I do nae care if ye are a witch or no'," he muttered with a wave of his hand.

His men didn't like what he said, but Katherine wasn't relieved because the laird's lips rose into a twisted grin even more horrific than the enjoyment sparkling in his eyes. It chilled her blood.

"I wondered why I've lived this long…" The hall went quiet as the laird continued to speak. "Bhaic MacPherson laid me son, Lye Rob, in his grave. I do nae care why, only that Fate has delivered a woman to me that Bhaic and Marcus call sister." Colum fingered one of the bear claws. "They took me family, and I will take a member of theirs. Blood for blood."

"You are insane." She didn't mean to speak, but the horrified words slipped past her lips. There was no going back, so she stiffened her spine and took a brazen approach. "You would leave your clan with a feud started for the sake of vengeance?"

Colum scowled at her. "No English bitch is going to lecture me."

"Someone should," Katherine insisted, raising her voice so it carried through the hall. "For it will be the women of your clan who are left to mourn their husbands and sons when the MacPhersons extract vengeance for you spilling my blood."

"Well, now." Colum leaned forward and pointed one gnarled finger at her. "The good Earl of Morton will be ordering them to stop. The MacPhersons do what that man tells them to, sure enough."

There was a gleam of unholy victory in his eyes, which sickened her.

"The earl is a long way from here." She meant it as a warning, but it also served as one to her, because the men around her were not shifting in their stances. There was no hint of any of them questioning their laird.

Colum didn't miss her rising fear. He chuckled at her, still smiling brightly. "And the beauty of it all is that even should me descendants find themselves answering to the earl, this will be a matter of a witch being burned. Put her somewhere where she can see the courtyard. I want her to watch the pyre being built."

Tyree was the one who hooked his hands into her hair and dragged her away. Katherine held back the cry of pain and stumbled as he half threw her ahead of him, only to then recapture her and toss her forward again.

But she saw them at last. Those Gordons who did not share in their laird's bloodlust. They were near the back of the hall, many of them looking away from her, shamed by her circumstances and the fact that they didn't dare go against their laird's will.

And then Tyree had hold of her hair again. She'd braided it tightly to keep it under her bonnet. He dug his fingers into it and jerked her along until she heard a door grinding open, the hinges stiff with rust.

"This will do well enough for a witch."

Tyree kicked her to get her to move inside the dank room. Katherine faced him instead.

"At least I do not make excuses when I am laid low."

His face twisted with rage and he raised his hand, but something flickered in his eyes. He was suddenly loosening the rope that bound her, pulling it free, and then in the next moment, he stripped her down to her shirt before pushing her into the room.

"A witch does nae need clothing to stay warm."

Tyree closed the door after his parting shot. Katherine started to tremble as she heard the bar being lowered into place to secure the room. It was pitch-black, raising the tiny hairs along the surface of her skin.

Alone...

She struggled against the memory of being helpless and alone, but in the darkness, there was no defense. She sank down and pulled her arms inside her shirt to try to keep warm. But the true battle was against her circumstances. This time, she'd brought them on herself.

She didn't regret it.

Couldn't, because to do so would make her a creature like Colum or Tyree and his followers. Better to center her thoughts on the men she'd saved. Wasn't it wiser to lose one life instead of five?

Well, perhaps she was just trying to ensure her plight had a purpose that was more than a life full of unkind circumstances. She refused to tumble into that pit of despair.

Refused...

❧

"I'm thinking ye need to be knocked on the back of yer thick skull again," Adwin said. "The Gordons will ransom her."

Rolfe sent him a warning look. "And if they do no'? I am nae content to turn me back on the lass. She put herself between us and trouble. Honor demands we make sure she is no' harmed."

Rolfe was silent for a long moment because they all knew there had been plenty of time for her to suffer through the night. He didn't linger on the thought of what the Gordons might already have taken from her. What mattered was the moment at hand, and there was no way he would be riding home while a woman sat in the Gordon stronghold because she'd shielded him.

"Aye," Adwin admitted. "Ye're right, we can nae be leaving the lass's fate unknown. But who knows what manner of welcome we'll receive from the Gordons?"

"Leave that to me," Rolfe informed his men.

They waited until midmorning before they mounted and rode toward the gate of the Gordon stronghold. Rolfe heard the bells being rung at a frantic pace, summoning the Gordons to arms. He pulled up and waited for their war chief to ride out to meet him.

Diocail Gordon hadn't been raised at the castle. It was only after Bhaic MacPherson had killed Lye Rob Gordon that Colum had brought his nephew Diocail down from the north country because he needed a clear blood heir. No one knew just what to make of the man, except that he was a Gordon—and that was something Rolfe needed to remember. Clan allegiance ran bone-deep in the Highlands. Men who failed to heed that fact often ended up dead.

"Come calling, have ye, McTavish?" Diocail asked.

"No' on me own account." Rolfe offered a similar tone of disgruntlement. "Me father is seeking an answer to his letter concerning the matter of me youngest sister wedding a Gordon."

"Christ," Diocail muttered. "That father of yers enjoys his alliances."

"Ye Gordons do nae live as close to the Lowlands as we McTavishes," Rolfe explained. "Morton is a bastard, and me father wants to ensure he stays off our land."

Diocail nodded in agreement. "I've no' been told to send ye on yer way, but I'd advise ye to lay yer head some place more Christian."

It was a warmer welcome than Rolfe had been expecting. The Gordons closed ranks behind them as they rode toward Gordon Castle. But Rolfe's stomach twisted when he made it into the courtyard and spied a pyre being built.

"Aye." Diocail came up beside him. "Colum has it in his mind to burn a MacPherson witch." He pointed toward a small window at ground level. "Even wants her to watch the stake being readied for her."

Rolfe reached out and grabbed Diocail when the man went to step away. "Are ye mad, man? Colum will be long dead when the MacPhersons come for their vengeance. Ye will be the one who has to live with it."

Diocail sent him a hard look. "Ye'll learn something about Gordons, McTavish, and that is that the laird's word is law. Perhaps ye'll be better off getting back on yer horse."

Rolfe made a scoffing sound in the back of his throat. "Me own father expects no less from his men, and being his son means I'd better lead by example. I'll see Colum."

"We all do what we must in this life."

❦

"I'm impressed." Adwin spoke softly as he stood near Rolfe. The laird of the Gordons had yet to rise from his bed, so they were waiting for him while the Gordons contemplated them.

"I did nae think ye could manage to get us through those gates without lying," Adwin finished. "No' too bad."

"Me sister will likely not agree with ye," Rolfe answered. "I believe she prefers a convent to a Gordon."

Adwin glanced back toward the stake being raised in the yard. "I can nae say I disagree. Nasty bit of business. No lass deserves it."

Rolfe nodded. He was tense as he held back the instinct to fight. There were too many Gordons and too many retainers on the wall for a straightforward attack. No, this was a fight he'd have to win with his wits first.

But he would win, or he'd be dead before they lit the pyre. His father would likely argue with his impulse to interfere, but his sire had also taught him that honor wasn't something a man could turn his back on. Whoever she was, her plight was a result of shielding him.

So he wasn't going anywhere.

❦

Katherine slept past dawn.

Considering how many hours she'd sat in the darkness shivering, it wasn't any wonder her body had taken as much rest as it could.

But she awoke to the sound of men building.

The sounds of wood being broken and something being dragged in behind a team of horses.

"Wake up, witch!"

There was a clang as someone hit the bars over the small window. Now that there was light, she could see the mold blackening the walls of the cell. It was no more than four feet by four feet, and she had to stand to see out the window because the cell was mostly below ground.

No wonder it was as cold as ice.

Tyree was peering down at her, fresh stitches running along his jaw where she'd sliced him. His eyes narrowed as he noticed where her attention was. "I brought ye a good stake. Sturdy and strong enough to last long past yer last breath." He smiled at her. "I'm going to make sure the lads set it deep, so when ye burn, it will hold fast and keep ye there for the flames to lick. We'll keep the fire low enough to ensure ye are alive for a good long time."

She felt the blood drain from her face, and he laughed at her horror. A moment later, she saw his knee as he pushed up and went back to the yard.

Do not look.

Katherine wanted to deny her captors the entertainment of her fear, but she couldn't seem to stop herself from moving toward the window. She had to lift her chin so she could peer out, and when she did, she felt as if her heart had stopped.

But Fate was not so merciful.

No, as she took in the sight of the Gordons digging a hold for the stake, she felt her heart begin pounding hard and fast, as though her body was trying to force her to keep living. She turned around, looking at the cell, frantic for any means of escape. Suddenly, the bitter cold was banished from her limbs as she sought the strength to survive.

All she faced were stone walls. She could see the places around the bars in the window where others had tried to scratch their way to freedom. With only the bars, she heard every sound of the pyre going up. Just as Colum wanted.

Well, she had to think hard and not abandon hope. Marcus had allowed her to train, and she would be more than a frightened female.

She would.

෪

Colum peered at Rolfe, but didn't speak until one of his men brought him a mug of ale. He drew off a long sip that left foam in his beard before he cleared his throat loudly enough for the kitchen maids to hear.

"Aye, I have the offer," Colum exclaimed. "What I do nae have is a son."

Bitterness was thick in the old man's tone. He drew off another sip before slamming the mug down on the table in front of him.

"May the MacPhersons rot in hell for taking me Lye Rob." Colum's eyes brightened. "I'll be paying them back for the loss. Ye're in time to see it, McTavish. I've been handed the means to even the score."

"If ye are speaking of that stake yer men are putting up in the yard," Rolfe said clearly, "I want no part of it. Especially since ye're telling me the woman is no' a witch, only a MacPherson who had the poor luck to be brought to ye."

Colum's face twisted in rage. "She was wearing men's clothing and…using a dagger like a man. What is that if not the doing of Satan?"

"Spirit," Rolfe declared. "I think I'd like a look at her."

"Ye can watch her burn," the old laird snapped before going back to his drink.

"I meant what I said," Rolfe replied. "I'll not have any part of it. The McTavish name will not be associated with any witch burning where there has been no trial."

"She cut one of me men."

"More than one lass keeps a dagger in case of men who try to do them harm," Rolfe explained. "I assure ye, me sister does, and I'm the one who showed her how to use it. That is no' witchcraft. It's good sense."

"Aye." Diocail Gordon surprised Rolfe by adding to the conversation. "One man's pride should no' be a deciding factor. Tyree should learn to drink less when he's planning on riding out."

There was a roar from the retainer. Tyree stomped forward, a few of his friends closing ranks behind him to make their support clear. He faced off with Diocail, leaving no doubt that the clan was headed for a split when Colum died. The strongest contenders for the lairdship were gathering.

"No one wants ye here," Tyree informed Diocail. "Go back to the north where ye belong."

"My father was Colum's brother," Diocail declared loudly. "I am a Gordon."

"Yer mother took ye away," Tyree declared. "Ye have no' served this clan."

"And ye call burning a lass a service?" Diocail asked quietly. "Only to yer pride, man. I'm wise enough to know it will start more trouble than the Gordons need. Ye are a fool to dismiss such facts."

Tyree snarled and lunged at Diocail. For all his quiet demeanor, Diocail moved quickly. He dove and dipped and came up with Tyree locked in a choke hold.

"Enough!" Colum roared.

Diocail hesitated for a long moment before turning Tyree lose. The retainer gasped, rage flickering in his eyes.

"I'll write yer father," Colum informed Rolfe. "And ye can take the message and be on yer way before I get on with Gordon business."

There was a crack of thunder so loud it nearly shook the walls. A moment later, rain started to pelt the windows of the castle. The women ran to close the shutters as hail started to come down. A frigid wind gusted through the open doors of the hall, blowing the tapestries. It was bone-numbing, with more than one woman lifting her hand to cross herself.

Colum visibly shivered. For a moment, he looked frailer than before, his joints locking up as he tried to stand but fell weakly back into his chair. And still, the gleam of hatred burned in his eyes. Rolfe offered him a nod before he turned and left.

If the lass was going to live, he'd have to find another way to free her.

❧

The Gordons took full advantage of their laird's frailty and the storm that kept them inside. Drink flowed freely, and before long, the retainers clustered around Colum were drunk. Rolfe only played at drinking. It was a game a wise man perfected early in life if he didn't want to wake up in a ditch with an empty sporran and no boots.

"It seems to me…" Tyree said, "that the witch shouldn't die a virgin."

There were snickers in response.

"I think I should give her a taste of a real man," he continued.

Rolfe knew enough of the man to know he wasn't going to stop, and there was no one willing to interfere. It was clear the majority of the clan was hanging back, waiting to see whether Tyree or Diocail would eventually be laird.

Rolfe looked at the fading light and exchanged a look with Adwin. His captain nodded and left.

"Finally leaving, McTavish?" Tyree asked. "It was only a bit of rain."

"We're going," Rolfe declared. "I'm tired of waiting on yer laird's letter."

"Piss off," Tyree declared. "Keep yer sister."

Rolfe turned and left. His men fell into step beside him as he waited in the lengthening shadows of the passageways. Gordon Castle was an older fortification that clearly hadn't seen much in the way of improvements in the last two decades. Bits of rubble lined the walls, and the stench was strong from the men urinating on them instead of using the jakes. More than one clan still clung to medieval ways, but Rolfe was grateful the McTavishes didn't.

Today, though, the conditions of the Gordon clan would be to his advantage. The retainers were lax and allowed to do as they pleased. For the moment, that meant a great number of them were drinking in the hall with Tyree.

The staff seemed accustomed to such evenings, because the older women had ushered all the younger females to places unknown hours ago. That left the passageways empty and the wind still howling through them through broken shutters that should have been repaired. But with no one insisting that the men put in a full day, many of them didn't.

There was a burst of laughter from the hall, and Rolfe recalled himself to his purpose. He sent half his men toward the stables to saddle the horses. The rest stayed with him as he made his way to where the cells were. In the semidarkness, he had to slow down, because water was pouring in through the windows, making the floor muddy.

❦

She was freezing.

Katherine laughed at the twist of fate. How very perverse to be saved from burning by an ice storm. The wind came through the window in frigid blasts, the hail hitting her no matter where she moved. There was an added cruelty to the place: whoever had built it had made it face north, toward the coldest weather.

Mud and water and debris from the yard came down the wall, filling the room until she was shin-deep in freezing muck. Time crept along, losing its meaning because she couldn't tell what time of day it was with the clouds so dark. Outside, the stake was in place, but all work had stopped as the hail came down with fury.

She found herself looking at the door, willing it to open. When it did, she stared at it in disbelief. Clearly she'd gone mad, and that was disappointing, because she should have liked to believe she was strong enough to last more than one day before insanity claimed her.

Yet it had, because as the door opened, she blinked, seeing Rolfe McTavish before her.

She shied away from the thought, wanting to cling to sanity, to life. He lifted his hand, beckoning to her.

"Come with me, lass."

His voice was soft now, enticing. It was so tempting.

"Tyree will be coming next, and what he plans is not pleasant."

It was Tyree's name that cut through to her. She jerked and blinked, and Rolfe was still there. She was still so cold it hurt, which made her realize she was not awash in the fold of insanity.

The insane did not feel pain.

But she did. So much of it that she clamped her jaw shut to keep from moaning. It was true agony, but Rolfe was waving her forward and she leaped toward him, slipping right through the door before he moved, without a care for how improper it was to brush against his body.

Freedom from the cell was the only thing that mattered.

"Hold up, lass."

Rolfe was right behind her. He reached out to cup

her shoulder and she wrenched free, stumbling along the passageway as her heart pounded with the need to escape. There was no other thought in her mind, and her blood was roaring in her ears now.

He jerked her back, pulling her into the shadows as he listened for any approaching footsteps.

"Easy now," he offered in a low voice.

His body was hard and warm. It broke through the strange bubble surrounding her mind, allowing her to think. The impulse to run was still strong, but she clamped her jaw tight and forced herself to stand in place as she listened.

The Gordon stronghold was as close to hell as she had ever been.

She turned and looked at the man behind her. She'd wondered if she'd imagined how big he was, but her head didn't quite reach his shoulders. The night was new, and the moon hidden behind the clouds made him seem even more a creature of shadows than the previous times she'd encountered him.

She wondered what he looked like in the light of day.

A hoot and a round of laughter sent a bolt of dread straight through her, for she recognized Tyree's voice. He was coming down the passageway, heading for the door of her cell.

"Witch," he declared as he pulled the bar up. "I've come to make yer last night a memorable one!"

He was laughing, but the laugh died as he looked into the cell. "Bloody—"

The shadows shifted, and Tyree was suddenly slumping onto the floor with a splat as he hit the mud and muck. His companions had a similar fate. Rolfe's hand had tightened on her, keeping her in place.

Diocail Gordon locked gazes with Rolfe for a long moment before he looked ahead of him and walked on as though they were not there.

"Go." Rolfe pushed her forward, breaking her thoughts as she once more focused on the task of escaping.

It wasn't hard. They emerged from the cells with the use of a narrow set of stone steps that led up into the courtyard where the stake was standing silently in the darkness. Katherine's belly roiled, making her grateful the Gordons hadn't fed her because she didn't want to have to take the time to retch.

She welcomed the cutting cold. With only her shirt on, it was bitter, and she decided she loved it because it meant she was still alive.

"There, lass."

Rolfe pointed toward his men. They stood beside their horses, many of them swinging up into the saddles as they saw their laird coming. Katherine flexed her fingers, praying they wouldn't fail her now. She was so close to freedom, something she hadn't thought would be hers.

She grasped the side of the saddle, pushing off the ground and using the muscles along her midsection to help pull her up. Rolfe didn't seem to trust her strength, staying beside her and pushing her up with one big hand on her backside that sent a rush of heat across her cheeks.

He was gone a moment later, appearing again on top of his horse. The animal was a full two hands

taller than her own, and it danced as its master reached
down to pat its neck. Rolfe looked forward, raising
his fist into the air. His men reacted instantly, closing
ranks around her and riding toward the gates.

Katherine felt time slowing down again. She felt
the connection of each hoof as it hit the ground and
moved with the motion of the animal beneath her,
leaning forward with the need to urge the horse faster.
Yet their progress seemed slow, as though the space
between her heartbeats was a small eternity where she
was left to endure the torment of seeing the open gate
while knowing the stake was behind her.

And then they were through the gate. Relief rushed
through her, leaving her sagging in the saddle.

She couldn't collapse now. She drew on the horror
that had squeezed her tight during the day, pulling
from it the strength she needed to taunt the specter of
death and Colum's vengeance. It was a sweet thing. A
victory unlike any other.

Of course, she hadn't done it alone.

Not that it mattered.

In fact, she discovered she didn't care a single bit for
the circumstances of her deliverance. Life was sweet,
and she preferred to revel in the knowledge that hers
wasn't going to be ending any time soon.

The rest of it... Well, the devil could take the
details.

❧

"We need to rest the horses."

Rolfe pulled up several hours later. His men cheer-
fully slid from the backs of their mounts and lifted

their kilts to relieve themselves. Katherine left her horse drinking from a stream and moved off a way to deal with her own business.

But Rolfe was watching her when she started to return. He'd stopped and directed his attention enough away from her to afford her some measure of privacy, while making it impossible for her to move past him without being seen. Of course she needed to have words with the man. It was only decent, and having so recently tasted the manner of treatment she might be subjected to at the hands of men who held themselves to no standard of conduct, she was loath to lower her standards, even if all she longed for was to swing back up into the saddle and ride until she was back at MacPherson Castle.

"I owe you my gratitude." She spoke clearly, making sure she did not flinch in tone or posture.

"Ye're a bloody fool to have ventured out again in male clothing," he cut back, turning to face her. He was on the high ground, making him appear even more hulking and imposing.

Katherine set her shoulders, refusing to be intimidated. "If I had not, you and your men would have been discovered, and would likely be dead now." She maintained a respectful tone of voice, but that didn't mean it was lacking in strength. She would not allow him to undermine her confidence.

"Me men fight very well, lass."

"You were outnumbered more than two to one," she reminded him. "And the Gordons were looking for blood."

He was still for a moment and offered her a nod of

agreement. Katherine returned it and started to move past him. He stepped into her path.

"Who are ye?"

It was a question, yet edged with the tone of a demand. She decided it was simply his way, for the man had a presence about him. Tyree thirsted for that kind of respect, but would never have it because the Gordon retainer didn't understand that respect, true respect, was earned.

Rolfe knew that fact, and he didn't care for her silence.

"Ye wear MacPherson colors, but ye are English."

"I am."

Rolfe was suddenly too large. She didn't care for how aware of him she was. It was unseemly, and the timing was horrible. Fine, she would accept that she was a woman and perhaps prey to the feelings all females seemed to have trouble controlling, but not at the moment. Such things would simply have to wait.

Her emotions paid her no heed.

"Yer name, lass." He'd crossed his arms over his chest. "Do nae make me ask again."

"Katherine."

She didn't care for how quickly she answered, but chided herself for allowing her temper to rise. It was her name, and there was no reason to deny him such—unless she was simply being peevish. She owed him better than that for the service he'd provided her.

Which stirred a memory.

"Diocail let us go."

"Aye," Rolfe agreed. "I was glad of it, too. I would no' have enjoyed killing the man."

"Tyree would have been a different matter entirely."

Rolfe snorted at her words. "What the devil is Marcus MacPherson thinking to train ye like a lad?"

She tried to go around him, but he stepped into her path again. "Do nae insult the man by denying it. No one wears MacPherson colors or rides a horse out of their gates without his knowing, and I'd say ye've been training for a good many years. Why does he allow ye in his training yard? There is no way he is ignorant of it."

A tingle went down her spine, one that was pure enjoyment. Words were easily spoken, but she'd impressed Rolfe with her skill. Something she'd earned.

"I might ask why not?" Katherine responded.

Rolfe chuckled, only it wasn't a happy sound. It was a male one that offered her a promise of his opinion being different from hers.

"For one reason: the facts of what happened there in the Gordon stronghold. Being a lass means ye are prey to more than a man might be."

"You mean to a man's bruised pride."

"Tyree's was bruised indeed," Rolfe agreed with her. "And it nearly got ye burned at the stake."

A lump decided to form in her throat right then, and it wasn't easy to swallow. Rolfe didn't miss her struggling to cast off her horror.

"Aye, it should stick in yer throat, lass. Ye're damned lucky I was here to go in after ye."

She scoffed at him. "You are the fortunate ones, for without me, there would have been plenty of McTavish blood spilled under the moonlight. I distracted them so they never saw you."

"That stubborn nature of yers is going to get ye killed yet." It was a grudging agreement. Something she had come to expect among burly Highlanders.

"It kept me alive for the last day, so I'll be content and bid you good-bye. I've a mind to make it back to MacPherson land."

"I do nae think so."

"It is not for you to consider at all," Katherine replied. "I belong on MacPherson land."

Rolfe shook his head. "Nae, ye're English, and ye have nae told me who yer sire is. The MacPhersons took ye from somewhere."

"They saved me," she said, her voice full of emotion.

"From what?"

Katherine felt a tingle on her nape. For all that Rolfe McTavish had rescued her from a horrible fate, the fact was that he'd been creeping about in the night, looking to toy with the MacPhersons, and he had held Helen for ransom just after her wedding to Marcus. As far as Highlanders went, he was a rogue—in every sense of the word. Standing firm was the only way to keep a man such as him from making her his next prize. Well, and making sure he didn't have any reason to believe she was worth anything.

"I have thanked you, and now I tell you good night," she said firmly, attempting to end the conversation.

"Tell me yer name now or later." He closed the distance between them, sending a twist through her insides. "I will know who ye are."

"Not if I am on MacPherson land."

"Ye won't be," Rolfe informed her. "Ye are coming back to McTavish land with me."

"You have no right to do any such thing."

"That is exactly the point ye need to absorb." Rolfe edged closer. "When ye venture out away from yer home, ye have no rights, except for the ones ye can ensure through force. There is strength in numbers. Marcus should have taught ye that, woman."

He really was a beast, both in size and thinking. She stepped to the side, but he followed her, unfolding his arms to make it harder to evade him.

"Forgive me." She tried a different approach. "I thought you a man of honor, unlike the Gordons."

His lips curled up, flashing his teeth at her. "Compliments already, Katherine?"

"More of a reminder," she offered softly. "As a hope that you shall not disappoint me by continuing with this rough treatment. I wanted to thank you, and I have. The fact of the matter is, we are both in each other's debt. An honorable man would accept that and allow me to depart."

"Honor comes with knowledge." There was a hard edge to his voice that Katherine knew came from bitter lessons learned the hard way for all of the best reasons.

"Marcus MacPherson has done ye a disservice by no' teaching ye to think of others before riding out into the night alone. Even I was no' out by meself."

That was a hard truth. She nodded and tried to let it be enough of an admission to soothe his need to instruct her. The urge to leave was growing, making her restless and suddenly so aware of the fact that she was standing there in nothing but a shirt and boots, with a man who seemed to notice far too much about her.

"Ye'll taste rougher treatment if I allow ye back to a place that clearly lets ye do as ye please without any regard for the men who might have to fight to defend ye," he stated firmly, his tone telling her he was becoming more and more set in his thinking.

"Stop it," she instructed him. "I am not any of your kin, so concern yourself with those you share blood with. They are the ones you owe your attention to. Not me."

"As ye said, lass, ye did keep me men from having to fight."

"And you have freed me from the Gordons," she was quick to point out. "We are even."

"No' while I know ye are returning to a place where ye will be free to venture into danger whenever ye take the whim to," he declared. "Ye can get on yer horse or I'll put ye on mine, but ye are coming to McTavish land."

"I most certainly am not."

In her agitation, her speech reverted back to pure English pronunciation. But her actions… Well, those she'd learned during her time in the Highlands. Katherine stepped back, widening her stance, and prepared to defend herself.

She was not going anywhere with the beast.

❧

Tyree came awake as a bucket of water hit him in the face. He jerked and snarled, flipping over and knocking his knees against the stone floor of the passageway before he gained his feet.

"So," Diocail Gordon greeted him, "ye thought so

little of the lass's powers that ye decided to have a go at her?"

Tyree looked around, trying to decide if he'd finished what he'd set out to do by coming down to the cells. The door was open, and Diocail was not alone. Some of his men had torches that allowed Tyree to see into the cell.

"Oh, aye," Diocail said. "She's gone, and I doubt Colum is going to be too happy about it. Or pleased with the men who lifted the bar."

"Someone laid me low," Tyree responded. "I never had the bitch."

"Ye deny that ye left the hall after declaring ye were intent on making sure she did nae die a virgin?" Diocail questioned.

Tyree hesitated. His wits were clearing, but he recalled his brazen words well—along with the fact that someone had knocked him in the back of the head. But Diocail was smart. The man had plenty of witnesses.

Tyree decided on a new tactic. "Told ye she was a witch."

"I am no' the fool who thought to let me cock get near her."

Tyree snarled at the word *fool*, but the men surrounding them only shook their heads at him. Diocail had planned the moment well, so Tyree would have to suffer through it.

But he would gain his recompense. On that Tyree was very sure.

Diocail had better sleep lightly.

⚭

"What the devil?" Cedric declared.

Rolfe pressed Katherine into his man's arms before he swung up and into the saddle.

"Let's ride, lads." He gestured to Cedric. "Hand her up, and mind her feet. She has a wicked kick."

"Is that what happened to ye?" Adwin asked as he held the horse steady by the bridle and Cedric lifted Katherine up while she fought. Her arms were bound tight to her torso by one of Rolfe's wide belts.

"Never mind what happened to me." Rolfe scooped Katherine's writhing form out of his retainer's arms and clamped her in front of him on the horse. "Just know we've got us a prize to show for our time away. An Englishwoman to ransom."

Katherine snarled around the strip of wool that he'd used to gag her, and his horse danced in a circle as she struggled. Rolfe clamped his arms around her tightly as his men mounted their horses. He set his heels into the sides of his horse, and the animal happily took off toward home.

Katherine was the only one who argued against it, grumbling against her gag. Rolfe ignored her, keeping his arms locked around her as he headed away from MacPherson land.

"Hate me as ye like, lass," he offered next to her ear. "But I'll not close me eyes and wonder if ye are suffering some horrible fate because Marcus MacPherson allows ye to behave like a hellion."

⁂

"Gone?" Colum's eyes bulged. "Curse and rot yer prick! I should have it cut off ye!"

Tyree faced his laird, his hatred festering as he was forced to remain silent while the rest of the clan looked on, feasting on his humiliation.

"She'd transformed into a white stag," he declared. "Ran me into the wall."

There was a ripple of fear from those watching. Colum clamped his mouth shut, taking a moment to think.

"A witch for certain." Tyree spoke directly to his laird. "Now ye know the truth of why the MacPhersons are undefeated in battle. They have a witch."

"I'm a man, no' a lad," Diocail spoke up. "And I'll no' be frightened by tales best left to old women around a winter hearth. Ye were in yer cups and went down to rape her. More than one saw ye stagger out of the hall. She managed to cut ye when ye were sober. It's little wonder she left ye drooling on the floor when ye tried her while drunk."

"She transformed!" Tyree declared louder. "Unless ye are calling me a liar, Diocail Gordon."

"I call ye a fool," he replied calmly. "And if ye want to fight over it, I am yer man."

"Enough," Colum said. "Ye've both failed me."

The hall went silent, people leaning forward to see what the laird would say. Colum pointed at Tyree. "Ye were in yer cups. Too many say so for it not to be true. Ye'll get fifty lashes on that stake, and ye…" Colum pointed at Diocail. "Ye'll get the same for no' making sure the gate was secure, for the walls were yer duty last night."

There was a shift in the hall as those who had pressed forward subtly moved back in an effort to withdraw from their laird's direct sight. Colum sniffed as he noticed it.

"I will no' be made a fool of!" he declared, his voice cracking with age. "I am laird of the Gordons! Me son will be avenged! I demand it of ye!"

His voice was only an echo of what it had been in his youth. All around him, his hall was falling to ruin, just as Colum himself was. His clan was thin and tired of his cries for vengeance.

But Colum Gordon still drew breath, so they followed his commands. Diocail felt his stomach turn. He'd been raised by his mother to dream of the day he returned to the Gordon towers and took command of them. He was glad she hadn't lived to see the ruin the clan had fallen into. Some men didn't live long enough, and others—such as Colum—lived too long.

Let the old man sentence him to some lashes. Diocail would never be sorry he'd made sure the little lass was free.

※

Rolfe McTavish was warm.

Deliciously so, considering Katherine wore only a shirt.

She tried to avoid thinking about how he kept her warm, but as the miles dropped behind them, her temper cooled as exhaustion took command of everything in her world. She simply didn't have any strength left to nurse her wounded pride. For certain, she was furious with him for taking her hostage, but it paled in comparison to the fate that would have been hers at the hands of the Gordons.

So by sunrise, she faced the first rays of light with gratitude.

Rolfe kept them moving with only short breaks for the entire day.

He lifted his hand and called a halt once the light began to fade. He handed her down to one of his captains and slid off the back of his horse next to her.

She'd never seen him by light of day. The sun showed her a head of blond hair that complemented his green eyes. His face was cut and chiseled, declaring him a man who didn't sit at the high table indulging his appetites while his men toiled through the daylight hours. She knew the difference better than most because England was more forgiving to such nobles. They became fat and slow, two things Rolfe McTavish certainly was not.

His captain released the belt holding her arms, and she stepped away from Rolfe, shooting him a scathing look as she yanked the gag off. Her jaw was stiff from the thing and her tongue dry as ashes.

That comparison tempered her thoughts, keeping her silent as she decided not to blister his ears.

She would be ashes without his aid.

So she turned and walked behind an outcropping of rocks to relieve herself.

But her restraint didn't last when she caught sight of Adwin taking a position on the high ground above her. The captain had his back to her, but he was clearly there to ensure she didn't make a run for it. Coming back around the outcropping, she watched as Rolfe tied her horse to his with a length of rope. He finished with a hard motion of his hand and turned his back on her before hiking over a ridge to seek his own privacy.

It would be a long walk, but she shifted back a step and then another, intending to drop back behind the outcropping of rocks that she'd just come around.

Adwin caught her by the upper arm and pulled her toward the other men.

"Release me," she insisted.

"No need to be so agitated, lass," the captain said before allowing her to shake off his hold. "It's just a bit of ransom. Unlike with the Gordons, no harm will come to ye. Now sit down and rest while ye can."

One of the men patted the ground next to him.

"I didn't think you were feuding with the MacPhersons."

"We aren't." Rolfe had returned, and she jumped because the man was right behind her. She ended up facing him and took a step backward.

Katherine felt her eyes narrow. Christ! Fate was having a merry time with her, it would seem! Why now, of all times, did she suddenly develop an awareness of men?

"We're needling them," Adwin informed her in a voice edged with experience. "Ye'll be well and treated fine. Ye've put up a decent fight, enough to satisfy yer honor. Now sit. No one wants to truss ye up."

"Excellent," she responded. "In that case, I will be on my way since we seem to be finished with this 'needling.'"

Rolfe was watching her, a glitter in his eyes that promised her an argument.

Or something else that she wasn't all too certain of.

She decided she didn't want to know because her belly was twisting as though she was anticipating something.

"Can nae expect an English lass to understand," Cedric spoke up. "Best keep a sharp eye on her."

There was a murmur of agreement among the McTavish retainers. Many of them had lain back and rolled themselves in their plaids to catch a bit of sleep.

"Settle here, lass." Adwin tried to cajole her once more. "We've no plaid to spare, so we'll put ye between us to keep ye warm."

"I will not—"

The last word was barely past her lips when Rolfe scooped her off her feet. Another one of those startled, feminine sounds escaped her lips before he put her exactly where he wanted to. What grated on her nerves was the amusement his men gained from it. But flipping over in her agitation only made her shirt ride up her thighs. She froze as she tugged it down, and Rolfe took advantage of the moment, lying down next to her. He turned his back to her, and Adwin started scooting toward her until she was wedged tight between them.

Oh, it felt good.

She tried to find some reason why she should resent it, but the truth was that she would be peevish if she continued to suckle her anger.

Not that she had much choice. Now that she was warm, exhaustion took over, ripping her away from everything except her need to rest.

∽

The McTavish stronghold had two main towers. A long building connected them, and once Rolfe pulled her inside, Katherine realized that the great hall was inside it. There were more refinements here, making her think of England. More tapestries on the walls, the scent of beeswax candles lingering in the air, and chairs with backs. There were still a good number of benches to help accommodate the large number of retainers sitting at the tables for meals, but there were also clusters of chairs with wide seats and armrests placed around the hall.

She understood the reason for those chairs when Rolfe brought her before his father. Laird McTavish was missing part of his leg. The wooden peg was only visible when he stood because the rest of it was hidden inside a boot.

Only a laird would have a boot made for a peg. It was an extravagance, but Katherine admitted that the hall appeared to suggest that the McTavish could afford such things.

"What have ye brought me, Rolfe?"

Katherine found herself facing a man who was clearly Rolfe's sire. He had the same huge frame along with green eyes. His people began to gather around, aiming curious looks at her, and she resisted the urge to tug on the bottom of her shirt.

"Katherine," Rolfe answered his father. "I found her wearing the MacPherson plaid like a lad and she will no' tell me her father's name, but she is English. So I brought her home after stealing her from the Gordons."

There was a round of laughter from the McTavish.

"You have neglected to mention how I prevented you and your men from being taken by those same Gordons." Katherine kept her voice even.

Laird McTavish's eyes narrowed as he looked at his son. "Ye were seen by the Gordons?"

"The lass stepped between us," Rolfe explained. "The Gordons should be grateful for that. Instead, they decided to burn her as a witch as a strike against the MacPhersons for Lye Rob's death."

Laird McTavish grunted and lowered himself into one of the chairs. Katherine caught a flicker of distaste in his eyes as he was forced to remove his weight from the peg.

"Colum is a fool to be seeking vengeance. Lye Rob lost a fight he started. When ye steal a man's wife, ye have to expect any decent Highlander to come look- ing for yer blood. Bhaic MacPherson was within his rights, and I'd have called him a dishonorable coward if he'd failed to meet the challenge of having his wife stolen. An unbedded bride is one thing, a wife alto- gether different."

There was a ripple of male agreement around them.

"Do ye have a husband?"

Katherine realized where Rolfe gained his sense of authority. Laird McTavish embodied the same, and she found herself shaking her head immediately. Unlike Tyree Gordon, neither Rolfe nor his sire struck her as undeserving of respect.

"A contract?" Laird McTavish leaned forward as he pressed her.

Katherine discovered herself hesitating to answer. He didn't care for it and slapped the arm of the chair.

"Either ye do, or ye do no'. Speak up."

The McTavishes didn't care for her silence. There were hard looks sent her way as more men arrived.

She resisted the urge to squirm. Wearing men's clothing was something she'd willingly decided to do. There would be no shrinking from it.

"I have not seen my father in over ten years," she answered smoothly. "I am bastard born."

There was a reaction to that announcement, but it was not as great as it might have been in England. The Scots were a bit more practical when it came to what side of the bedsheet one was born on. To their minds, blood was blood. With or without the church's blessing, it was still a tie that could never be broken.

"Who is yer sire?" Laird McTavish asked bluntly.

"It does not matter. His newest wife was quite clear that I should expect naught from him."

Laird McTavish slowly smiled. "The fact that ye are no' willing to tell me says the man is important." He considered her for a long moment, sweeping her from head to toe. "Aye, ye have the look of nobility with that fine pale skin. And the MacPhersons have allowed ye to run wild. That tells me no one wants to cross yer blood."

"You are simply disappointed," Katherine spoke softly. "It is understandable, yet I have spoken the truth."

Laird McTavish was chuckling. He suddenly slapped the arm of the chair and looked at his son. "When ye brought Helen Grant here, was no' there some mention of Morton trying to force a bride on Marcus MacPherson?"

Rolfe shifted, his expression darkening. "Aye. A girl too young for marriage."

Laird McTavish contemplated her for a long moment, his lips slowly curling into a grin of victory.

"Well done!" Laird McTavish declared. "The Earl of Morton may be willing to pay more for her than the MacPhersons. Put her abovestairs."

Katherine felt hollow. The security she'd felt in Scotland melted away as easily as sugar in the rain. Someone gripped her bicep, and she didn't bother to look at who it was. The two towers were on either side of the hall.

"Oh for Christ's sake, point the way. I certainly have no wish to go back to your hall," she groused at her guide as she was smashed next to him in the narrow stairway.

A thick finger appeared in front of her in response. She forced her feet to move, recalling Marcus's words that choosing one's battles was wisest. If there was no clear path to victory, better to bide your time and wait for better circumstances.

She'd be ready when they arrived.

❧

"Ye should have told me who yer sire was."

Katherine wasn't expecting Rolfe.

She turned and found him standing behind her in the chamber. His men were outside in the hallway.

Waiting to bar the door.

She couldn't stop the shiver that went down her spine in response.

He contemplated her for a long moment, looking as though it bothered him to see her upset.

"Why?" she asked. "So you could celebrate your victory sooner?"

"I would have risked taking ye back to Marcus."

His expression implied that he was serious, but she only saw what she longed for. "I doubt that."

His jaw tightened as she questioned his word. Katherine stared straight at him, making it clear she wasn't going to shirk from his displeasure.

"I would no' have risked ye being given back to the Earl of Morton," Rolfe said softly.

"It is ever so simple to apologize once deeds are done." She'd meant to cut him with her words, but all she did was send another chill across her skin as she recognized how dire her circumstances were. She had spent years having nightmares about the Earl of Morton and the way he viewed her as a thing to be traded for what he wished.

It is better than being burned at the stake…

She held tight to that thought, yet it was difficult to accept that as a blessing. She turned her back on Rolfe, needing to maintain some sort of poise.

"Ye know why I did no' take ye back to Marcus." Rolfe wasn't willing to be dismissed. "He allowed ye to act foolishly."

"No more so than you." She turned back to face him.

Rolfe shook his head, his expression serious. "Yer fate at the hands of the Gordons would have been horrible, but over soon. The repercussions of it, well, they would have claimed lives for years. Marcus could no' have let it pass, no' when ye were under his personal protection. It's becoming clearer why he trained ye. The man is no fool, and he knows the English have few friends in the Highlands. There would have been a feud."

He started for the door but stopped before crossing the threshold. "If ye can nae think of the men who would fight to avenge ye, then ye are still a child, Katherine."

He sent her a hard look before he let his men close the chamber door.

He was right.

She detested the facts and the harsher side of Fate for not making her see the truth in some easier fashion. But life had never taught her any lessons the easy way.

Today was no exception.

❦

The crack of the whip was a sound every Gordon knew.

As Colum grew older, whippings had become more frequent. Tyree watched as Diocail took his punishment first. The damned bastard had boldly jerked his shirt off and walked up to the stake without waiting to be ordered to it. He was holding on to it, his back crisscrossed with red stripes.

Somehow, he'd managed to transform a punishment into a reason to gain respect.

Colum sat in his chair, which had been moved outside for the spectacle.

He needed to die…

Laird or not, it was time for Colum Gordon to join the son he couldn't seem to forget. The Gordons needed a strong laird, and Tyree planned to be that man.

"Fifty."

Diocail let go of the stake and turned to face the men watching. His face was red, but he growled before striding off as though nothing pained him. The blood dripping down his back should have made a liar of him, but the men who watched him leave all wore expressions of respect for his stamina.

An idea started to form in Tyree's head. Fortune favored the bold, and the Lord helped those who helped themselves. So maybe it was time to plan Colum's death and make certain Diocail was the one blamed for it. Without a clear successor, the matter of choosing the next laird would come down to a vote, and the Gordons would not vote for a murderer.

Yes, it was time to plan his future.

Which would begin with Colum's death.

                            *

"Ye're no' pleased with me."

Rolfe considered his father and nodded. "The Earl of Morton is a bastard. Ye know it. I would no' have brought the lass here if I'd thought ye'd be doing business with him."

Inside his father's study, Rolfe could speak his mind. His father eyed him, torn between admiring Rolfe's courage and being annoyed with his son for questioning him.

It was a look Rolfe saw more often than not.

"Look around ye." His father opened his fingers and fanned them around the room. "Ye have a fine inheritance, and make no mistake, it came from yer kin making choices with their business sense." His father tapped the top of his desk with his forefinger. "But that is no' what is eating at ye, boy."

Rolfe stiffened, earning a chuckle from his sire.

"That's what I thought," William McTavish declared. "Ye've got a whiff of her in yer nostrils."

"Father—"

"Do nae deny it." William snorted at him with a grin. "Truth be told, she stirred me member as well. What with her in naught but a shirt so that every man among us might glimpse those tempting tits."

"That is no' what we are discussing," Rolfe insisted.

His father roared with laughter, throwing his head back and letting his voice hit the ceiling. Rolfe made a sound under his breath that was less than respectful.

His father sobered. "Aye, back to the business. She is that, my son—business. Do nae go soft on me."

"Ransom her to the MacPhersons, and ye'll have yer gain."

"And what will ye get from that bargain?"

Rolfe was caught off guard by the question. His father was serious.

"Ye brought her here, and I'm grateful for the respect ye show me beyond that door, but she's yer prize. The clan will expect ye to get as much as ye can for her."

"I've told ye what I want done with her." Rolfe knew better than to answer quickly. His father had a razor-sharp mind.

"But no' why ye argue with me," William responded quickly, a suspicious look in his eyes. "If she did step between yer men and the Gordons, why did ye no' allow her to go free? I can see that ye would have decided it was an even exchange. Yet she is here."

His father knew him well. Rolfe stared back at the gleam in his sire's face.

"The foolish chit almost started a feud," Rolfe replied. "She needed to be taught a lesson."

"Ye're no' her kin or her husband to be thinking of her education. Here, she is a prize."

Rolfe drew in a deep breath and let it out slowly. "She did put herself between the Gordons and me men. We were outnumbered, and that's a fact."

His father absorbed the knowledge and held silent as he contemplated what it meant.

"So," Rolfe continued, "I would appreciate it if ye did nae contact the Earl of Morton. Katherine needs a lesson, but I owe her a measure of gratitude."

His father nodded. "Off with ye, then."

Rolfe tugged on the corner of his bonnet before he left the study. William McTavish waited until his son was gone before he looked up to see his half brother emerging from the shadows.

"What say ye?" William asked.

"I think ye needs be careful how ye go," Niul responded. "Rolfe will nae forgive ye for forcing this issue easily."

William snorted. "He barely knows her."

"Does nae matter," Niul replied. "Ye know Rolfe has a sense of honor that is no' going to be pushed aside."

His half brother sent him a knowing look that made William shift in his seat. William remembered well his desolation after losing his leg. His pride has been damaged as well as his body. His son had been the one to force him to emerge from his chambers.

"Aye, and yet Morton is the regent. The man rules Scotland in all but name. We have more to lose than the

MacPhersons if the man is angry with us. The march from Edinburgh to McTavish land is much shorter."

"James is growing up," Niul replied.

"But he's been raised by Morton," William cut back. "And do nae forget that Morton is a Douglas. Even if the man loses his head, there will be plenty of his kin to remember who their enemies are. And before ye tell me that Morton knows naught of the girl, remember that secrets never stay hidden for long. Rolfe snatched her from under the Gordons' noses."

Niul nodded. "Aye, that tale will spread far and fast. So discover who her sire is. He must be important, or Morton would no' have tried to force her on Marcus."

William's face suddenly lit. "Brenda Grant would know. She was there. Go up to Grant land and see what that woman has to say."

Niul scoffed at his sibling. "The way I hear, Brenda Grant answers to no man since her escape from Morton and court."

William waved his hand. "Use that handsome face of yers. Let her think ye've arrived to pay her court. Her damned cousin will no' make a match for her that she does nae approve of. For all that I hear, Symon Grant is a man to be reckoned with. I wonder why the man is soft concerning the women of his house. And if she's fool enough to be completely taken with ye, bed her quick."

Niul grinned. "Ye can be sure I will. Wedding her, on the other hand... I'll leave the business decisions to you."

William chuckled at his brother's humor. Niul liked women, and he had the devil's luck when it came to his features. The lasses flocked to him. Niul enjoyed it full well, as any man should. William was forever having to deal with Niul's cast-off lovers trying to gain recompense and acknowledgment of his bastards. None of them had succeeded so far, because William would protect his bloodline for Rolfe. Recognizing bastards would only lead to splits in the clan.

And he would do what was best to ensure his son inherited more than William had. It was the truest test of a laird: to increase his holdings and make certain his son inherited.

But there was one thing William didn't have, and that was a noble title. Indeed, it was fine to be a laird in the Highlands, but in the more modern world, noble titles carried weight. Morton might bestow one of those, and that would be worth a great deal.

Even worth a fight with his son.

Anger faded, but a noble title... Well, that was something that stayed. William rang the small bell sitting next to his desk. A few moments later, there was a shuffle of feet as his secretary came into the study.

"I need a letter written to the Earl of Morton."

Three

CLEAN.

Katherine sighed and stood in front of the hearth in naught but her skin while she looked at her fingernails. They were chipped and broken—unlike her stepmother's, which had always been carefully shaped and buffed.

But for the moment, Katherine was absorbed by the fact that there wasn't a bit of dirt left under her nails or on any other part of her body. She sighed and turned so the fire could dry her hair. She had distant memories of bathing in a shift, but those habits had fallen away in Scotland.

The Scots were far more practical. The purpose of a bath was to get your skin clean, and cloth was expensive, greatly so. No coin was spent on a garment whose only use was to shield modesty while sitting in a bathing tub. She'd gladly discarded the often-tedious ceremonies of England as she'd settled into the Highlands.

Katherine smiled as she felt the warmth from the fire drying her bare skin. In England, the Highlanders were labeled savages and wicked.

Well, that suited her rather well.

Thanks to Marcus.

Her thoughts darkened. He'd been more of a brother to her than any kin she had ever known. He'd made certain she grew strong, and that was a gift she treasured. It pained her to know she would cost him.

Rolfe was correct; she'd been acting like a child who didn't consider what her actions wrought.

Well, no more.

She moved across the chamber and picked up a shift that had been laid out for her. She couldn't fault the McTavishes, because they had provided her with good clothing to wear. The shift was made of soft linen that felt good against her skin. There were stockings for her, too. She pulled them up her legs and secured them with garters before putting on her boots.

She really had been thinking like a child to believe the cobbler hadn't sought payment for the fine footwear, or that the man hadn't noticed they were men's boots. They closed all the way up to just below her knees with the aid of antler-horn buttons that she wound a leather lace around. She'd certainly been grateful for them in the Gordon stronghold.

Well, now she had another place to escape from. Marcus had taught her to be strong, and the best way to repay that was to take care of herself.

There were two sets of skirts for her to choose from, both made of sturdy wool. She chose one that looked as if it was hemmed correctly for her height and slipped it up and over her head. The waistband was worked with several eyelets that she threaded a lace through. Next, there were bodices. Her McTavish guards had been unwilling to allow any of the maids to stay and help her dress.

Katherine smiled as she recalled how the men had stood guard over her while the tub was filled. In the past, she'd taken pleasure in revealing her strength and ability. Now, she realized it would have been far better if the McTavishes had believed her to be helpless. So she'd bitten her lip and stood quietly, trying her best to appear meek. Perhaps they thought their clansmen were exaggerating the tales about her abilities.

The bodices had boning in them so that once she laced one up, her breasts were supported. It had become harder over the last year to bind herself. She'd hoped that her breasts simply wouldn't grow because of the wide strip of cloth she used to flatten them. But nature seemed to be determined to have her way, and the bodice cupped two rather large mounds.

Katherine looked at herself in a mirror, enjoying the sight of herself in a dress. Sometimes, she longed for a life that didn't make her choose to discard her gender. It was just that a woman's place was so very difficult to stomach. Such as her current circumstances. She was expected to be submissive and accept that she would just have to wait to be ransomed.

Perhaps that might have been acceptable if the idea of being returned to the Earl of Morton wasn't a possibility. Or to England, for that matter. It had been a long time since she'd been under her father's roof, and she would be an unwanted mouth to feed.

So she had to use her wits and her skills to escape.

The chamber was on the second floor. She looked out of the window, but it was too high to descend from, even if she knotted the sheets. The knot might give or her hands fail to hold her.

But she suddenly looked back at the second set of clothing as an idea formed in her mind.

Maybe she needed to fight smart and dupe her captors with the aid of their own fear.

∞

Someone screamed.

Rolfe looked up, as did a dozen or so men. There was a commotion coming from the new tower, and it took him about two seconds to decide Katherine was the likely cause. He went running around the gate and into the yard, just in time to see a woman dangling from a crude sort of rope from the third-story window.

"Bloody fool," he snarled as he pushed people out of his way to try to get to her faster.

She was dangling from the rope, twirling around and around, and he suddenly stopped, realizing there was no weight on the rope, at least not the weight of a person. It was flapping like a child's toy. There were men in the window of her chamber, tugging on the bedsheet to pull her up. They stumbled out of sight as they tugged too hard, anticipating a person's weight.

Rolfe scanned the area. Everyone was hurrying into the courtyard to get a glimpse at what was causing the commotion.

Katherine would be heading the other way. He turned and ran toward the stables. He caught sight of a skirt as she went around a bend in the stalls toward the back door that was open to let in fresh air.

"Katherine."

She turned on him, her eyes wide as she realized he'd caught her.

"Ye're a bloody hellion, woman!"

Her eyes narrowed in response. She reached out and picked up a pitchfork used to move hay.

"Yes, and I am more trouble than you need."

"On that we agree," Rolfe stated.

"Your lesson is well learned," she argued. "Now, leave me be. I do not wish to hurt you. I am simply set on going home."

His lips twitched into an arrogant grin. "Put that down so I do nae have to hurt ye."

"You said you would not risk me being turned over to the Earl of Morton."

That made him stop edging toward her. "I did."

"But your father is laird here."

He drew in a deep breath. "He is."

Katherine felt a much-needed breath of relief fill her lungs. "Good. Go back the way you came."

He shook his head. "As ye have learned, lass, the McTavishes are no' the worst ye might run across. I will no' allow ye to leave alone."

"I will go straight back to MacPherson land," she offered. "I promise, no more rides at night."

Katherine tightened her grip on the pitchfork, but she was loath to use it.

"Ye'll have to trust me, Katherine."

Her name came across his lips in a deep tone that send a shiver down her spine. It mixed with the way her heart was racing, producing a very unexpected sort of excitement.

"You owe me a debt," she reminded him.

"No' at the expense of yer safety." Rolfe stepped closer, eyeing her weapon. "No honorable man would let ye take the risk of crossing all the clans between here and MacPherson land."

She lifted the pitchfork, shooting him a clear warning. Rolfe didn't back down. He was edging toward her, backing her into a corner. She twisted away, bringing the pitchfork up before the wall behind prevented her from using it. For a moment, she hesitated, wishing things might be different between them.

That was her undoing. Rolfe launched himself at her, pushing her back, and claiming her weapon in a motion that knocked the breath from her. But she went with it, turning back so he stumbled past her. He took the pitchfork away with him, while she gained a few steps of freedom.

It wouldn't be enough. She knew that. She'd have to disable him or submit to his will. She lifted her foot and kicked the back of his knee.

He let out a curse and hooked his hands into her skirt as he went down. He twisted and turned, tumbling her as she tried to get her feet braced beneath her.

"Curse and rot this dress!" she exclaimed as it trapped her legs.

"I preferred ye out of it meself."

Rolfe landed on top of her in a hard, panting mountain of muscle that she was powerless to move. She flattened her feet beneath her and tried to heave him off her. All he did was roll over and take her with him, until she was beneath him once more with her wrists held captive in his hands as he pinned them to the ground near her head.

"However"—his breath was close enough to tease her lips—"I believe it's better that ye have more than a shirt on right this moment."

"Get off…me…" She was breathless and panting, her heart hammering as she shuddered.

He seemed to feel it, suddenly lifting a bit of his weight off her as he stroked the insides of her wrists with his thumbs.

She shuddered again, this time twisting away not because of any conscious choice but because the sensation was too deep somehow, too purely intimate to endure.

"I should," he rasped, drawing her attention back to him. There was something in his tone that stroked another place inside her, one she hadn't known might be touched by another human being.

In his eyes, she caught a promise that made her belly twist. It was so deeply personal that she withered, straining against his hold on her wrists.

"No' just yet, lass," he said. "I'll be claiming a prize from ye first."

She knew he was going to kiss her before he angled his head and fitted his mouth against hers. She moaned softly, unable to remain silent as sensation went flowing through her as if a dam had ruptured. She'd never realized what it held back, and now it swept her up in its grip, tumbling her with its power and rolling her completely within its current.

The kiss was hard, just like his body. He didn't

allow her to keep her mouth closed, but pressed her lips open with the motion of his own as he moved his mouth over hers. It was overwhelming, like a clap of thunder directly overhead. She was left with her ears ringing, off balance as she reeled, and all the while, the storm continued.

And then she was free.

One moment, she was full of the taste of him, every inch of her body prey to the sensation of his contact, the bite of his hold on her wrists confirming how much stronger he was than herself, and then the air brushing over her was cool because he'd withdrawn. She rolled over, frantically trying to recover her poise, and found him facing her as he balanced on his haunches just a foot away.

They stared at each other for a long moment. She thought she saw uncertainty in his eyes, although she wasn't really sure her mind was working. But the stall where they'd landed was full of the raspy sounds of their breathing.

"Has no one ever kissed ye before?"

Of all the things he might have said in that moment, his question caught her off guard. She looked away, realizing that it bothered her to have to admit that no one had.

She heard him mutter in Gaelic and looked back toward him. "Just because I didn't kiss you back doesn't mean—"

"It is no' a shame," Rolfe informed her softly. "At least no' yers. It's mine to admit that I let me temper get the best of me. For that, ye have me apology."

He straightened up, reaching back down to offer

her a hand. She was crouched in the corner, watching him warily, when her senses cleared enough for her to realize she must look like a trapped fox.

She didn't take his hand but rose under her own power. He nodded slowly, admiration in his eyes that granted her some measure of poise. Was it for the way she failed to cry? She wasn't sure. But she did know she wouldn't be showing him any sort of weakness.

There was a pounding of feet. Rolfe looked out into the stable and whistled. "I have her, lads."

She was grateful he was looking away during that moment of crushing defeat. She clamped her jaw tight as she felt her fingernails digging into the wall behind her. The impulse to turn and break it down was strong but senseless.

So she set her shoulders and faced the men who skidded to a halt in front of the stall. They took her in, shock registering on their faces at the sight of her.

Which pleased her at last because she knew she'd given them hell.

And she planned to do it again.

⁓

Helen was wringing her hands. She didn't question Marcus when he came in because she knew his body. He was stiff from long hours in the saddle. Dirt was caked onto his skin, and his boots were covered in mud. His horse eagerly took off toward the stable and a warm stall.

Bhaic stood on the top steps, waiting for his brother to reach him.

"The Gordons had her, planned to burn her as a witch."

Helen sucked in her breath, as did Ailis. Marcus cut her a quick glance. "Somehow, she managed to escape. Rumor is there were McTavishes in the Gordon stronghold as well, but I've no solid proof of it."

"Rolfe McTavish?" Helen asked in a ghost of a whisper.

Her husband nodded.

"I pray so." Ailis spoke up, gaining the attention of her husband and brother by marriage. "They'll just want ransom again."

"We can nae be certain of that," Bhaic informed his wife.

"It's better than the Gordons," Helen offered, but she knew her husband. He took the welfare of all MacPhersons personally.

He trudged toward the bathhouse, and Helen followed. He shed his clothing as she readied a tub for him.

"I failed her," he said at last.

"We share the blame." Helen rubbed a lump of soap across his back. "I should have argued with ye when ye allowed her to train."

Marcus grunted. "The good Father Matthew should have said something about that."

"I'd like to have heard it." She worked the soap into his hair. "Let me see, it is a sin for the wife to argue with her lord and husband…and yet it is a sin to allow a young girl to run wild like a lad."

"Aye," Marcus agreed. "It would have been a very interesting conversation."

One they would never have. He sighed. "We'll have to wait, to see what news comes."

He'd taught his son not to lie.

Just as a father should.

William McTavish watched Rolfe tug on his bonnet and leave his study.

"Are ye sure ye need to send the lad out?"

It was his senior captain Boyd who asked the question.

"Ye saw her." William reached for his mug and downed what was left in it. "Hay stuck to her skirts and hair."

"She was trying to escape. To tell the truth, I can nae recall when I saw such determination in a lass before. Stuffing the bedding into those clothes and sending them out of the window was a fine idea, sure enough. Fooled the men into thinking she'd gone out that way, and all the while, she was just waiting on them to leave the door open for her... Clever."

William snorted. "I still remember what a woman looks like when she's been kissed." He pointed at Boyd. "That lass looked startled down to her garters. Which means she's a maiden, and Rolfe is... Well...he's..."

"A man to be proud of," Boyd offered.

"Aye."

"An honorable man," Boyd continued.

"Which is why I've sent him off to the Robertsons," William replied. "I'll no' have him near that wench. If she was nae worth something, I'd turn her out and let her make her own way back to MacPherson land. But know this, I will not have me son wed to an English chit."

Boyd nodded. "It would nae be good, unless she brought a dowry worth overlooking her English blood."

"There are things more valuable than coin."

Boyd lifted an eyebrow at his laird's words. William looked around first, making sure no one was inside his study. "The Earl of Morton stole that girl to use in an alliance with England. She's a woman now, ripe for marriage. I sent a letter to him to see if he will ennoble me line in exchange for her."

"The man might just insist ye have Rolfe wed her," Boyd cautioned.

William grunted. "I'll see her wed to Niul first."

"Ye think ye'd have a choice in the matter?"

William merely shrugged. "The man might just have to take what alliance I give him."

Boyd didn't correct his laird, but he had his doubts. The Earl of Morton was king, or at least he might as well be, and from what news came up from Edinburgh, it was clear the earl was intent on making sure he maintained power.

"For now, put that wench in the cellars."

Boyd was shocked. "Ye'd do that to a lass?"

William nodded. "I need her more submissive, ready to do me bidding, and too a-feared to cross me. Make sure Angus knows I'll cut off his balls if he fucks her. The earl might have her inspected."

"Well now, taking an English bride is bad enough," Boyd agreed. "Getting saddled with another man's leavings... That's downright pitiful."

William made a low sound of agreement in the back of his throat. He pointed at a pitcher, and Boyd refilled his mug. He detested having to ask for help. The damned wooden leg he was saddled with was almost more than his pride might bear. It had been

Rolfe who refused to let him stay abovestairs, and it had proven that Rolfe was a man grown. William would be wise to listen to him.

Yes, he was a fine son. More like his mother when it came to his honor, but a woman could afford to be devoted to things such as honesty and integrity. A laird had to temper that with the will to improve his clan's lot. A noble title. It was a fine thing to want. The regents surrounding the young king made sure to not hand out titles to the Highlanders, preferring to keep them all beneath their higher stations. The Earl of Sutherland was one exception, and William planned to be another.

Rolfe would come around in his thinking.

⤸

Grant land

"Ye are very fetching," Niul complimented Brenda Grant honestly.

The woman was breathtaking and a few years past the first blossom of her youth. He decided maturity suited her even better, and wondered just what skill she had when it came to riding a man. Virgins were tiresome with their shyness.

"And ye"—Brenda looked straight into his eyes and fluttered her eyelashes—"are clearly accustomed to yer handsome face melting the hearts of the women on McTavish land."

Niul chuckled. "Perhaps I'm the lucky one to be sent up here after all. And here I was thinking it was another duty thrust upon me by me brother."

"Happy to be proven wrong?" Brenda asked him in a lyrical tone.

Niul took the opportunity to lean closer to her, but froze when he felt the point of a dagger against his thigh. Brenda's eyes flickered with hard purpose.

"Brenda," Symon Grant spoke his cousin's name in warning. "Tell the man ye are no' interested and be done with it."

Brenda withdrew the dagger and looked at Symon. "Men such as…him do nae listen to a female. They think us all creatures to serve their needs."

Brenda rose and lowered herself before the new laird of the Grants. In a motion that was so graceful that Niul discovered himself enchanted by it, she turned and left the hall.

"Why do ye allow her to behave in that manner?"

Symon angled his head so he could make eye contact with Niul down the head table. "Brenda did her duty in wedding her father's choice of husband for her. The Earl of Morton used her cruelly, and me own father arranged a match for her that was distasteful, so…" Symon sent him a hard look. "It was me father who decided she would be her own woman on account of the service she's done for the Grants. Make no mistake, McTavish. I will be keeping me promise to me father. If ye want her, best learn a thing or two about courting."

Niul didn't care for Symon's words, especially when the Grant captains were listening in. "I've heard rumors of the way it is here on Grant land now that ye are laird." Niul took a deep drink from his mug. "Heard ye spent a year following that Lindsey wench about before she agreed to wed ye."

Symons knuckles popped as he curled his hand into a fist. "Never"—his voice was as tight as his body—"speak of my wife again."

The Grant captains were shooting Niul hard looks. He wasn't willing to back down, and not just because he wanted to pick a fight. There was a chill in the air in Grant Castle. It raised Niul's hackles and made him want to kick Symon Grant in the arse. The man had a full mourning beard on his face, growth that was over two years old.

"This place needs life," Niul began. "Ye and yer cousin are the only members left of yer line. Ye need some weddings here."

Symon slammed his fist onto the tabletop. "I did so and buried me wife before a year had passed. No more talk on the matter."

He'd loved her. Niul drew off a long sip of ale and contemplated Symon. Since Niul was a bastard, William had made sure his half brother never wed. Never produced another branch of the family tree. The laird had no idea how much Niul resented his ways or how Niul longed for a son of his own. One he might recognize and raise up. Without one, he found himself seeing Symon as a younger man in need of guidance. Everyone around the new laird was too intimidated by his position to do what needed doing.

Being a bastard had its advantages at times.

"Women die in childbed, man. Ye sound like me brother, cursing Fate for the loss of his leg when he is hardly the first man to suffer a wound that festers."

"I said—"

"I heard what ye said." Niul raised his voice. "And

I see how yer captains are looking at their suppers and letting ye seep yerself in yer mourning. I'm no' afraid of ye, boy... She is dead. Long cold in her grave, and it's far past time someone found the balls to tell ye to notice how long it's been."

"Bastard!"

Symon roared as he came up and out of his chair. Niul met him, the pair of them rolling over the long head table as they grappled.

"Ye aren't fit...to speak her name..." Symon snarled.

Niul staggered back under a hard hit, but raised his leg and drove his knee into Symon's belly when the Grant laird tried to follow his first blow with a second one. "Ye are nae dead, man." Niul smashed his elbow into the side of Symon's jaw, sending him staggering away. "Stop expecting her to rise up and give ye children."

Symon wasn't ready to listen yet. He charged at Niul, and they collided like bears. There was grunting and curses, but everyone stayed away. Niul finally broke free and threw his hands wide.

"Look at yer men, Laird Grant!"

Symon stiffened, his rage cracking as he did indeed cast a look around him.

"They are no' stopping me because they recognize the truth of me words." Niul softened his tone. "Do ye think it brings me pleasure to say them? I nearly watched me brother die abovestairs when he lost his leg and would nae be seen. Bastard? If I truly were less of a man, I'd be after yer cousin in the hope that our children will inherit after ye leave the Grants without an heir." He spat blood on the floor and wiped his mouth across his sleeve. "Instead, I'm trying to kick yer arse and drag ye kicking and screaming back into the light of life."

Symon slowly grinned. "Well, ye are no' the smartest man, are ye?"

Niul opened his arms wide and performed a courtesy, lowering himself. "The lot of a bastard—to please as often as I might while still being expected to fail at it due to me lack of breeding."

Symon nodded and slowly walked toward him. He offered his hand, and Niul grasped the Grant's wrist.

"We all have our lots," Symon said as he finished shaking Niul's hand. "I thank ye for reminding me of mine."

⚶

Symon turned to see Brenda walking down the passageway with a tray in her hands.

"Ye're going to tend him?" he asked, surprise thick in his tone.

Brenda only smiled at him. "Yes."

"Why?" Symon asked in a quiet tone.

Brenda moved up next to him and cast a look at the portrait he'd been staring at. His wife looked back at them, the paint making her appear almost lifelike.

"Because I could no' give ye the thrashing ye needed to keep ye from following Tara into the grave."

Symon tore his gaze from the painting and looked at Brenda. She watched the pain still flickering in his eyes.

"This is for ye." She held out a razor. "I sent a maid up to yer chamber with hot water and soap."

Symon drew in a stiff breath and fought the urge

to look back at the portrait. He took the razor and offered Brenda a stiff nod. He started to walk away, looking as though his feet were heavy, but he stopped and turned back toward Brenda.

"Ye are right," he said firmly. "I will shave this mourning beard off."

Brenda inclined her head.

"And I am no' the only one who needs to start living again, Brenda."

It was her turn to stiffen. Symon offered her no mercy as he nodded. "For all that I have no' been able to move past that moment when Fate decided to take the woman I loved from me, I would no' have learned what it is to love without her. It changes a soul, enriches the world around ye in a way, and no one can understand until they allow themselves to love another."

He pointed at her. "Ye need to move past yer history too. Let someone touch ye, and hopefully teach ye the pleasure of being a woman."

"Symon," she hissed in a low tone.

"I am correct." He cut her off by holding up the razor between them. "Just as ye are right about me needing a thrashing. Ye've never chosen a lover. It can be more than duty, Brenda, and it falls to me to say so bluntly since yer parents are gone, and ye and I are the only kin we both have left. Do nae squander the years ye have on the ones who treated ye cruelly. We are both here and we must begin living, no' simply going through the motions while we are chained to the dark elements of our pasts."

Brenda felt his words cut through something inside

her. To be certain, she'd never thought to discuss such personal things with a man, yet he was correct. They had only each other, and the castle was a sad place because of it. Life was merely an echo in the stone hallways.

"I will…will…think upon the matter…" Her composure failed her as her tongue felt graceless inside her mouth.

"As will I," Symon said. "We must both begin living again."

Symon pointed in the direction of their guest's chamber. Brenda found her belly knotting as she began to move toward Niul. Did she desire him? Would she even recognize passion if it gripped her? Her thoughts were full of questions, and she felt an odd heat teasing her cheeks.

Blushing?

It stunned her and made her smile at the same time.

Because it had been a very long time since she had felt so alive.

❧

McTavish land

"Where is Katherine?"

William McTavish turned and eyed his son. "I've never had an Englishwoman at me table."

Rolfe considered the captains on his father's right who were sending him cutting looks. "So, she is just locked away until the matter of her ransom is resolved?"

His father took a bite of his supper and chewed it before answering. "It worked well enough for the other one ye brought home."

"Helen Grant was only here for a week."

"She did nae cause such a fuss, either," one of his father's captains declared with a frown.

"That was good fun," Adwin shot back from his place beside Rolfe. "Clever lass to stuff a dress with the bedding and send it out the window. Nice to see Scotland has influenced her. Ye can wager she did nae learn such spirit in England."

There were some chuckles in response, but Rolfe was more focused on his father. "I've been gone nearly a fortnight. Are ye saying she's been locked in her chamber all that time?"

"Nae," another of his father's captains answered. "We'll no' be wasting men on the guarding of that hellion. She's down in the cellar, where she'll not be—"

Rolfe didn't wait for the man to finish. He shoved his chair back and gave his father a single, hard tug on the corner of his bonnet before he was striding away.

"Hey." Adwin caught Rolfe by the bicep in the passageway between the hall and the kitchens. "Are ye certain ye want to be showing so much concern? The lass has a purpose, and so do ye. Or did ye no' notice that yer sire sent ye out because of yer little tryst with the lass?"

"It was a kiss," Rolfe defended himself. "No' a tryst. For Christ's sake, what are ye all so concerned about? Do ye think she has the pox?"

"Worse than that. She's English, Rolfe." His man gave him a hard shove in the shoulder. "Ye're no' daft. It matters. To some more than others."

"She's a lass," Rolfe cut back. "One I'm sorry I brought here."

But she was there, and he'd been gone a long time. Rolfe made his way through the kitchens, startling the women working there. The closest thing McTavish Castle had to cells were the cellars next to the buttery where the casks of ale were stored. Cells were generally unnecessary; the worst thing that could happen to a person on clan land was to be put out of the castle without his colors. Rolfe turned and descended belowground where the air was chilly year-round.

"Angus?"

There was a shuffled step on the hard floor. The massive form of the butler came into sight. A ring of keys hung from his belt, but his collar was open and the skin of his neck wet.

Angus reached up and tugged on his bonnet, except that it was missing, so he settled for touching two fingers to his temple.

"Where is the English lass?"

Understanding dawned on the butler. "In the back. The laird said it had to be so. For meself, I would have placed her near the stairs, to keep her warmer, as well as give her more than bread and water. The laird was firm in his orders, though. Very clear. Bread and water, naught else. And only once a day at that."

"Of course he was."

Rolfe went down the dark passageway. Below the tower, it was narrow, the walls composed of rough rocks that were not plastered to make them smooth. He caught sight of a maid hurrying away before he recognized her, only half of her hair shoved up into her cap. At the end of the passageway, there was a very solid door. It was barred and locked. Angus came up behind him, the keys jingling as the butler sorted through them for the correct one.

Rolfe peered into the darkness and cursed.

❧

Time had never moved so slowly. Of course, it was difficult to grasp it when there was no sunlight. Katherine began to know the day by the visits from her jailer. Angus wasn't unkind to her, at least not after their first meeting, when he'd made it clear he knew a great deal about causing pain, should she be any trouble and need a lesson in minding him.

She believed him. The butler bore the marks of too many fights to count and seemed to enjoy his battered appearance. As far as choices for guarding the buttery, she had to concede that Angus was a fine selection. No one would be getting into the stores of ale and grain without permission.

Every house had such strictures, lest gluttony deplete the storerooms before spring arrived with a new harvest to fill them again.

He came once a day and unlocked her door. If she wanted to be fed, she would be against the far wall and stay there. He left her plate and changed her toilet bucket before locking her back in. A crude sort of grayness made it into the room during the daylight, but by night, she couldn't see her hand in front of her face.

And so the days passed slowly, because she could only sleep so much and the chill kept her from ever being comfortable. She passed the time by coming up with escape plans or at least attempting to concoct a means of escape. Just because she hadn't succeeded didn't mean she wouldn't.

"Jesus fucking Christ."

"So, you have come to see me." Katherine recognized Rolfe's voice and did her best to sound as though it meant little to her.

"I've been gone," he said. "On me father's orders."

She liked the sound of that. A ripple of relief went through her, and she didn't bother to question it. Beggars couldn't be too particular, and she was starting to smile when she heard the squeaking of the mice as though they were companions.

"I did nae know me father put ye here, lass."

But he sounded as if he was sorry. She did bristle a little, straightening her back and setting her chin. "I've weathered it well enough."

He extended his hand. "Come, lass."

She started to reach for his hand but stopped when she noticed how filthy her nails were. They were a testament to how she'd crawled around the room, testing every stone for loose ones that might lead to a secret tunnel. His jaw tightened when she folded her hands together instead of taking his.

"Truly, I did nae know, but I promise ye, I will be having words with me father."

He'd stepped out of the doorway, and she took the chance to leave the cell behind her. Rolfe seemed larger than she recalled, and she shied away from his form as she drew in a deep breath, but froze when she noticed Angus was watching her.

The burly butler reached up and tugged on a tuft of his hair. "Do nae be cross with me for doing me duty."

"Yer duty is finished." Rolfe reached across and grasped her by the upper arm.

But now that she'd left the cell behind, she realized she reeked and pulled away from him. He stiffened but released her.

"I'm filthy." She wasn't sure why she spoke; it was just another one of those impulses that seemed to take command of her thoughts when she was near him.

Her admission earned her a softening of his features. He truly was a handsome man when he relaxed. Heat teased her cheeks as she walked beside him.

"Well, that is something I can remedy."

He took her down the passageway and into the kitchens. She drew plenty of notice from the staff, who must have known what her fate was. The scent of food was strong, and her belly rumbled.

Rolfe frowned again. "I'll feed ye better than Angus did."

"I don't want to be pitied." There was a humph from one of the women working at a table near enough to hear. "I can make do when I must."

That earned her another grin from him, but this one was more knowing. "Aye, I can see that ye do nae take delight in wielding yer gender like some sort of weapon against us poor men."

"You're so defenseless against me, after all," she mocked him in return. But it stirred the memory of the last time that she'd seen him.

And felt his kiss.

Her pride was still tender from the encounter because she was not a match for him.

"Here." He'd stopped in a doorway. "It's the

bathhouse. There will be soap, and I'll set one of the women to finding ye some fresh clothing."

There was a snap of fingers before an older woman came forward. She lowered herself before Rolfe.

"I'll see to her."

Rolfe nodded but locked gazes with Katherine. "I'll be right here."

It was a warning and a reminder of her plight. Katherine ordered herself to move forward and take advantage of what she might. It would be foolish indeed to shun a bath simply because she didn't care for her circumstances.

"Having you waiting on me is a surprise I didn't expect."

Katherine caught the flash of surprise that went across his face before she disappeared through the doorway. The woman behind her was snickering and trying to hold her breath to muffle the sound.

"Lord, ye've a fine wit," she said as she stopped in front of Katherine. "I'm Ceit, and I'll tell ye straight that I did nae care to hear ye'd been locked in the cellar."

Katherine shrugged. "I suppose I frightened someone."

Ceit leaned her head back and chuckled. The sound was balm for Katherine's lonely soul, bouncing around the room and lifting her spirits until she was returning Ceit's smile even as her belly rumbled again.

"Well, now," Ceit said as she rubbed her hands together. "Let's get ye bathed so ye can get on to having some supper. It's the truth that I was after Angus for taking ye naught but bread and water." There was a splash as she emptied a bucket of water into a tub. "The brute claimed the laird gave instructions for ye to be tamed."

"It will take more than that to break me." It would likely have been wiser to remain silent, but Katherine didn't much care. The tub was a large, round half of a barrel, coated with pitch on the inside to hold the water. The room itself was very warm, making disrobing a pleasure. They were behind the massive hearths the kitchens used to roast the meat for the tables in the great hall.

But there was another novelty that gained her interest. There was a long trough running along one side of the wall. Water glistened in it, and Ceit was refilling the bucket from it.

"A fine luxury, is it no'?" She poured more water into the tub. "There's a longer trough outside that is fed from the water wheel. No fetching the water up from the river. Saves the hands."

"It does indeed."

Katherine hesitated and looked behind her, but Rolfe wasn't in sight. He wouldn't be.

No, for all that she might think ill of him for bringing her to McTavish Castle, she could not accuse him of being dishonorable.

So she stripped down and climbed into the tub with a shiver because Ceit had yet to add any hot water. Katherine didn't care. She started to rub a lump of soap across her arm, delighted to feel the grime being washed away.

❧

"Do ye nae worry about yer hair being wet after the sun's gone down?"

Katherine emerged from the bathhouse to find Adwin keeping watch. The captain was enjoying a thick piece of cheese he'd placed on a hunk of bread. His beard sported crumbles of bread as he chewed.

"I find myself more focused on the fact that it may be a long time before I am able to bathe, so it's best not to waste my opportunity."

Adwin swallowed. "It's yer head, I suppose." He jerked his toward the kitchens. "This way."

She didn't care for being under guard, but Adwin led her away from the cellars, so Katherine moved along without complaint. She heard him smacking his lips as he chewed, and the sound was nearly her undoing. Her mouth began to water as the ache in her belly became painful. The scent of meat had never struck her as so delicious before.

But Adwin didn't stop in the kitchens. He led her through them as she fought to control her disappointment.

Such seemed her lot among the McTavishes. Well, she'd weather it. Take what Fate was forcing on her. Just as she always had. The only true choice she had was how she stood up to it all.

Hellion?

It sounded far better than *pitiful*, so she would embrace it.

❦

"Ye countermanded me orders."

Rolfe stood firm in the face of his father's displeasure and looked him straight in the eye. "I did."

William snorted and lifted his mug, but he stopped

short of drinking from it. "Ye brought her here for gain."

"Ye wanted to break her," Rolfe replied. "I told ye, I owe her a debt of gratitude. She should be treated as her station demands."

"It was a necessary action, brought on by her own escape attempt," his father responded firmly. "I'll no' have that hellion turning me house on its ear."

"The MacPhersons will no' be happy to hear how she's been treated," Rolfe said softly.

"Lecture me on that, will ye?" his father demanded. "Was it nae ye who told me that she needed a lesson?"

Rolfe nodded, earning a grunt of satisfaction from his sire.

"Ye are the one who tumbled her. Why do ye think I sent ye away?"

"I did no' tumble her."

His father choked on his amusement. "Everyone saw the hay sticking to her."

"I stopped her from escaping," Rolfe explained.

His father smiled brightly at him. "Mind ye, I'm rather relieved to see that shell of honor ye've always worn cracking. There are times a laird must employ a bit of deception to gain what he seeks. It's canny."

"I am not deceiving ye."

William shook his head. "I'm missing part of me leg, no' one of me eyes, boy. I saw the way that lass was looking at ye, her eyes wide and her lips swollen. Ye kissed her. Deny it, and I'll call ye a liar."

Rolfe snapped his jaw shut. His father roared with amusement.

"It's no' that I blame ye—she's a fine sight—but I'll no' have ye taking up with any English chit."

"Good night, Father."

His sire slapped the arm of the chair he was sitting in. "Did ye hear me, Rolfe?"

Rolfe had started to turn away, but he stopped and made eye contact with his father. He gave him a hard nod before he left the study behind.

He had kissed her.

And he had scarcely stopped thinking about it since.

Perhaps the rest of the clan saw him as honorable, but the truth was that he'd been less than respectable in his dealings with Katherine.

He stopped in the passageway, quelling the urge to hit the wall out of frustration.

His position gave him a view of the great hall. Adwin was playing dice with Cedric and others. As it was late in the evening, supper had been cleared away and many had sought their beds. Rolfe looked toward the stairs that led to the top of the tower. He didn't doubt that Adwin had made certain Katherine was secure in a chamber.

But he wanted to make sure.

The urge was strong, so much so that it made him hesitate.

But that was the extent of the hold his better judgment had on him. He was halfway up the tower stairs before he finished thinking the matter through. Was it truly a case of wanting to make certain she'd been treated fairly, or was he standing outside her chamber door because he just couldn't stop thinking about how much he'd enjoyed the taste of her?

❦

Someone knocked.

Katherine turned in time to see the chamber door opening. The stairwell was dark, but the candle she had burning in the chamber cast a yellow light over Rolfe. He found her quickly, his jaw tightening.

"Ye do nae have to be against the wall when this door opens," he informed her.

"I was looking out the window." She wasn't sure why she wanted to soothe the anger in him. In some way, his ire should have pleased her, provided balm for her wounded pride. But it didn't.

He crossed into the room as the door shut behind him. She watched his body go tense as the sound of it meeting the doorjamb hit their ears.

Katherine ended up smiling. "I don't believe my reputation could be in worse condition."

"So I should just dispense with correct behavior?" he demanded.

"It wouldn't be the first time," she answered. He drew himself up stiffly in response. "I meant that as much for myself as you."

She'd surprised him once more. He crossed his arms over his chest and contemplated her. Something rippled over her skin, an awareness of him, or maybe it was more correct to say that she was conscious of how aware he was of her. She couldn't recall feeling so exposed to anyone before.

"Why were ye allowed to be a lad?"

It was a personal question, and yet she didn't shy away from answering. Maybe that was because she had been alone for so long, or perhaps it had more to do with her feeling that he saw deeply into her soul. All she knew for certain was that it was very nice to be asked a question like she was more than a prisoner.

"I'm English."

Rolfe rolled his eyes at her. "I had no' noticed."

Katherine discovered herself sharing a smile with him. "Marcus knew there would be times I might be faced with difficulties over my blood."

"So he took ye into his training yard?" Rolfe's tone was disbelieving.

She smiled brighter, feeling her pride returning. "Not exactly."

Rolfe snorted at her, admiring her daring. "Ye snuck in."

She nodded, not bothering to hide how proud she was.

Rolfe's grin faded. "But Marcus is no fool. For all that I do nae profess to call the man a friend, I know him. He does not miss details. No' for as many years as ye must have been training to be as good at mounting as ye are."

"In truth, I failed to think about it myself, but it seems he did know. Only recently did it become a matter he was unwilling to ignore any longer." Lament crept into her tone.

"Ye should no'…dislike yer own gender, Katherine. Ye're a fine-looking woman."

He'd moved closer. Somehow, she hadn't noticed, or perhaps she was simply becoming at ease in his presence. She felt more aware with him there, and it was a relief after so many endless hours alone in the darkness. She craved the sensation, even though it felt as if everything was heightened. Her sight, hearing, even the way her skin registered the air moving in the room. All of it was intense, and Rolfe was the most overwhelming of all. The span of his shoulders, the way he pushed his sleeves up to expose his forearms.

His gaze was enchanting.

"Green eyes," she muttered. "I don't believe I have ever seen them before."

He took another step toward her, angling his head down now that he was so close to her.

"I've never seen a woman pull herself up into the saddle."

She started to smile, but froze when he leaned down toward her.

He was going to kiss her.

The thought felt frozen in her mind, becoming the only thing she could manage to think about. There didn't seem to be anything but him and the way her insides felt as if they were twisting with anticipation. Even the surface of her lips was eager, and Rolfe didn't disappoint her.

He pressed his lips to hers with a softness that delighted her. Unlike the last time, she wasn't crushed by his strength. No, it was intoxicating. Her wits dulled until there was nothing but the motion of his lips against hers. Naught except for the impulse to lift herself up onto her toes so she might kiss him in return. He guided her with a gentle hand on her nape, his fingers sending a ripple of excitement down her spine that spread out over her skin, raising gooseflesh and drawing her nipples into tight little points.

She gasped, and he sealed her mouth beneath his

once more as he moved with her. She was twisting, unable to remain still, so she grasped the front of his doublet, holding on to the only steady thing in her world.

Him.

He made a low sound that rumbled through his chest. It was a mixture of promise and enjoyment that made her heart accelerate and her thoughts fall completely away. She found a new place inside her mind, one where impulses bred and combined and were ruled by nothing.

In this state of mind, she pulled him to her and opened her mouth so the kiss might grow deeper, harder, more intoxicating. Rolfe bound her to him, delighting her with his strength. She craved it, craved him, and she simply wasn't close enough. There were too many layers of clothing between them when what she wanted was to be pressed against his bare skin.

It was a shocking urge that knocked her back to her senses for a moment as she pulled away, breaking their kiss so she might drag in a ragged breath and think.

Rolfe simply kissed his way down her face and onto the side of her neck.

Delicious…

She had never understood why women were called creatures of enchantment. Now, she felt that way herself, only she was the one falling under the spell. It wove its way through her mind as Rolfe's lips sent ripple after ripple of pleasure down her body. She heard herself crying out. Little sounds of breathless wonderment that she scarcely believed came from her.

She had never been so wanton.

Never realized her body could feel so much delight.

And then she was alone, stumbling back a step to lean on the wall. She was grateful for the support because her knees trembled and threatened to fold.

Rolfe was stepping farther away from her, his jaw so tight that the muscles running down his neck were corded.

His agitation slapped her straight across the face, shaming her with just how willing she had been, while he appeared furious to have fallen for her charms. He was gone in another moment, leaving her to battle the guilt that tried to tear her flesh from her bones.

But that wasn't what sent tears into her eyes. Hot, stinging drops that spilled over and onto her cheeks. What broke her was the way he'd retreated from her.

From the Englishwoman that she was.

❧

How could she crave him?

Katherine woke to that question in her mind.

Marcus, Robert, Rolfe… They were correct. She was a woman grown now, and she was far from innocent of what went on between men and women.

In some respects, it was better to know, because that helped her find her balance as she tried to sort her feelings into something that could be managed.

Her newest chamber was high in the top of the tower. It had a curved ceiling with exposed arches. What she enjoyed most were the windows. She walked toward one of them, carefully opening the glass that was set into shutters to seal out the weather. The morning chill came in, but she welcomed it after so many days sealed in the cellar, where the air never stirred and all she did was sit in her own stench until she didn't notice it any longer.

The chamber was a single one, without a partition between receiving and bed space. She cared not at all about the lack of modern appeal, because the room afforded her windows that overlooked every direction. In the distance, she heard a church bell tolling and the McTavishes beginning to rise and greet the day.

She had been a child. Or, at least, childish.

The thought of what Marcus was thinking now was a burr in her underbelly. One she admitted she deserved full well for riding out without a care for what might become of her. Rolfe had done her a service in forcing her to see that.

Her cheeks burned scarlet as she thought of Rolfe. So many emotions rolled through her, like bubbles beginning in a pot of water as it neared the boiling point. First, there was one or two, then eight, and then the entire contents were boiling.

She enjoyed his kiss.

Craved his touch.

Wanted more.

And yet she'd be damned if she would throw herself at a man who detested her for her blood.

At least being loathed because of her parentage was something she understood well. Oh yes, she recalled that so very well from her childhood. Had tasted a different version of it when she'd encountered the Earl of Morton, and finally, it seemed she must face it again in the form of a man she longed for.

Cursed Fate.

She had been its plaything for too long. Frustration

nipped at her as she combed out her hair and straightened her bed.

Well, she'd have to cultivate resolve. Wasn't that the true difference between adult and child?

❧

Boyd listened to his laird chuckle with glee. He'd served William McTavish for a long time and knew the different sorts of laughter that came from him. Today, it was a sound rich in victory, confirmed by the satisfaction brightening his eyes.

"Ye see?" William declared. "The English do have uses!"

Boyd took to stroking his beard. His laird didn't care for the lack of camaraderie.

"Well, speak yer mind," William said at last. "I'm growing old waiting."

Boyd gripped his wide belt before choosing his words. "I do nae think yer son will be happy about taking the lass down to the Earl of Morton. Rolfe was clear when he brought her here that it was to teach her a lesson."

"I am no' the chit's father," William announced with a wave of his hand.

"Well, now, the earl would likely no' be interested in her if ye were."

William scoffed at Boyd. "What matters is that we have her, and the Earl of Morton values her."

"Perhaps ye should be more concerned about what yer son will say when he learns that ye plan to give the little lass back to a man who tried to have her wed when she was too young."

"She is a woman grown now," William argued. "It's time for her to wed."

"Wedding too young is no' the only sort of ill that a bad match can bring to a woman," Boyd responded. "Yer son will be quick to tell ye so. He feels responsible for the lass, make no mistake."

William took to drinking. It was a long moment before he lowered his mug and contemplated Boyd. "Ye're right, and yet I am proud of Rolfe. He's now a man to be reckoned with, so I'll not shirk from telling him. I'm doing the best I can for me clan. He'll have to reconcile himself to it in the end."

"Ye're certain of that?"

William lifted his mug but paused with it in the air between them. "Aye. For I'll tell him in front of the men, at the same time that I inform the English wench of her fate. Rolfe will nae cross me in front of the clan. His honor would no' allow him to."

It was a bold strategy, but he was a Highlander. William drank long and deep before he set his empty mug aside and stood. He was going to dress well for the moment, taking care to ensure that he looked every inch the laird of the McTavishes.

❧

It was one of Laird McTavish's captains who knocked on her door next. Katherine turned toward the sound, anticipating supper. All she received was a curt nod and a jerk of the man's head.

"The laird wishes to see ye."

Her belly knotted, and at the same time, she was hopeful that perhaps Marcus had arrived to fetch her back. She wasn't sure how she would repay the MacPhersons, but she would worry about that after she was home.

The great hall was full of McTavish retainers. They filled the long tables as supper was served to them. She heard them before she reached the hall and realized how much she missed being part of conversations. Her debt to the MacPhersons was mounting as she appreciated how welcoming they had been.

And now, there would be the matter of a ransom.

Guilt heated her cheeks as she turned and stood in the large double doorway that opened into the hall. Men grew silent as they spotted her.

"Aye, bring her up."

It was the laird who spoke, and his people quieted as they waited to hear what he wanted with her. Rolfe looked up from his seat beside his father.

"Katherine Carew," the laird began with a satisfied tone. "Natural-born daughter and recognized bastard of the Earl of Bedford."

"I have not seen him in over ten years."

Eyes narrowed at her, as it was clear many believed she should remain silent.

"Blood is blood," William McTavish declared. "And yers is blue. The earl recognized ye at yer baptism."

"A fact that has brought me nothing but grief."

William frowned and pointed a thick finger at her. "It gains ye men who are interested in taking ye to wife because of the alliances with yer father's house." He slapped the table in front of him. "Do nae be ungrateful. A place is a place."

"I was stolen from mine," Katherine replied.

"Hold yer tongue," William warned her. The captain beside her gave her a shove to emphasize his laird's command.

"I will not," Katherine declared firmly. "For I will not have it said that I deceived you about what I am worth."

"Which ye still say is naught?" William asked.

"I have been in Scotland for too many years for any of my blood kin to believe I am unsoiled."

"Well, as to that matter…" William waved his hand. "It is no' me concern, for the Earl of Morton has interest in ye. He can see to the matter of having ye inspected by a midwife."

Katherine paled. She stood strong, but she felt the blood draining from her face.

"Do nae look so stricken," William continued without a shred of mercy for her. "Ye are nae too tender for marriage now, and ye have thrived in Scotland, so a marriage with a Scot will likely suit ye well enough." He paused to take a drink, the sound of the mug hitting the tabletop like a pistol exploding. "No' that I care. What matters is that Rolfe has brought his clan a fine prize that will see me ennobled and the McTavish raised up above others."

Katherine was numb as she locked gazes with Rolfe. "You promised to ransom me to the MacPhersons."

"There was no promise made by my son." William hit the table with his fist and struggled to stand. Once he was on his feet, he pointed at her. "Call him a liar again, and I'll have ye beaten for it. No English chit will be making up tales about the McTavishes."

He leaned on his hands once he was done, daring

her to voice a complaint. She battled the urge, but it wasn't his threat that kept her silent. It was the hostility of those watching her. All of that hate, and for what reason?

Her English blood.

It destroyed the foundation of her life, that wonderful existence she had been living with the MacPhersons.

No, what had smashed her life was Rolfe McTavish with his desire to claim her as a prize.

The McTavish started to chuckle at her silent form, enjoying her moment of submission.

The captain behind her grabbed her by the arm and swung her around. She went willingly enough, telling herself there was nothing for her in the hall.

And she repeated that again and again as she climbed to her tower chamber.

Rolfe McTavish was nothing, and she would take that to heart.

Because her private thoughts were the only thing she had left.

⤜❧⤐

"Stay where ye are, son."

Rolfe curled his fingers into fists as his father settled back into his chair.

"She is a prize that will net more than ye thought."

"Since when do we play into the hands of the bloody Douglas?" Rolfe demanded softly.

"Since the man can bestow a title on me." William turned his head to lock gazes with his son. "One which ye will inherit and pass on to yer own son one day. A laird always thinks of his clan first. Every McTavish will benefit."

Rolfe disagreed. He shot his father a hard look but kept his jaw tight.

"Women are meant to wed for purpose," William offered softly. "Why do ye think the MacPhersons allowed her to turn hellion? They do nae want the burden of providing a dowry for her. The Earl of Morton will find her a husband with a position, and her children will have better lots for it."

Rolfe couldn't fault his father's thinking. It was the way the world was. A solid truth that only a fool argued with.

So label him a fool.

⤳

"Do nae let me father's words wound ye."

She hadn't thought Rolfe would follow her into the chamber, much less touch her, but she felt him cup her shoulder. It was so tempting to indulge in a moment of bliss. Linger in the sensation that seemed to result when he touched her. It was a mystery—in many ways, an alarming one—but her pride refused to allow her to take shelter in it.

"Your father"—she made sure to enunciate every syllable exactly the way she'd been taught by her tutors in England—"does not have the power to frighten me."

Rolfe knew she was lying. The look in his eyes told her she could not hide her emotions from him.

"So…go on with you." She tried to make her tone one of disdain. "Or are you looking to gloat over what profit you have gained by bringing me here?"

"That is no' why I am here," he replied softly.

She shifted away from him, her belly twisting in response to how close he was. Her craving for him was undermining her ability to recall why she had to shun him.

"I meant what I said when I brought ye here, lass." He spoke each word in a tight tone that sent a warning through her. "It was for a bit of ransom, and so ye might learn the value of thinking before ye took to acting rashly and placing men in peril."

She nodded, in spite of her temper. It pleased him. For one small moment, there was peace between them. But she closed a door inside herself, refusing to let him see any more of her feelings. She had to do it or be flayed alive.

"But me father..." Rolfe's tight expression crumbled for just a moment, allowing her a glimpse of his frustration. "He is laird here. I failed to think about how he'd treat an Englishwoman."

Englishwoman...

Katherine stiffened but Rolfe cupped her shoulders, keeping her near him as he aimed a hard look into her eyes.

"I do nae share his feelings, Katherine."

"Oh, really?" She twisted away from him, stumbling because of how much force she used. "Do not coddle me. I know your true feelings on the matter."

His face was a mask of determination. "I've a mind to kiss ye again, woman." He pulled her close enough to feel his breath on her lips. "So ye do nae forget."

"Kiss me?" she demanded. "Why? So you can jerk

away from me once more, to make certain I know you cannot stomach the fact that you lust for me?"

He sealed her against him with an arm around her waist, while his other hand captured her nape and he pulled her the last remaining inches toward him.

"So ye know I must have ye."

She was melting, cravings rising up from inside her, but she jammed two knuckles into the soft spot where his neck and torso connected. He recoiled instantly.

"Your father is laird here." Her anger had drained away, leaving her tone nothing more than a soft lament.

Rolfe drew himself up stiffly. "I can nae be a man of honor if I do nae agree with ye on that."

Somehow, she'd still been clinging to hope. The look in his eyes made her release it. He turned but paused at the door.

"I should no' have brought ye here, Katherine."

∼

"I know that look," Adwin said when Rolfe emerged. His longtime friend was shaking his head in warning. "Ye're plotting."

"Ye'd rather I acted like a dog?" Rolfe asked. "Accept what me father does with me prize like a hound being tossed a table scrap? She is me prize."

Adwin contemplated him seriously for a long moment. "This is likely no' going to end well. Ye know that?"

Rolfe shot him a cocky grin and made sure it remained on his lips. He wasn't going to admit how many doubts he had.

Four

"Boyd will take the chit to Morton."

His father was making sure his voice was heard by half the men in the hall.

"And give that Douglas the opportunity to take the payment without giving us what is due?" Rolfe inquired. "Better that I go. He can raise me up in yer stead, in front of witnesses, and I'll make very certain no' to let him even see the wench before he seals the patents of nobility in front of men he'll think twice about crossing."

His father was suspicious. Rolfe watched him weigh his words along with the looks on his men's faces.

"Morton is a Douglas, sure enough."

"Send only yer senior captain, and ye might be waiting until the end of time for yer title," Rolfe said.

William grunted. "Aye, and aye." He slapped the tabletop. "Ye've a fine head on those shoulders, right enough. Take the English girl down there, and if that Douglas does no' keep his end of the bargain, bring her back, and we'll ransom her to the MacPherson."

There were nods of agreement from those watching.

Rolfe caught Adwin giving him a curious look, but he didn't linger in the hall. He offered his father a tug on his bonnet before going to make preparations to leave.

His father enjoyed the fact that he had a good head on his shoulders? Rolfe hoped so, because he was going to test that.

❧

She shouldn't have any feelings for him except loathing.

Katherine intended to lecture herself firmly on the merits of cultivating a deep dislike of Rolfe McTavish, but all of her words seemed to slip away once she was in his company again.

He was too handsome, but it was more than his exterior that she found attractive. The man had honor in the truest sense of the word, and it took self-discipline to maintain such a thing. So she was drawn to him, both in flesh and spirit.

The fascination would only do her harm. Rolfe would obey his father. It was his only option if he planned to maintain his honor, and she would rather suffer being handed over to the Earl of Morton than watch Rolfe McTavish become less than he was.

She fought to keep her attention off him as they rode. At least during the day, it was simple enough. His men were over forty strong, and they clung to her hem in groups of four anytime she was out of the saddle.

Which wasn't often.

At least that thought offered her a twinge of distaste for Rolfe at last, but it wasn't in the form she wished. Instead, what she felt was a sense of impending parting that was going to leave a scar on her heart.

At last she came to a hard truth, one that nauseated her.

The Earl of Morton was a man, like many nobles she had encountered among her father's sort. They were men who had been raised believing they were elite, placed in their positions by God himself. There was no arguing with such men. They expected submission, and she suspected they enjoyed the odd person who didn't give it immediately because it offered them the amusement of breaking that person.

Today was different, though. It drew her from her thoughts as Rolfe took them near a village and up to the doors of an inn.

She was grateful to him for it.

And chided herself for thinking of him in any way that was positive, but she simply couldn't seem to loathe him.

More the fool her. He was driving them hard in an effort to deliver her to the man willing to pay the McTavish the most for her. She'd be wise to remember her purpose, because Rolfe certainly would.

Still, it had been raining the entire day and the opportunity to lay her head down in a dry place was too enticing. There was also something to be said for knowing when to see one's blessings and enjoy them before they were gone. Katherine slid from the back of her horse and happily went toward the front of the inn. The McTavish retainers crowded around her, but tonight, she decided that they were just as eager to get out of the rain as she was.

Once they were inside, the scent of supper drew a rumble from her belly. Conversation filled the great room where trestle tables were crowded in with benches for travelers. A buxom woman by the hearth wore an apron sporting numerous splotches. She wielded a ladle and called out a greeting to them.

"Plenty of bread and supper for all!"

Rolfe still stole Katherine's breath.

It was an admission she couldn't avoid as she caught sight of him sending a smile toward the woman before he turned to her husband and began to discuss the details of business.

With the rain, the tavern was full. Katherine ventured toward the hearth, only to be pushed back by two large Scots.

"Excuse me."

It was an ingrained response, polite manners that had always served her well. Tonight, they had the opposite effect. The two men turned on her, their expressions dark.

"English bitch."

One of the men reached out and started to shove her away from him. Another response came from the years she'd trained with Marcus. She stepped to the side at the last moment, so that his own motion sent him stumbling past her. His companion roared with amusement.

The first man snarled and flipped around to face her. "Think ye'll be getting the best of me? No English will ever live to see the day."

"Causing trouble already?"

Rolfe was suddenly there, pressing her behind him as he shielded her with his body. The two clansmen faced off with him.

"What are ye doing with an English wench, McTavish?"

"Better still, why are ye bringing her into our taverns?" The second one spat on the ground at Rolfe's feet. "Let her bed down in the stable."

"But apologize to the horses first for making them suffer her presence," the first man added with a grunt.

"I'm on me father's business," Rolfe said firmly. "And I'm no' one to question him."

Rolfe hooked Katherine by the upper arm, turning and pushing her toward the back of the room where there was a narrow flight of stairs. The woman from the hearth was in front of them, and she pushed open a door at the top of the stairs.

"In here." She was flushed and gestured Katherine inside, as though she were stuffing someone with a case of the pox out of sight before word got out and her business was deserted.

Katherine made it inside and heard Rolfe snort. She turned on him. "Don't think I will be apologizing for keeping that man from putting his hands on me."

Rolfe had paused in the doorway. She looked past him and realized her two tormenters had followed them.

"Well, now," the one who had tried to touch her declared. "I've misjudged ye, McTavish. Seems ye are putting the bitch to the only use she truly has. How much for a turn on her?"

"She belongs to me," Rolfe said firmly.

Boyd and Adwin suddenly appeared to haul the two away, and Rolfe started to close the door but hesitated. He finally cursed in Gaelic before shutting the door and turning to level a hard look toward Katherine.

"If I leave, there is going to be a fight, and no mistake about it."

Katherine was still standing in the middle of the room. Her belly had decided to twist with excitement, a very inappropriately timed sort, too.

"Unless ye prefer to sleep in the rain, lass, I'll have to stay here, no matter the damage it will do to yer reputation." He spoke softly but maintained his position right in front of the door, as though he was loath to venture any farther into the room without her permission.

Which was ludicrous, since she was his hostage.

She suddenly laughed at their circumstances. He raised an eyebrow at her.

"I've never seen you uncertain, Rolfe McTavish," she explained.

He rocked back on his heels for a moment. "Enjoying it, are ye?"

She shrugged and moved a little farther into the room. Her memory offered up a fine, perfect recollection of what had happened the last two times they were alone together. And exactly how much she'd enjoyed it.

Her cheeks heated.

She turned and looked into the small hearth the room was furnished with.

"I suppose ye're due a bit of enjoyment," he said quietly. "'Tis the truth that I've missed seeing ye smile."

Katherine turned back to face him so quickly that her skirts swished in a wave of wool. "I have little to be pleased about, thanks to you."

"Me father is the one responsible for ye being taken back to Morton."

"If you had not insisted on taking me to McTavish land in the first place," she argued, "I would never have met the man."

Rolfe was watching her and suddenly came to some sort of conclusion. He stepped into the room, and she fell back instantly. The heat in her cheeks doubled, her breath catching in her chest.

Why did it have to be Rolfe McTavish who had suddenly awakened the woman inside her?

He placed his sword on the table and walked over to the hearth. It was strange the way he drew her attention. She was fascinated by his motions. The way he knelt so easily and sat there, poised on a knee as he placed some wood into the hearth and struck a flint next to it. She'd done the same many times, but had never enjoyed watching someone do it. The man mesmerized her.

The only saving grace was that he detested her English blood. At least he would prevent her from succumbing to his touch.

Yet was that a blessing?

With the fate she was bound for, was she wise to squander her opportunity to enjoy the touch of a man she craved?

Wicked…

Perhaps she was everything she'd been accused of being recently, and more.

There was a knock on the door, and it swung open a moment later as the woman returned with her arms full. She bustled over to the table and set several dishes on it. Rolfe had turned to watch her, but he was looking through the open door at his captain. Adwin didn't smile often, and tonight his expression was dark.

"We'll be at the base of the stairs."

Rolfe nodded as the woman lowered herself and hurried out.

"I'll sleep by the fire, lass."

"Of course you will." She should have sounded more grateful, but the sting of that moment when he'd jerked away from her was still too sharp.

Rolfe slowly chuckled. The sound wasn't one of amusement, though. There was a dark promise in it, one clearly expressed on his face when she looked toward him.

"Ye think I pulled away from ye because ye're English?"

Part of her recognized that she might be far better off ignoring his question, but the wound that had yet to heal from that moment refused to allow her to suffer in silence any longer.

"Yes."

He rose and closed the distance between them. "I am a man of me word, Katherine."

His comment caught her off guard, but she was having trouble thinking again. He was too near, too large, too imposing, and her flesh was far more interested in responding to him again without any interference from her thoughts or sense.

"I did bring ye to me land to ensure ye did nae meet a foul end due to yer foolishness."

She bristled. "And I have told you that you were justified. Is it so terrible to say I felt at ease in the Highlands and never suspected that there would be men who harbored hatred for me simply because of my blood? Is it so very wrong to see the world as a good place? Inhabited by men of honor? I never had a reason to hate the Scottish and didn't see any reason to distrust the MacPhersons when Marcus brought me north. They gave me every reason to embrace their kindness."

"Ye were old enough to have heard about the strife between our two peoples."

She lifted her hands into the air. "Aye, and yet young enough to decide to embrace a life that seemed free of such hatred." She finished with a sigh, realizing how desolate her life was now that she'd been forced to face the hard reality of hatred. It left her so lonely. "There must have been a time when you were forced to face such harsh facts. Wasn't there a time when you viewed the years ahead with hope instead of duties to be fulfilled?"

He paused, brought up short by her words. She glimpsed a moment of surprise flashing through his green eyes.

"Aye," he offered with an honesty that felt very personal. He locked gazes with her, and she knew she was looking at the boy he'd once been. The one who had believed in hope. The one so similar to herself that she felt a kinship with him that was nearly soul-deep.

It made her realize how alone she'd felt since Robert had decided to see her as a woman instead of his companion.

"When me father lost his leg, he took to his chamber abovestairs." Rolfe moved back toward the hearth, leaning on the mantel as he relived the moment.

"I thought the worst of it was when the surgeon took off his leg. I've heard men scream before, but this was my father. I wished it were me own limb, and that's the truth. I cursed the bloody Hays to hellfire because it was a skirmish with them that had festered."

Rolf took a deep breath. "But that was no' the worst of it all. Me father lived, and yet he was no' alive in those months after the fever passed. He kept to his rooms, refusing to be seen." Rolfe shot her a hard look. "Thought his men would no' respect him with a leg missing."

"He strikes me as that sort of man."

"Aye, he was raised to be laird and does nae have anything but his clan." Rolfe moved back toward her. "That time, I was forced to shoulder the weight of the clan. Made to face the fact that I'd been living the life of a man who was no' completely a man because I had nae been forced to make choices. I chose me father's life over me honor, told him I'd leave him to starve abovestairs. Ordered the staff to obey me over him, and the McTavishes followed me. I understood I could no' play games any longer. Everything I did had consequences, repercussions."

"You are better for it." She could not deny that she admired the man he was.

"Well, no' so perfect." He was looking at the fire now, but turned to lock gazes with her. "I should have thought harder upon the matter before bringing ye back to McTavish land. I overlooked yer English blood. That was a grave error."

The moment shattered into a thousand tiny shards that felt like they sliced her on their way to the floor. "I am sorry you find me so. Yet you are the one who kissed me."

His lips curled into an unpleasant grin. It sent a shiver down her spine because it was pure intention.

"And I pulled away from ye because I was acting like a youth who had no concern for the harm it would do yer reputation. Preaching to ye of honor when I was forgetting that a decent man does nae ruin a woman. If we'd been seen, ye'd no' only be English but branded a slut as well."

He'd closed the gap between them again, reaching out to stroke his fingers across the crimson surface of her cheek.

"Ye captivate me, Katherine," he whispered, looking down into her face. Only a single step remained between them.

"Yes." The word slipped out as she shivered. Strange how a sensation such as shivering could have more than one purpose in the body. She wasn't cold, wasn't horrified; no, that same little jolt of awareness was now a beginning of her response to him.

He slid his hand along her cheek and into her hair. Never once had she realized how sensitive the skin of her face could be. Beneath his touch, it felt as if she'd never been fully awake.

"A lass should no' be kissed as I kissed you in the stable." He took that last step while he cradled the nape of her neck in his hand. "No' the first time."

He leaned down, easing her against him when she shifted, full of uncertainty. It wasn't a hard hold, but his body was so solid that she sighed as he moved so she was in contact with him from knee to head. She felt his breath teasing the delicate surface of her lips before he pressed his against them. The moment while she waited for the contact seemed impossibly long, while anticipation twisted her insides.

Then he was kissing her, controlling her head with his hand as he pressed his opposite one against her lower back to keep her in his embrace. Sensation went swirling through her, touching off a hundred different points of awareness inside her. Her heart was thumping in hard beats that drove her blood faster through her body. Her breathing increased, and she caught his scent. Before, it had merely been a small part of him, but now she felt intoxicated by the combination of his kiss and scent. Her thoughts were falling away, leaving something else exposed, some part of herself that had been dormant in her heart.

"That's the way a first kiss should be."

Her eyelids felt heavy, but she lifted them and found him watching her. There was a flicker in his eyes that unleashed a ripple of need inside her. She'd laid her hands on his chest, and it was suddenly not enough. She curled her fingers into his doublet, trying to pull him closer.

His expression tightened, the look in his eyes brightening. He leaned down and kissed her again, but this time it was harder, more demanding, as he abandoned his need to handle her like a fragile bird.

It suited her perfectly.

She rose onto her toes, kissing him with every bit of desire flowing through her. He rocked back, absorbing her motion before his fingers spread wide and he clasped a handful of her hair to hold her in place.

A half sound of delight escaped her lips before he was taking them in a searing kiss. There was no gentle exploration. He wanted a taste of her and intended to take it.

But she wanted one of him as well. She opened her mouth as he teased her lower lip with the tip of his tongue, unleashing a new sensation that gripped her with a need that went rushing down her body to clench her belly. A throbbing began at the top of her sex, an awareness of that part of her she'd never encountered before.

And she didn't want to think about it. Didn't want to contemplate what was right or wrong. All she knew for certain was that she hated their clothing. She pulled at his doublet, pushing the buttons through the holes as she tried to make contact with his skin.

"I'll not ruin ye," he rasped, pulling her back and keeping her away from him as she let out a frustrated sound.

"No one believes I am not soiled."

His lips twitched. "That does no' mean it is acceptable for me to take ye, lass. Surely ye see that?"

Standing still seemed impossible. She wrenched herself from his embrace, her body tight with frustration. "Aye. And yet, I wonder if it is foolish to save myself for the fate Morton would plan for me. Any man who will agree with his plans is only concerned with power and gain. It seems such a poor pairing, maintaining my virtue so it might be bartered to a man who merely wishes to collect Morton's approval." She ended up facing the fire. "As you noted, maturity holds more moments of duty than anything else."

Along with disappointment.

But she didn't loathe the frustration nipping at her

insides, at least not completely. No, she was enjoying the flickering of heat, recognizing it as passion, along with the more blunt reality of what acting upon it would entail. What made it worse was the certain knowledge that she was savoring her time with Rolfe because she knew her future would be dim indeed. Although she'd accepted that the world was not always a pleasant place, she hadn't wanted to give up on happiness completely.

But it seemed that she had.

❧

The Earl of Morton was the regent for King James the Sixth of Scotland.

Mary Stuart's son was Scotland's monarch, but the boy was too young to rule, and there was no way the lords of Scotland were going to allow the boy to be raised by his mother. In a way, it was sad, because Mary had been raised in France from the time she was five years old. She'd been crowned as an infant and smuggled out of the country to save her from the English.

Morton took a moment to enjoy his success. Scotland was Mary's country once more. The English stayed on their side of the border, and he wouldn't apologize to anyone for the means he had employed to make it so.

He was Scotland's leader.

His only true fear was that James was growing into a young man. His blood entitled him to the crown, but Morton couldn't help but wonder if it might be better if the boy never succeeded.

Well, he must, at some point.

And Morton would serve Scotland until the boy was a man.

Morton recalled his thoughts to the issues that needed his concern. There were the Highland clans, a topic that took a great deal of his time. For years, he'd invested his time in quelling the fighting between them. Scotland needed to be united if she were to remain strong. England's Virgin Queen had shown him the value of letting go of wars in favor of trade.

England flourished under the rule of Elizabeth Tudor, in spite of the fact that she had not wed. In fact, she had ignored all of the rules that should have applied to her as a woman.

Morton admitted to admiring her, because her country was strong and her people fat. It made them forget she wore the crown alone and seemed in no hurry to produce an heir. In fact, the nations of Europe were all loath to make advances on her realm, so they sent suitors to try to win England by way of marriage to its queen. Elizabeth played her part to perfection, never granting a clear answer to any of those men, and so she maintained her throne without firing a single shot. The battle for England was being fought in the queen's court, with dances and flattery.

He wanted the same for Scotland. A state of peace that would produce a society with time to invest in producing goods for trade. So the clans would cease their feuding. He'd begun on that path years before, forcing a union between the Robertsons and MacPhersons to stop their fighting. He smiled as he looked at a letter from one of his spies in the

Highlands. That feud had truly been put in its grave. He wasn't fool enough to think that the Robertsons and MacPhersons were friends, but the bloody skirmishes had ceased. They contented themselves with stealing cattle now.

That brought him to the matter of Katherine Carew.

Strange how Fate delivered matters into his hands at the proper time. Marcus MacPherson had taken the girl home with him instead of wedding her as Morton had ordered the man to do. True, she'd been too young, but when it came to securing Scotland, Morton couldn't afford to be too particular. He had to use the means available. Katherine was the natural daughter of the Earl of Bedford, one of Elizabeth Tudor's privy councillors.

Scotland needed alliances, and Morton wanted the Highland clans to be aware of the power of the crown. He looked over the demand from Laird McTavish. He didn't care for it, but he admitted to admiration for the man's ability to see the girl's value.

Which was her father's blue blood.

Morton snapped his fingers at his secretary. "We will send a letter to the Earl of Bedford."

His secretary never questioned him. The man withdrew a sheet of parchment and dipped a quill into his inkwell, waiting for Morton to begin. The chamber was full of the scratching of the quill until Morton was satisfied. He had the secretary read the letter back before moving over to the desk and waiting while the man lifted a small silver ladle sitting beneath a candle flame to keep the wax hot. The secretary poured it carefully onto a place at the bottom of the letter. It beaded, while the candle flame glittered off its surface. Morton curled his fingers into a fist and pressed his signet ring into the wax. It stung his knuckles, but didn't burn because his skin had been toughened by the numerous times he'd sealed letters. When he lifted his hand, the crest of the King of Scotland was firmly displayed in the cooled wax.

Yes.

It was a good plan. The secretary rolled the letter and placed it in a leather case, ready for a messenger to carry to the border. Part of the Earl of Morton didn't care for the English any more than his fellow Scots did, but countless centuries of war had yielded nothing and he'd be a fool to ignore that fact. Perhaps it was more a matter of better the devil he knew. The English were demons, and it would be better to have alliances with them than to deal with their armies marching onto Scottish soil.

So Morton chose the alliances.

And he would have one with the Earl of Bedford.

❦

Rolfe didn't ride to Edinburgh.

Katherine found herself in yet another stronghold, with another clan filling the yard to stare at her curiously.

A huge man came out to greet them. "Rolfe McTavish, what has ye darkening me day?" he asked.

Rolfe slid from the back of his horse and turned to offer Katherine a hand down. He pulled her away from her horse once her feet had touched the ground.

"Duncan Lindsey, Katherine Carew."

Duncan's eyes narrowed as he considered her. He was every bit as large as Rolfe, but they were opposites because he had devil-dark eyes and midnight hair.

"I've heard that name before," Duncan said as he considered her.

"Ye have," Rolfe responded as he took her up the steps to a tower. "Morton tried to force Marcus MacPherson to wed her a few years back."

Duncan chuckled, his eyes sparkling. "Morton is a fool more times than not. He should have known he was on borrowed luck after forcing Bhaic MacPherson to wed Ailis Robertson."

"And he learned that lesson when Marcus left with a different wife and the lass in tow as well."

Katherine felt Duncan contemplating her. "And now the McTavishes have ye."

Inside the tower, the scent of supper was thick in the air.

Duncan gestured to a woman, who came bustling over to him. "See to the lass."

The woman lowered herself before propping her hands on her ample hips and looking Katherine over from head to toe.

"A bath first," she said.

Katherine started to lower herself but quelled the urge. Instead she moved away, determined to ignore Rolfe. It wasn't a matter of what she wanted. No, it was a necessity that might protect her from the moment when he delivered her to the man she feared the most. Her feelings strengthened with every moment she was with him. It would be hard enough to leave him as it was.

Better to remind herself of her fate. At least that way, she would not cry.

❧

"I'm thinking ye should be thankful the little lass did nae have a dagger," Duncan observed as he settled himself in a chair inside his solar. The Lindsey stronghold wasn't as large as McTavish Castle, but that was because there was more than one fortification on Lindsey land. "The look she sent ye was sharp enough to draw blood, man."

"Best make yer men aware that Katherine knows how to use a dagger," Rolfe responded as he settled in beside Duncan.

Duncan had been lifting a mug to his lips, but he paused and locked gazes with Rolfe. "Ye're planning on leaving her here?"

Rolfe nodded. "Ye owe me a favor."

A memory crossed Duncan's eyes, his expression drawing tight. "I do. Now tell me what is so important about this girl that ye're calling in that favor."

Duncan placed his mug on the table and ignored it. Rolfe didn't blame him. It had been years before, but Duncan owed Rolfe his life. Rolfe didn't have any doubt Duncan would pay the debt, but that didn't mean the man would be fool enough to think Rolfe would call it in for anything frivolous.

"I'll be straight with ye," Rolfe said. "And no' be surprised if ye tell me to take her and get off yer land."

Duncan's eyes narrowed. "It's been too long since ye've come down out of the Highlands, man. Ye seem to think me cock has shriveled up and I'm less of a Highlander than yerself. I might be closer to the border, but I've not taken to kissing Morton's ass along with that lot clustered around him and our boy king."

Rolfe enjoyed Duncan's brassy humor. "Katherine is English."

"Now I'm insulted ye think I am blind as well," Duncan responded. "To think I'd overlook how fetching that lass is in favor of her blood. Now that wounds me, Rolfe, truly."

"I'll be the one wounding ye if ye do more than notice," Rolfe warned.

Duncan's eyebrows rose. "Is that so?"

Rolfe nodded. Duncan picked up the mug and drew off a long sip. "Interesting, considering she looked as if she wanted to gut ye. I might just do as ye say, all in the interest of enjoying the spectacle of ye trying yer hand at changing her mind. That little lass does nae like Scots."

"That is no' the reason she is thinking of drawing me blood," Rolfe responded.

Duncan tapped the tabletop. "I'm growing old waiting for ye to explain the matter."

Rolfe nodded. "Marcus MacPherson took Katherine up into the Highlands. He trained her."

Duncan absorbed those words. "Why?"

"Because she's English, and Marcus… Well, the man is ever practical."

Duncan nodded. "I suppose it makes sense, even if I doubt I'd be brazen enough to tempt the Church by doing something similar. Now tell me why ye think I'd send ye on yer way empty-handed after ye saved me life."

"Because me father has a mind to trade her to Morton for a title, and I plan to leave Morton with naught."

Duncan took a moment to consider the matter. His lips started to rise into a grin that Rolfe recognized from their younger days, when they'd been hell-bent on embracing their wild natures.

"I can nae wait to hear how ye plan to do it."

Rolfe's eyes brightened. "I plan to have ye help me dupe the man."

Duncan chuckled again, only this time the sound was crusty and full of anticipation. "No one will enjoy it more than us Lindseys."

❧

There was a rap on her chamber door. Katherine turned and watched Rolfe enter. She cursed the way her heart leaped in response and then regretted her fickle emotions. There would be plenty of time to be unhappy in the future. Best not to impose such things upon herself.

"I've business for ye to attend to, lass," Rolfe said softly.

There were men with him. They came through the door and tugged on the corner of their bonnets as they crossed into the room. One of them placed a writing desk on the table, lifting its lid and withdrawing a sheet of paper. He placed it on the top of the desk and withdrew the waxed rope stopper used to keep the ink in the small pottery jar.

"Ye remember Duncan Lindsey?"

Katherine nodded. The man offered her a grin that

was as devilish as the color of his hair. There was a gleam in his eyes that set her on edge, because Rolfe's jaw was set and his expression guarded.

"Yes."

She started to venture closer to the page, intending to read it. Rolfe stepped into her path. "I am no' taking ye to Morton."

To say she was surprised was an understatement. Katherine absorbed his words as she looked again at Duncan. The man was enjoying the moment far too much for her comfort.

"So just where are you planning on taking me?"

"To church," Rolfe replied. He tapped the page of paper behind him. "I've had a contract drawn up."

"And I'm here to witness ye signing it," Duncan added.

They appeared to be well pleased with themselves. A tingle touched her nape as Katherine debated asking Rolfe what he meant. She stepped closer to the table to see what sort of contract he had brought with him.

"Are you insane?" she demanded. "A contract of marriage?"

Duncan Lindsey was choking on his amusement, his knuckles turning white as he gripped his shirtsleeves over his upper arms. "Might be, at that. He just might."

She tore her attention from the contract to glare at him briefly before looking back at the desk. It was there, in bold, black ink. Rolfe William Brian McTavish and her own name, clearly noted as the parties entering into holy wedlock.

"It's the perfect solution," Rolfe said, trying to soothe her.

"Perfect?" She looked up to find him watching her intently. "Perfect until you take me home to your father as his daughter-in-law. I doubt he'd consider your actions very favorably."

A gleam appeared in Rolfe's eyes that drove home just why he was as arrogant as he was. The man had more daring than was healthy for a single soul. Of course, she'd come to realize that more than one Highlander suffered from that same affliction.

"Me father will appreciate me cunning" was his confident response.

Katherine settled her hands on her hips and scoffed at him. "Right before he has me smothered."

"Ah…she's met yer father, I see." Duncan was doing a poor job of containing his snickers.

"There is nothing for you to witness. Get out." She was being overly daring to order the man about in his own tower, but Katherine didn't really think about her words.

Duncan's dark eyebrows rose with surprise before he opened his arms wide and lowered himself in a mocking display of courtesy. "One of the fine things about Scotland is, now that he's offered to make an honest woman of ye, I really do nae need to stay to protect yer reputation."

"So I'll sign that contract or face being labeled unpure?"

Duncan nodded without a hint of remorse for the blunt fact that he was trapping her.

Katherine pointed at the door, her temper straining against the hold she had on it. "I don't much care if your people say I've sampled half your men."

Duncan had started toward the door, but he turned and cocked his head to one side. "And ye did nae think to share any of yer honey with me?"

"Duncan!" Rolfe growled at his friend. "If ye do nae mind, I need to woo me bride."

Katherine snorted, eliciting another round of snickers from Duncan.

"I'll tell the surgeon to expect ye shortly."

Duncan held the door wide for his men and let it swing shut the moment the last of them was past the threshold. He closed the door with a solid sound that shattered Katherine's anger, letting it fall to the floor like ice, and leaving her to look at Rolfe in pure, unguarded uncertainty.

He was watching her now, determination glittering in his eyes, his jaw set stubbornly.

"I would never allow me father to harm ye, Kat."

He meant it. Part of her didn't care to insult him by arguing, but that left her far too aware of the marriage contract sitting on the table near her and the fact that there were only her own arguments to overcome. Ink and quill were at the ready while Rolfe McTavish stood waiting for her to accept his suit. It both astonished and confounded her. No one had ever wanted her, not merely for herself. The contract was only a single page long, because no one was promising him anything.

Did she dare?

Christ, wasn't Fate done toying with her?

"You don't question your father," she began, trying to find some patience. No one chose their parents, after all, and the scriptures bound all children to obey their parents.

"Which can lose its shine when I fail to consider what my father is ordering done," Rolfe explained. "Ye reminded me the other night of just how important it is for me to question him from time to time."

She shifted away from Rolfe and the contract. Her heart was thumping hard beneath her breastbone, pushing her blood through her veins too fast. That made it hard to concentrate and form calm thoughts.

Katherine pointed at the contract. "That is not an answer to anything."

Rolfe slowly grinned, giving her a glimpse of his teeth. It made him both menacing and delectable. He stepped toward her and she retreated, earning a soft sound of victory from him.

"It's an answer, sure enough," he offered in a soft tone edged with promise. "I want to take ye to bed, and by Christ, I will wed ye first. For I will no' act like a brute who sees ye as a prize."

Was it so simple?

Katherine scoffed at her own thoughts. Life was never so easy.

"We cannot do any such thing," she told him firmly.

He crossed his arms over his chest and faced her with his feet braced shoulder-width apart. He was only two paces from her, making it necessary for her to look up to lock gazes with him.

"And why no'?" he asked seriously. "Are ye contracted to another?"

She shook her head.

"Promised?" he pressed her.

"I am English," she argued. "And your father detests me for it."

Rolfe closed the distance between them, and her breath caught. He reached out and gently tapped her on her chin. So simple a touch, and yet she jerked because it felt as if lightning had just struck her.

"Are…ye…promised? By the MacPhersons' word or yer own?"

He had that sense of purpose, the one he'd so often used when dealing with her. Part of her was melting in response to it, the need to just sag against him and allow him to shelter her nearly overwhelming.

She drew herself up straight instead. "You would respect a private promise I may have made?"

"I respect ye enough to insist we take the Church's blessing before I take ye to bed." He tilted his head to one side and offered her an arrogant grin, with no apology for how personal his words were. "I'll be happy to allow ye time to pen the man a letter explaining why ye chose me over him. If he does nae have the blessing of the MacPherson, the man has nae the courage ye deserve in a husband."

"That is not funny," she exclaimed. "And you are too sure of yourself by far, sir."

"I'm sure I crave ye." His voice had deepened, stroking something deep inside her. He reached out and caressed her cheek with the backs of his fingers.

She shuddered, sensation flooding her. The simplest of things, such as breathing, had becoming difficult with him so close.

"And very sure ye want me to touch ye."

He moved close, slipping his hand around the back of her head to cradle her nape.

"So," he muttered, just a bare inch from kissing her, "I am going to wed ye."

"But your father—"

Rolfe sealed her protest beneath his lips. It was a firm kiss that pressed his will upon her. She shifted but honestly couldn't say if what she felt was the need to get closer to him or to move away. They were twisting against each other, her hands on his chest as she tried to use his clothing to pull him closer. She rose onto her toes, pressing her mouth against his as she kissed him back.

Heat flared between them, stealing her breath and turning her thoughts into vapor that dissipated in the flames of need. There were so many new sensations, things she'd never associated with passion before. Such as the way her nipples contracted into hard little points. It wasn't from a chill and they didn't hurt, but there was a definite ache that had her pressing forward, seeking out some sort of comfort from his body.

Rolfe tore his mouth from hers and kept control of her nape to keep her from following him.

"Sign the contract." His voice was raspy, his eyes glittering with hard purpose. He released her and backed away, as though he doubted his own control. He paused at the door and sent her a look that left no doubt about how determined he was.

"I will have ye," he declared. "And I will no' do so without giving ye the respect ye have earned." He looked past her. "Sign it."

"And if I do not?" She questioned him, or maybe her own need to quarrel with his will. Honestly, she did not know for certain.

"Ye are a coward." He pulled the chamber door open. "For I will stand firm in the face of me father's displeasure because ye are a woman of rare spirit, and I willingly admit I want to bed ye nearly more than I want to continue drawing breath. Refuse to meet me in church, lass, and ye are afraid of yer own body—and that is a solid fact."

He closed the door, the sound like a stone dropping in the chamber. She flinched, wrapping her arms around herself because she felt chilled without him against her. The surface of her lips was tingling and still moist from his kiss. Her heart was racing, and she felt more aware of her body than she ever had been. Wave after wave of sensation was washing over her, and as her thoughts returned, she faced the hard truth that Rolfe had awakened something inside her.

It was rare.

Perhaps it was also wicked.

For certain, she knew the way lust was spoken of in church, and yet she couldn't help but feel elated over the sheer intensity of the feeling. To think she might have gone through life without ever feeling it horrified her, making her sure she would have missed out on something very special.

Intimate…

Yes, that was the correct word, or at least when such feelings were sanctioned by the Church. Katherine came to a stop near the table, looking down at the contract. The black ink on the creamy paper would serve to legalize her relationship with a man and take it from murky, slanderous terms such as *fornication* into the realm of holy wedlock.

One a sin, the other a duty.

Rolfe was correct: if she refused, she was a coward. Frightened of her own gender and unwilling to embrace everything that being a woman meant. That knowledge burst upon her as she stood there, looking past the table to where the bed was.

It would have been simple for him to claim her, and not many would have reprimanded him for it.

She was English. Her blood deserved to suffer recompense.

Rolfe wasn't that sort. She smiled as she contemplated his character. His nobility was more than a word spoken by men who didn't care for the struggle it might take to uphold it. Rolfe embodied it.

She dipped the quill and signed her name on the bottom of the contract. Only after she'd laid the quill aside did she realize she'd held her breath.

The ink was shiny at first, slowly drying as Katherine smiled at the sight of her name.

Embrace her fate?

Indeed.

That was exactly what she would do after all.

Five

"YER FATHER IS GOING TO HAVE YER BALLS CUT OFF," Adwin warned.

Rolfe reached for a lump of soap and started to wash his chest. "He might curse me, but he'd no' want to see his bloodline ended by castrating me."

Adwin had been worrying the edge of his bonnet. He stopped and threw the wool hat to the ground in frustration. "Ye are no' going to talk yer way out of anything, Rolfe. Yer father will no' forgive ye for wedding an English lass."

Rolfe slipped down in the tub until he was submerged and came up as water went streaming down his face. He wiped it out of his eyes before working the soap into his hair. "If me father was so worried about it, he should have arranged a match for me."

"And that is how ye repay yer father's kindness in no' swearing ye into a contract with a woman ye've never laid eyes upon?" Adwin reached down and scooped up his bonnet with a motion full of repressed anger. "Ye're fortunate beyond measure to have a sire who thought to let ye have a look at the fillies before deciding on one for ye to marry. He has them brought up every summer, and ye know it well."

Adwin put his bonnet back on, glaring at Rolfe.

"She's the one I want, the one I crave."

Adwin's fingers went still as he locked gazes with Rolfe. The chamber was silent for a long moment before Adwin let out a snort.

"Ye would settle on an English lass."

Rolfe went back to working the soap into his hair. "Is no' marriage for alliances?"

His captain gripped his wide belt and scoffed at him. "Do nae think I don't know ye are just saying what ye think will gain ye me compliance."

"True." Rolfe sent his captain a cocky grin. "But I'll admit, I do nae want to be known as the man who gave Morton what he wanted, when he demanded it. There is only one way to ensure he can nae wed her to someone else for his gain, and that's if I take her as me bride before he knows about it."

Adwin fought it, but he ended up grinning in response. "The earl does make a fair number of demands when it comes to us Highland clans."

"He does," Rolfe agreed. "And I am no' going to have him thinking I will be less difficult to bring into his plans than Marcus MacPherson was."

Adwin's grin widened. "No, we can nae have that. Still, it's a dangerous game. The earl is a Douglas and will nae be duped easily, nor will he be fool enough to not see exactly what game ye are playing."

"That's why I'm wedding Katherine before I ride down to meet the man. I want him to know the

McTavish will not be dancing to his tune like those who inhabit his court."

Adwin's expression became serious. "He might still dissolve the marriage, consummated or not—or worse yet, clap ye in irons. The truth is, the girl's family has no' agreed to the match."

"Aye, I thought of that meself." Rolfe slid down and submerged his head to rinse the soap from it. When he came up and wiped his eyes free of water, Adwin was waiting for an explanation. "So I hope Marcus shows up soon to attend the wedding. I sent him word of me plans."

"Ye did...*what*?" Adwin was back to throwing his bonnet onto the floor. "He's as likely to kill ye as give ye his blessing."

"With the MacPhersons, it's one and the same." Rolfe leaned forward and started washing his feet. "But it beats being fool enough to ride down to Morton with Katherine, hoping the earl plans to treat the McTavish well."

Adwin made a low sound under his breath. "The earl has no liking for the Highland clans, and that's a well-known fact."

"So," Rolfe continued, "better my father's displeasure over what I've done than returning home with naught."

"But..." Adwin was stroking his beard. "Ye do nae have to wed her. The contracts would do the trick."

Rolfe looked toward his captain. "She did keep us from having to fight the bloody Gordons."

"And sending her home with Marcus will even out the debt."

Rolfe shook his head. "I can nae let her go."

It was an admission, one Adwin wouldn't dismiss because he knew Rolfe very well. Adwin still held Rolfe's gaze for a time before shaking his head. "Well, ye're no' the first man to be taken by a lass and no' able to separate business from yer cravings."

"And I can no' refuse to go to see Morton, since me father has ordered it so." Rolfe inhaled deeply.

"So ye'll wed her to deny Morton an easy path to claiming her," Adwin said.

Rolfe slowly smiled.

"Get in one of those tubs, Adwin. Ye know there is naught like a wedding to make the lasses more receptive to a man's charms after the feast has been finished. A few of Duncan's housemaids watch ye as if ye're something they'd like a taste of."

His captain slowly grinned, a flicker of wicked knowledge in his eyes. He left the bonnet on the floor and unbuckled his belt. "That's a solid fact, and I won't have to be worrying about them following me home."

Rolfe heard his friend shucking the last of his clothing before taking one of the kettles hanging over the fire and pouring the hot water into a tub. Then there was a splash and a sound of male enjoyment as Adwin settled into the bath.

❦

It was over so quickly.

Katherine still heard her blood roaring in her ears, while each breath took effort. Her fingers felt like ice, while her body was hot, and her thoughts jumped about like rabbits after a spring rain.

"She's going to wilt."

Katherine stiffened and turned her head away from Rolfe to look at his captain. "I will do no such thing."

Adwin was cleaner than she'd ever seen the man, his shoulder-length hair brushed and tied back, while his bonnet looked as if someone had brushed the dust of the road off it. Even his beard was trimmed and free of crumbs. He tilted his head to one side and fixed her with a narrow-eyed look. "Are ye doing that on purpose? Sounding more English?"

"She's nervous," Rolfe answered his captain.

Katherine returned her attention to him.

To her husband.

The word felt odd as she contemplated the look of satisfaction in his eyes. Many would tell her it was lust and the knowledge that he would have satisfaction now that the priest had finished the blessing.

She wanted to believe it was more.

Perhaps she was doomed to be cut deeply in the morning when Fate showed her again how little she seemed to be worth to those around her and Rolfe proved he'd wanted to bed her naught more. But for the moment, she enjoyed the way Rolfe gently captured her hands and warmed her icy digits.

"Nervous." Duncan spoke smoothly from where he stood near Rolfe. "Nothing a good drink will nae soothe."

Duncan's people were enjoying the excuse to celebrate. The hall was full of music and good food. Although the Head of House had been given very little warning of the wedding, the woman had done a fine job in laying out a feast.

"Come, my friend." Duncan indicated the two chairs in the middle of the head table. It was the place of honor reserved for the laird, but Duncan made it clear that Rolfe and Katherine would preside over the feast.

Katherine shuffled up the stairs, feeling all eyes on her and blushing because she was so ungraceful in the gown she wore. The lessons of her childhood paled against the reality of dealing with a boned farthingale and two skirts that had more fabric in them than anything she'd ever worn.

Two Lindsey women leaned over behind her and tugged the whole ensemble up when she sat down, tucking the fabric around her before two retainers pushed her chair forward toward the table.

"So lovely to see yer mother's dress being used."

It was the Head of House who spoke, and she sent a firm look straight at Duncan that made the man pause. Katherine gained a rare glimpse of the burly Highlander being taken down a peg before he masked his emotions and resumed offering the first toast to them.

The music was a fine treat, and servant after servant presented trays loaded with meat, fruit, cheese, and other delights.

Rolfe looked toward her after she stopped eating. "Ye do nae care for the fare?"

She discovered her breath catching. Suddenly, she was unbearably conscious of the fact that he had the right to touch her, and the rather firm knowledge that she wanted him to exercise that right.

He pointed at a platter, and a maid hurried over to carry it to him.

"No, really, I cannot eat another bite."

"Ye've barely touched yer supper." Rolfe contemplated her plate. "Me reputation could use a bit of a shine from everyone saying I made ye forget to eat in yer haste to get to the bedchamber, but—"

She lifted her hand and delivered a light blow to his arm in reprimand. "Honestly," she said under her breath. "Keep talking like that, and you will spend your wedding night in the stocks for pride."

Rolfe grinned at her and pointed at something off to her left. When Katherine turned her head, she caught sight of the clan priest. He had his head tipped back to empty his mug, and when the man finished, he licked his lips, to the delight of those sitting near him. A maid was already lifting a pitcher to refill the man's mug when he started singing.

"The man seems to feel morality has been well and truly served by our wedding." Rolfe spoke close to her ear.

Katherine shivered at the feeling of his breath against her skin, and he reached out and stroked the gooseflesh that rose along her neck. She felt her eyes widen as she locked gazes with him, lost in some sort of connection that made everything around them disappear.

A loud burst of laughter broke the spell. Duncan Lindsey was out of his chair and pounding on the tabletop with his fist.

"The lass is finished eating, Rolfe!" Duncan declared in a voice that shook the rafters. "Only a fool would argue with her about lingering at the table!"

The hall erupted into merriment. Men tipped their heads back as they laughed, and women shot her knowing looks. A few of them were downright catty as they cast longing glances toward Rolfe, making it plain they envied her.

"Off to bed with ye!" Duncan declared with a raised mug.

Katherine felt her eyes widen at the blunt mention of what her night would include, but she had little time to linger over it as her chair was pulled back and she was lifted right out of it. The Lindsey retainers never let her feet touch the floor, hoisting her high above their heads and carrying her toward the passageway, to the delight of the Lindseys watching.

But she was happy enough to go, because the suggestions being called out set her cheeks on fire more than the fact that she was being taken abovestairs to consummate her vows.

The Lindsey women weren't going to be left out of the fun, either. They flooded the chamber, taking delight in kicking the men out before they turned on her.

"Let's get ye out of that dress."

"Aye, 'twould be a terrible shame if it were to be torn."

"No man knows how a fine dress like that is laced."

"It would be damaged for certain."

"And ye do nae need it anymore."

Katherine twisted and turned, but they still managed to get at the lacing that went down the back of the dress. They laughed at her as they lifted the bodice away, and Katherine felt hands on the hooks that secured the waistband.

"I really can tend to myself," she implored them.

"Nonsense," an older woman said from where she stood supervising the entire madness. "A dress like that, well now, it's a noble one. Ladies do nae do anything themselves."

"English ones," someone added as the overskirt came free and was taken across the chamber.

"My stepmother ran the house," Katherine said.

Some of the women stilled, fixing her with critical looks.

Katherine merely shrugged. "From what I recall, she kept the books and oversaw the kitchens and social events as well as keeping up with correspondence."

"Sounds as though she set a decent example for ye," the woman in front of her offered before she snapped her fingers and pointed at the underskirt. "But did she tell ye what yer duties are as a wife?"

There was more than one giggle in response as the women took away the underskirt and Katherine's farthingale puddled around her ankles when the drawstring was released. Her hip roll was next, leaving her in her corset, smock, and stockings.

"I know what...well...how it all fits together."

There was a fresh round of amusement at her expense as the women took to pulling every last hairpin from her hair.

"If a lass is lucky, it fits together very nicely."

"I'd enjoy having Rolfe McTavish fit his parts to mine, and that's a fact."

"All right then." The woman in front of Katherine raised her voice, and there was the unmistakable ring of authority in her tone. "Enough of that. Ye've had yer fun. Off with ye."

There were sounds of disappointment, but the chamber began to empty, making Katherine realize how tightly she was clenching her fists. Her fingernails had pressed deep into the skin of her palms.

The older woman waited until the rest of the Lindsey women were gone. She offered a kindly smile before she picked up a comb from the dressing table and came toward Katherine.

"There is no shame in admitting ye do nae know what is to come tonight." She was pulling the comb through Katherine's hair, sparking a memory from a time when her own mother had once done so for her.

So very long ago.

"I know," Katherine said softly, not wanting to break the spell of the moment. "The MacPhersons allowed me to train, and, well…"

"Ye think ye heard everything there is to know?" The woman continued to comb. "Mind ye, if yer groom treats ye as men talk in the yard, I'll have the laundress pour salt in his washing."

"Salt?" Katherine turned a questioning look toward her.

The woman offered her a knowing smirk as she extended the comb. "Makes the fabric itch, especially on the tender spots beneath a man's arms and at the back of the neck. A gentle reminder that while a man is master of his house, only a woman can make it into a home."

She moved behind Katherine and began to work at the lace holding the corset tight. "Little wonder ye were finished eating. I have no idea why ladies wear these. If you're fortunate, you won't be able to fit in it come summer's end."

The woman eased the corset down Katherine's arms and knelt to untie one garter and then another. Her stockings slipped down as soon as they were free.

She hadn't thought about children.

Of course that was a duty of a wife, but she had not truly contemplated what it would mean to force her blood onto a child.

Was it cruel?

There was a rap on the door as the woman stood and nodded at Katherine's undressed state. Only her smock remained.

"That will be the midwife."

The chamber door opened, and two older women looked in. The woman in front of Katherine waved them forward.

"Off with that smock now."

Katherine gripped it instead, which earned her a raised eyebrow.

"It's better ye are inspected," the woman said softly. "Especially with ye being English and yer groom no' having the blessing of his father."

Katherine felt her mouth go dry. She had failed to consider just how easy it would be for Laird McTavish to annul the marriage. The women took advantage of her shock, pulling her last garment from her. She felt her hair flutter down to lie against her bare back as the two midwives lifted candles from the tables and brought them close.

They missed nothing, lifting her hair so that every inch of her back was seen. She felt the heat of the candle flame when they brought it close to check for witch marks or hidden nipples where she might suckle a demon. There was safety in submitting to the examination, and yet she felt unbearably exposed. The moment they nodded with satisfaction, Katherine plucked her chemise out of the first woman's hand and put it on.

There was a little sound of amusement from one of the midwives.

"Ye're no wanton," the other said with a nod.

"Come." The first woman was standing near the bed, with the bedding pulled down. "Yer groom will be on his way soon."

Katherine slid into the bed, feeling none of the comfort of the fine sheets. There was a teasing scent of rosemary and amber, sprinkled about for fertility and good fortune. The three women contemplated her before nodding again.

"Good night to ye."

⁂

Duncan slapped a book down on the table in front of Rolfe.

"There ye are, lad. Just what ye'll need tonight."

Rolfe cocked his head to the side and sent his friend a glare. Duncan wasn't impressed at all. He wiped his mouth with a linen before scooping up the book and opening it to a random page.

"English ladies enjoy poesy," he said.

There was a round of laughter in response.

"Ye'll likely have to read her most of this book to win her over." Duncan was searching through the pages.

"Be lucky to deflower her before dawn!" someone called out.

"Can't be showing her too much strength, or she'll wilt dead away!"

"A sleeping wife is no fun to tumble at all!"

Rolfe growled and started to stand. "I bid ye all good night."

He really should have been less trusting of his friend, because the moment he was on his feet, a plaid was tossed around his body and pulled tight.

"Duncan!"

"No need to thank me," his friend responded through his mirth. "Ye'd do the same for me."

"I've a long memory," Rolfe growled. "Ye can bet I will."

His struggles were in vain. The Lindseys had him surrounded and were rolling him in yards and yards of wool while Adwin looked on with a huge grin.

"A fine wedding present, the wool," Duncan replied. "Since yer bride retired so early, it's best ye take it on up to...her..."

Duncan was nearly doubled over with laughter. There was so much fabric that Rolfe was swaddled like a babe and reduced to glaring at his friend. The Lindsey retainers were clustered around him, admiring their work. The fabric was twisted around him from neck to ankles, so that he didn't dare move or he risked breaking his nose when he fell to the floor.

"Thank ye," Rolfe ground out. "I promise"—he stressed the word *promise*—"I'll no' be forgetting yer gesture."

Duncan heard him loud and clear but only grinned in cocky amusement as the Lindsey retainers hoisted Rolfe high and began to carry him toward his bride.

❦

Katherine was out of the bed the moment the women left her alone.

You are being silly…

Perhaps, but there was no way she could stay in the bed, just waiting for Rolfe to come and find her there. So she opened a wardrobe and found a length of Lindsey plaid. She wrapped it around herself as she pinched out several of the candles near the bed to decrease the light, in case the Lindseys decided to escort Rolfe to his nuptial chamber with the same amount of zeal as they had her.

The wedding dress was lying across several chairs. It shimmered in the candlelight, the soft silk looking like something from a child's dream. She moved toward it, gently stroking it with a single fingertip. There had been a time when she'd looked at her stepmother's collection of dresses and wistfully longed to wear such finery.

She didn't lament the past few years in Scotland. For certain, her life was nothing like those dreams, but she could never have imagined the adventures that she had been on.

And tonight?

Well, it was another sort of adventure, to be sure.

She became aware of the sound of men coming up the stairs. Her heart started to accelerate, making her breathing harsh. There was a rap on the door before it burst open, and she watched as at least fifteen Lindsey retainers came through the door in one mass, a chuckling, kilt-clad bunch.

They labored to haul something between them and left it in the middle of the receiving chamber.

"Night, ma'am."

"Felicitations!"

"Pleasant…rest…"

"Get out, the lot of ye savages." Adwin followed his order with a couple of kicks at the backsides of the men who were a bit slower in their obedience.

The chamber door was shut with a very firm sound that she felt as well as heard.

For it left her very much alone with her groom.

❧

"I wondered…when ye'd come for me."

Colum Gordon's voice crackled with age, but there was a clear note of victory in it. Tyree moved closer, noting the glitter of satisfaction in the old man's eyes.

"Always glad to be of service," Tyree said mockingly.

Colum's attention flickered to the pillow Tyree had in his fist. "I stopped sleeping in the bed years ago," he continued. "Because I knew one of ye would try to smother me."

Tyree grinned. "Easy enough in a chair."

He tightened his grip on the pillow and raised it.

"No' as easy as ye think, lad."

Tyree froze. Diocail's voice came from the far corner of the laird's chamber. As he watched, Diocail emerged from behind a tapestry.

Colum chuckled. "I still have loyal men who will no' allow ye to murder me."

"Loyal?" Tyree questioned. "He allowed the witch to escape."

Colum's face tightened. "Is that true?"

Diocail came closer and braced his feet shoulder-width apart. "It is."

Colum tried to say something but ended up hacking.

"And I will no' apologize," Diocail continued once his laird had quieted. "She was no' a witch, and I will no' feed the hunger for witch-hunting. 'Tis a nasty thing, that, breeding fear in folks who would have otherwise had the good sense no' to see the hand of Satan where there is only the unfairness of life. The Gordons do nae need to be suspicious of one another. Before ye fault me for me actions, remember who is here to defend ye and who has come to further his own lot by snuffing out yer life."

Colum had been digging his fingers into the padded armrest of his chair. His eyes were mere slits in his head due to his rage, but he only opened and closed his mouth a few times once Diocail finished.

Tyree paled, realizing he was losing the battle. "The Gordons need new leaders, Diocail. Help me open the doors to a new laird, and ye will be me war chief. It's hardly murder—he's got one foot in the grave already."

"Murder is murder," Diocail replied. "I have enough sins to bear without adding that sordid bit of business to me list of transgressions, and I will no' be standing by while ye do it. No' when I've sworn me allegiance to Colum as laird of the Gordons. A man is only as good as his word."

"Well, then." Tyree dropped the pillow and pulled his dirk. "It will be a fine morning, because I'll be greeting it with ye and Colum both dead." He began to move in a slow circle around Diocail. "After all, I came here and found ye murdering our laird. Such a shame I was too late to stop ye, but I dispensed justice."

Colum tried to cry out for help, but his voice was thin and didn't carry across the wide expanse of his huge chambers.

Diocail only bared his teeth and curled his fingers in a come-hither gesture. "Try me, lad."

Tyree grinned, but a moment later he was jabbing at Colum. Blood went spurting as the chair toppled and Diocail lunged at Tyree. They fell on the floor as Tyree turned the dirk on Diocail. It was what he'd intended, to make Diocail come at him so Tyree had the advantage.

The chamber was full of the scent of freshly spilled blood and the grunts of men fighting for their lives. Colum dragged his body away from the two men, leaving a path of blood behind him.

There was a bone-crunching sound, and the chamber went silent. Colum stopped trying to reach the door and turned to see what his fate would be. Both men were in the middle of the floor, a tangle of limbs and Gordon wool. The fresh blood was scarlet and covering both of them. For a long moment, Colum squinted at them, trying to find a hint as to which one had prevailed. It had been a long time since he'd tasted fear. Now, the taste was thick on his tongue as he felt his own blood slipping down his skin.

There was a heave and motion as Diocail sat up and pushed Tyree's lifeless body off him. There was a wicked slice down the side of his face that he didn't bother to wipe as he stood and came across the chamber.

Diocail opened the chamber door and let out a

whistle. Colum started to chuckle as he realized he'd been delivered.

❧

"It's no' something to laugh at."

Katherine shrugged. "You look like a bundle of sheep's fleece on the way to market."

He did, too, with his blond hair sticking up and the rest of him bound by the fabric. The Lindseys had left him standing on his feet and really quite helpless, if such a thing were possible.

Rolfe sent her a disapproving glare when she softly snickered.

"Duncan even included a book of poetry for yer enjoyment, but ye'll have to unwrap a few layers if ye want to find it."

"I'm astonished to hear he even knows what poetry is, much less has a book of it."

She was moving toward Rolfe, pulling one of the ends of the fabric free from where it was tucked into a fold. "There is a small fortune in cloth here."

"Aye," Rolfe agreed. "Although, for all Duncan's insisting that it is a wedding present for ye, I rather believe his true intent was to make it so I must wait on yer whim to release me."

Katherine stopped. She'd begun to circle him, unwinding the cloth, but froze as she remembered exactly what they were expected to do.

Her belly decided to knot as her hands started to shake.

Rolfe let out a very male, frustrated sound. "I suppose I'd be insensitive if I growled at ye to get on with it?"

"You would."

Of course, she'd be a coward to stand there behind him, shivering over consummating wedding vows she'd decided to willingly take.

"And if I plead for mercy?"

She laughed. "You would never do any such thing." But the break in the tension allowed her to get her feet to begin moving again. Katherine came around in front of him but kept her gaze on her work, succeeding in pulling a full measure of blue wool from him.

There were still at least three more lengths wound around him.

"Do nae doubt me, lass," he continued. "The truth of the matter is, I took a bath, but I am sweating like it's the dead of summer. So, if ye do nae release me soon, I believe I am threatening ye with the company of a man who smells less than sweet."

"Well, I shall take that under consideration."

She freed another length of wool, this one a brown color. "Is this a customary way to deliver a bridegroom?"

Rolfe snorted. "Only when Duncan Lindsey thinks I will no' get the opportunity to repay his…kindness."

"Hmm." She held up the third length of fabric and admired the dark-ruby hue. "Perhaps he wishes to soften the blow of my having no dowry."

"Katherine."

There was a firm note in his tone. He wanted her to look at him and she knew it, yet she still worried her lip before she lifted her chin and locked gazes with him.

"If I wanted a fat dowry, I'd have wed years ago."

There was a light in his eyes that made her tremble

deep down inside her body. The reaction defied her understanding, and yet she felt it so keenly, it didn't matter that she failed to make sense of it.

That was the way it was with Rolfe McTavish.

"I wanted ye," he muttered in a husky tone. "I wanted more than to bed ye. I wanted to know ye are mine."

She'd pulled another length from him and stood for a moment as she simply released it and let it settle to the floor. "There will be plenty who tell you how foolish it is to wed me for a tumble."

His lips twitched. She'd seen him grin before, but this was something different, something more intimate. It was roguish to say the least, cocksure as well, but there was a promise lurking in his eyes that made her breath catch before she circled behind him yet again and pulled another layer away from him.

He shrugged, dislodging the remaining layers and sending them down his body. She stepped back and enjoyed the sight of him emerging from the cocoon, because he was too strong a creature to be bound. There was a majestic quality in his strength that mesmerized her.

He kicked the fabric to the side and contemplated her. The Lindsey plaid she'd wrapped around her for warmth was lying discarded on a chair. She stood there in her smock, feeling as though the candles behind her made it nearly transparent.

Yet where she'd been nervous, she was now curious to see what he made of her.

Would he be disappointed in his bargain?

For all she brought to him was herself. If he stayed,

it was because he wanted to, and she found that idea endearing.

It felt as if the chamber had shrunk, now that he was free. He fixed her with a long stare before he grinned at her.

"Ye have the devil's own courage, Kat."

She lifted one shoulder in a shrug. "Some call me hellion for it." She plucked the book from where it lay nestled in the fabric and set it on a table before she turned to look back at him. "Best know I have no plans to adopt more submissive ways. If that displeases you, the door is behind you."

He snorted before laughing outright at her brazenness. The Lindseys had wrapped him up in all his clothing. He started to work the buttons on his doublet as he finished chuckling. He locked stares with her before he firmly tossed it aside.

Her mouth went dry.

But her insides felt as if they were heating.

"I am no' going anywhere."

"So I see." It had become impossible to stand still. She shifted slowly away from him, but her attention remained fixed on him as he pulled the end of his wide belt free.

You know what a man looks like…

Yes.

However, this was Rolfe. The man who made her breath catch. It was vastly different somehow. Time was moving very slowly as he tugged on that end of leather to release the buckle, and then it was free, the pleats of his kilts sagging and slipping down his hips.

It left him in his shirt and boots. Katherine found

that pleasing because they were somehow more evenly matched now, even if she'd be a fool to think he wasn't stronger than she was.

No, it wasn't about raw strength.

"Do nae fear me, Kat." His voice had become husky, but there was a genuine note of concern in it, too. One that warmed her heart.

"I wouldn't have signed the contracts if I did."

She wasn't sure she'd thought about her answer, only that the words were very true and they pleased him. She watched his expression change to one of enjoyment. Not the same as when he'd been laughing—no, this was a deeply personal sort of satisfaction.

He'd sat down to work his boots off. The fire popped, a log shifting and sending up a spray of crimson sparks while Rolfe finished getting out of his boots. He stood and faced her, contemplating the way she'd come to stop in the shadows between the bedchamber and the arched opening that led to the receiving portion of the chamber.

She likely looked frightened.

Well, at the very least, nervous.

Even admitting that wasn't enough to get her feet to move toward him.

It would be best.

Courageous.

And yet, she lingered in… Well, she wasn't exactly sure what to call it. Part of her was caught in a rush of anticipation, while the other seemed to be embracing doubts about what she was doing.

"Are ye hungry?" he asked. "Ye did nae eat very much."

Katherine shook her head. "The corset was snug."

He cast a glance at the dress where it was draped over the chairs.

"I hope ye did nae mind that the dress was nae made for ye."

"That sort of life was lost years ago when Morton stole me from England," she answered. "I have not longed for it."

"No' even now?" he asked quietly.

She ended up smiling. "Especially not now. There are some things that Scotland and England have in common, and one is the expectation of children wedding whom their parents choose."

Rolfe joined her in grinning. He was moving toward her, leaving the light behind, which suited her well. Of course, she had to tip her head back to maintain eye contact with him as he neared, and his size made her heart accelerate.

"Ye do nae think I would be yer kin's choice of groom?" he asked, a single step from her.

"No more than I am your father's."

Rolfe reached out and settled his hand against the side of her face. She shuddered with the contact, so intensely aware of him.

"Ye're mine."

He spoke in a raspy whisper before pressing his lips against hers. He'd intended it to be a soft kiss that wasn't too startling, but she rose onto her toes so she could kiss him back, and it felt as though something snapped inside her. A leash that had been holding her back, because now she reached for him, hooking her hands into his shirt as she tried to mimic the way he'd kissed her before.

The hard, determined way.

She didn't want soft.

She wanted him.

Rolfe didn't disappoint her. He took her kiss as permission to discard his attempt at being gentle. His chest vibrated with a growl as he closed his arm around her body and clamped her against him. His hand slid across her cheek and into her hair, where he closed his fingers into a fist that tugged the strands of her hair tight.

Then his mouth claimed hers in a demand that sent a jolt down to her toes. It was raw and hungry, the way he moved her mouth beneath his. There was a touch from his tongue, and then he was pressing her mouth open wide so he could thrust his tongue deep inside her mouth.

She let out a little moan.

He ripped his head away from hers in response, gaining another little cry from her.

"No, don't let me think."

He frowned at her, holding her head in place and keeping her from following him. "I am nae a beast. It does no' have to be this very moment."

But he was hard. His member was a solid length pressed against her belly. She'd seen them before, man parts, but now she felt something entirely new in regards to them. She wanted him inside her.

"I like your strength."

She wasn't entirely certain what she meant, but understanding flashed in his eyes a moment before he lifted her off her feet and carried her to the bed. It seemed perfectly correct, in all its wickedness.

Honestly, that wickedness made it even more enticing as Rolfe crawled into the bed with her. He was hot and heavy, and that felt so very good against her flesh.

So right.

As though she'd been made just for the purpose of fitting against him.

"I do…nae…want to hurt ye," he muttered against her neck, pressing tiny kisses against skin that was unbelievably sensitive. The kisses stirred the cravings inside her, making her writhe against him in an effort to get closer.

"It cannot hurt so terribly," she answered him. "Not with the way the maids defy the Church to tryst."

She slid her hands beneath his shirt, absorbing the way he felt. She had never thought she might enjoy touching another human being so very much.

"Where the devil did ye see that?"

He'd lifted his head and was glaring at her.

"You know I trained in the yard, as a boy."

Her answer hit him, making him blink, right before Rolfe McTavish did something she'd never thought to see him ever do.

He flushed.

She laughed at him and raised her thigh so his hips slipped between her legs. It felt so very right in a way that she had never imagined carnal intimacy might.

"Would you rather I lay here dreading this?" It was an honest question. Wives were expected to perform their duty in a dignified manner that she doubted included kissing him back. Uncertainty needled her, and she let her hands fall back onto the bed, feeling as if she were being denied the best food on the table in favor of devotion to piety.

"No," he answered sharply. "Sweet Christ, I think I'd agree to anything ye demand so long as ye put yer hands back on me."

It was what she wanted, and knowing he agreed was like striking a flint stone over a bowl of tinder. She felt the first teasing sparks hit her skin as she laid her hands on him, arching when it felt as if they were connected at some level of awareness she had never encountered before.

Enchantment?

Bewitchment?

All she knew for sure was that she was intoxicated, and happily so. He shifted, pushing their clothing aside as he settled between her thighs. She opened them wide and sucked in her breath when he touched her folds. The sensation was so acute that she wasn't sure if it was pain or pleasure.

Only that she wanted him to touch her again.

"Easy."

He was cooing to her, his tone soothing as he stroked her open sex. She was wet, and he teased the sensitive folds with delicate touches of his fingertips.

"I'll…no…rush…ye…"

Frustration edged his tone, but he seemed to be fighting the urge to get on with claiming her. She wanted that, too, and shifted beneath him, seeking out his member. She'd never felt empty before; now, it seemed to be the single thought she could manage. Everything had melted away beneath the feeling of his hard body.

"No…no' just yet."

He lowered more of his weight onto her, imprisoning her beneath him as he stroked her folds, drawing her wetness from where it emerged from the center of her body.

"Rolfe…"

He made a soft, male sound of amusement under his breath. "I like the sound of me name on yer lips."

He pressed a kiss on her, all the while teasing her spread sex. She writhed beneath him, gasping when he touched a spot at the top of her sex.

"I like that sound even more."

He sounded arrogant now, pleased in a very male fashion. Part of her recognized that, even if it defied her understanding completely. All she knew was that it was too difficult to keep her eyes open. She was lifting her hips up toward his hand, her lips parting because containing everything inside herself was completely impossible now.

There was too much sensation, too much tension twisting beneath his fingertips. She wanted something so badly that she was straining toward it. Desperation drew her muscles tight as she felt her abdomen ache from her effort to press herself more firmly against his touch.

Then it all burst, like a bubble above her face. She felt the tiny drops of water splattering all over her skin, in a hundred different places. Pleasure ripped through her, holding her in its grasp for moments that felt like hours before she was dropped back into reality, a panting mass of quivering flesh.

Her cheeks stung as she realized he'd watched her through the climax.

"Do nae be shy," he muttered as he kissed her softly. "If I wanted to wed for duty, I could have done so years ago. I crave yer passion, and I will nae be content without it in our bed."

They were in shadow, but she saw the glitter in his eyes, could see the way his jaw was tight, while his tone conveyed his determination. She relaxed beneath him, cradling him between her thighs.

"Then come to me." Her voice was husky, and she lifted her hips in invitation.

She watched the muscles running down his neck cord. He nodded, his teeth clenched as he moved, and she felt the first touch of his member against her sex. It was hard and yet slid easily into the slickness he'd drawn from her body.

The first thrust only drove his length halfway into her. She gasped as her passage stung, feeling as if the skin was being ripped. But he withdrew, granting her a moment to suck in a breath before he was thrusting deep, opening her wide.

He caught her hands when she raised them in defense, pressing them to the surface of the bed as he remained lodged deep inside her. What had been white-hot pain suddenly eased, like a scab jerked off the surface of a partially healed wound. One moment, it was agony, and the next, bearable.

The moment she sucked in a deep breath, the cravings returned. They were deep inside her, echoes of the intense feelings that had drawn her tight right before pleasure burst through her, but she knew what they promised now and was eager for the satisfaction that might be gained.

"More," she prompted him.

He let out a half bark of male amusement before she felt him shift his body above hers, withdrawing his length and driving it back into her with a smooth thrust that made her gasp when he lodged himself completely within her.

"I'll happily give ye plenty more."

He was as good as his word, moving with a pace that was slow and easy, helping her find the rhythm. He smoothed the hair back from her face and then held on to it as he began to move faster. His chest filled and emptied faster, his breath rasping between his teeth as she felt him growing harder. The bubble was growing tighter inside her, the approaching moment beckoning to her as she strained up toward him.

He was holding back; she felt him struggling as she clawed at his arms in need. It was all-consuming, the boundaries of right and wrong dissolving into a storm of cravings and demands from her flesh. She wanted to be taken and he didn't disappoint her, pinning her beneath him as he drove his cock into her over and over until she burst.

Pleasure wrung her body and tossed her against the wall. She was gasping, straining upward when she felt him slam his cock deep into her and groan. His hot seed flooded her, spurting against her insides as his hand tightened in her hair. For just a moment, there was pain, and it enhanced the moment in a manner she couldn't completely explain, but it unleashed another ripple of satisfaction. One born from the knowledge that he was stronger than her.

She didn't know what it meant, couldn't form

serious thoughts if she had needed to. Her body felt heavy and more satisfied than she'd ever imagined possible. So she didn't bother to open her eyes, but drifted off into sleep while wrapped in bliss.

Tomorrow would be soon enough to face her circumstances.

❧

Gordon land

"He'll no' last long."

Diocail nodded once in response to the healer before the man made his way out of the laird's chamber on shuffling footsteps.

"Bury that bastard in unhallowed ground," Colum growled from his bed.

Diocail only sent him a steady stare. Colum tried to rise, but the wound was weakening him too much.

"I am still laird."

"Aye," Diocail agreed. "And I've served ye dutifully."

"No' so well as ye think," Colum snarled. "I am still dying."

"Ye've lived a long life."

Two of Colum's captains eyed Diocail, waiting to see what Colum would make of his words. Their laird looked out from his bed, hate twisting his features. He even sent that same look toward the priest who had come to offer him last rites. Instead, he looked at his secretary and gestured him toward the bedside.

"Diocail is me chosen successor."

The secretary nodded and pulled a sheet of paper from his small traveling desk. Colum pointed at Diocail.

"And ye'll take the Hay lass as yer wife. Bring me the offer."

His secretary was off in a moment, going through the opening into the outer chamber and beyond it to where Colum kept his business papers.

"Ye'll do as I say," Colum informed Diocail. "I can see ye mean to argue with me, and I will no' have it."

"Better to wed the MacPherson girl and put an end to the bad blood between our clans."

"I…will…no'…have…it!" Colum growled, straining to rise from his bed, but his blood was draining from his body. Tyree's blade had sunk deep into the man's belly, and it was a better death to go with his blood than to linger as infection from the wound took him slowly with fever and rot.

So they had not bound the wounds, but laid him in his bed.

"My laird." The priest ventured closer, recognizing the look of approaching death. "'Tis time to repent, embrace peace, and be welcomed into heaven's grace."

Colum had no intention of embracing submission to the Church's doctrine. His eyes glittered with hatred as he pressed his signet ring into the wax his secretary had poured onto a document.

"The Hay girl…" Colum's voice was becoming weaker. "Bring me the offer…now…"

More of the Gordon captains filed into the room. Colum tried to lift his hand, but in the end, he couldn't press his ring into the wax. He slumped back against the bedding as the priest tried to gain a confession from him.

He died with hatred in his eyes.

"Do any of ye mean to challenge me?" Diocail asked the captains. They were men who had earned the respect of the Gordons, and they contemplated him for long moments before one of them shook his head and the others followed.

Diocail obviously hadn't thought it would be so simple. The most senior of the captains slowly grinned. "Ye're welcome to the burden. I have enough authority to content me, and ye will have to ride down and give yer vow to Morton. I want none of that, yet whoever takes up the mantle of laird will have to see it done."

"I will do it," Diocail declared.

The senior captain nodded before lowering himself to one knee and pulling his dagger. He pressed a kiss of allegiance against the blade before rising.

The other captains slowly made their way over to kneel before Diocail. Colum looked on in death, the priest finally closing his eyes once the last man had knelt.

His mother would have enjoyed the moment.

Diocail felt her spirit rejoicing to see her son, the unwanted whelp, being given Colum's blessing. She'd taken him into the isles to make sure he survived, and the harsh life had aged her. But he was strong and enough of a man to reclaim what she had always told him was his birthright.

He turned and left the chamber, going to face the first true challenge of his lairdship. It wasn't coming in the form of feuding clans that he needed to run his land.

No, it was in the form of the Earl of Morton, and

Diocail would have been a fool to dismiss how very dangerous the coming meeting was.

ҽ๑

Katherine's eyes popped opened the next morning while it was still gray.

"I thought they'd at least wait until dawn," Rolfe groused as he rolled out of the bed and found his shirt. "Best rise, lass."

There was a flutter as her chemise came sailing across the bed toward her.

She grabbed it and tugged at the sleeves to pull them right side out, her fingers fumbling as she heard the footfalls coming closer.

"Lord, it sounds as if half the Lindsey clan is coming," she muttered as she succeeded in getting into her shift.

Not a moment too soon, either. The door burst in without a knock as Katherine held tight to the covers. The chemise was puddled around her waist, and her bare bottom was still beneath the bedding.

"Ye are a dead man."

Marcus MacPherson stood in the doorway, wearing enough dirt to tell her he'd been riding hard for a long time. His face was coated with it, so when he flashed his teeth at Rolfe, they looked even brighter due to how much grime was on his face.

"Marcus…" Rolfe began, but that was all he got out before Marcus was lunging at him.

The chamber was full of people now. Someone drew her out of the bed, pulling her into the small antechamber to be dressed. Katherine fought against the women trying to shield her modesty as she heard the crashing and cursing coming from the bedchamber.

But the Lindsey women were too many, keeping her in place. She finally decided to help get her clothing on, because it was clear she wasn't going anywhere until she was dressed.

"Pull those two apart." Duncan arrived, and his men acted upon his command.

There was cursing and growling, but there were just too many Lindsey retainers, and Marcus ended up pushed against one wall, while Rolfe and Adwin were kept against another.

"I do love weddings," Duncan declared as he looked toward the bed. The soiled sheet was plain in the dawn light. "Looks like it was enjoyed by everyone."

Marcus let out a snarl and surged toward Rolfe again. "Ye should have kept yer hands off her!"

"Marcus!" Katherine slipped beneath the arms of the men holding him back. He drew himself up as she straightened up in front of him. The rage on his face cracked to reveal relief. "Christ, lass, it is good to see ye well."

He wrapped his arms around her, using so much strength that he nearly cracked her ribs.

"And ye do nae have to stay married to him," Marcus spat out once he'd finished embracing her. "Leave that sheet and get out."

The Lindsey women had turned their attention to the bed, pulling the stained sheet off. They looked at Marcus, clearly resistant to his order.

"Katherine is me wife," Rolfe declared. There was

a glint in his eyes that made it clear he would back his words with his body if necessary.

"We'll be seeing about that," Marcus promised in return. "Get out, the lot of ye. I will be hearing what Kat has to say when she is no' surrounded by those who have something to gain by forcing her hand."

The Lindseys bristled at the insult and looked toward their laird. Marcus glared at Duncan.

"Ye'd say the same if ye were standing in me boots right now."

No one moved until Duncan gave them a wave with his hand. The chamber began to empty, but Marcus had to yank the soiled sheet out of the hands of the Head of House when she tried to carry it past him.

"Ye'd have the lass shamed, then?" the woman declared. "If I appear below without that, there will always be rumors about her."

Marcus didn't lose his temper often. That iron control was a trait Katherine had come to admire about him. Right then, it was stretched thin, but she was distracted by the look on Rolfe's face. Her new husband was looking straight at her, waiting for her to make a choice.

"Take the sheet," Kat said.

Marcus shifted his attention to her, his eyes narrowing. The Head of House didn't wait for further discussion. She hurried out of the chamber, leaving Katherine feeling her cheeks burning scarlet as she realized everyone was there to discuss what she'd been doing with Rolfe.

But what made her belly tighten to the point of

nausea was just how determined Marcus was to see the marriage dissolved.

❧

Colum Gordon was interred beneath the floor of the church beside his son. His wife had been buried in the graveyard behind the structure in punishment for only providing one living son to her husband. If Diocail had his way, he'd have let the man rot in unhallowed ground for all of the hate he'd kept festering inside him. The Gordons were despised by the clans on all sides of them because of it, and it would fall to Diocail to change their ways.

That would be a difficult task, but one his mother had reared him to face. He would not shame her by failing.

Especially on the very first day.

The hall was unusually somber at supper. Diocail sat at the high table, contemplating his new clan. He finally stood.

"I will be heading down to swear fealty to the Earl of Morton."

There was a grumble among the Gordon retainers.

"The man is the regent for our king, and I will no' be frightened away by the tales of him. Even if I believe a great many of them are true."

There was a rumble of approval.

"I'd expect ye to toss me out on me arse if I were no' man enough to face the earl."

Now there were grins. A few of the retainers lifted their mugs toward him.

"And I'm going to say what is being said among ye."

Diocail braced his feet wide and faced them. "That I am no' a Gordon because me mother left this land."

He stopped for a moment and watched his words sink in. There was a shuffle among those eating at the long tables as they eased closer, wanting to hear what else he had to say.

"Me mother took me away so I'd live to see this day." Diocail spoke clearly. "But only after someone tried to poison her, while I was still on her breast. Me father died from it. Colum's ambition was stronger than his decency. Now that he is gone, I intend to speak clearly and truthfully."

It wasn't considered right to speak ill of the dead, but there was more than one nod among those watching.

Diocail came down the steps and stood on the hall floor. "So, if there are any among ye who wish to challenge me openly, now is the time. Any man who resorts to potions and daggers in the dark shadows is a coward and no' fit to lead the Gordons. For those whispering behind me back, I call ye out now. Make yer arguments here, before all, or have done with trying to split the Gordons. I will honor the choice made by the majority and leave this castle, but so too will whoever stands against me."

It was as silent as a graveyard. No one moved, and most of those watching held their breath as they waited. Diocail watched the looks some of the men made, quick glances toward silent members of the clan that told him exactly who was talking behind his back.

None of them stepped forward.

"It is done," Leif said from the high table. He was the senior captain, a man who had served the Gordons for over thirty years. "Aed can start with the swearing of fealty."

Aed was one of the men the other clansmen had looked toward. His jaw was clenched as he hesitated. He moved forward and drew his dagger. There was a long moment as everyone waited to see if he'd challenge or kneel.

He knelt and pledged as a line formed behind him.

Six

"I WOULD HAVE THOUGHT YE'D BE TALKING TO Katherine."

Marcus MacPherson offered Rolfe a menacing grin. "Ye can be very sure I will be having words with me sister later."

"She is no' yer sister," Rolfe responded. "At the moment, ye are acting far more like her father."

"At the risk of agreeing with ye, when all I want to do is choke the life from ye, aye," Marcus replied. "That's a fine, healthy way for ye to think of me. Because I swear I'll twist yer cock off if ye harmed that lass."

Duncan let out a snort, gaining him a glare from Marcus. "Perhaps I'll start with ye, Duncan Lindsey, for allowing this wedding on yer land when ye knew the lass was under MacPherson protection."

Duncan sobered. "The lass agreed, or I would no' have let it happen. And I do nae care for yer tone. A bit of ransom is one thing; rape under the guise of marriage is another. One I do nae hold with."

Marcus nodded.

"She did agree," Rolfe insisted. "So do nae insult me by suggesting I took her against her will."

"Ye're saying she went to McTavish land of her own accord?" Marcus questioned.

Rolfe drew in a stiff breath. "Nae."

Marcus's expression tightened.

"Colum Gordon had a mind to burn her at the stake," Rolfe said. "Ye should nae have allowed her to run wild."

Marcus bristled. "I made sure she could defend herself. Can ye tell me truthfully that the fact that she is English has no' caused trouble for ye? I'm no' so arrogant to think that, short of locking her abovestairs, there won't be times she'll have to rely on herself."

Rolfe nodded reluctantly. "I am no' debating the need for her to learn to defend herself. Did ye truly no' see the harm in her riding out at night? Christ, man, me own men caught her once, thinking her a lad."

"So," Marcus growled softly, "ye were on me land?"

Rolfe grunted. "Ye enjoy a good raid as well as I do. Kat learned a lot from ye, and it's me guess that she saw ye leaving on a raid she was no' invited to."

Marcus slowly cocked his head to one side. "Aye," he rasped out. "That much is true. I know what I'm guilty of, McTavish. That does nae mean ye should have taken her home to yer land and no' sent me a ransom demand." Marcus pointed at Rolfe. "Taking her to Morton is something I can nae forgive."

"Me father is the one who would nae allow me to send a ransom demand. It's true enough that I failed to think that part of me plan through. Me father craves a title and sees Katherine as the means to getting it from

Morton. I can nae refuse me sire any more than ye can," Rolfe argued. "But I wed her to make certain Morton can no' harm her."

"And she will be staying on Lindsey land under my protection," Duncan added.

Marcus looked from one to the other before he nodded. "It's a decent plan, I'll admit. However, neither of ye have ever faced Morton. I promise ye, the man will nae bend easily. He's dangerous. Very much so. Wedding vows will nae keep the man from taking her."

"This keep will," Duncan declared.

"Do nae be too certain of yer plan," Marcus warned. "Ye have kin the earl may strike at. I've seen him do it. The man has no honor. He'll find a weak spot and force ye to give her up. The man annulled me own vows without so much as a Hail Mary said in penitence. Go down there, and he'll slap ye in chains rather than ennoble ye if ye arrive without the payment yer father promised him."

"I am no' afraid of a few months in prison," Rolfe answered tightly.

"Morton will no' hesitate to chop yer head off and set it on a pike as a warning to the other Highland clans," Marcus continued. "He sent Robert Gunn into me own castle to make it clear that he can reach into every one of our keeps. He is determined to destroy our way of life, man. Taking yer head, when ye've wed without the permission of yer laird and father, will be the perfect opportunity."

"I will do what I've promised me father I would," Rolfe declared firmly. "Ye're right to be angry with me for taking her home without thinking about what me father might do with her. I took her there because she needed a lesson, one ye could no' teach her after letting her have her way so long."

Marcus let out a grunt. "Aye, true enough. It's me failing, one I admit."

"And I will do what me father ordered me to do," Rolfe continued. "Just as ye would. To do less is to be unworthy of leading me clan. Ye know that is true. It's the reason ye went to see Morton yerself."

Marcus slowly nodded. "In that case, ye'd best get on with being grateful that I managed to catch up with ye, because ye will need all the friends ye can muster. Even so, ye stand a fine chance of losing yer head."

❦

Katherine felt the world spinning.

It was fortunate she was leaning against a wall, because her knees felt weak.

Morton will no' hesitate to chop yer head off…

Rolfe was noble to his core, something she admired about him. There was no doubt in her mind that he would face Morton, because his father had ordered him to.

But Marcus never spoke in jest when it came to matters of life and death.

And then there were her own dealings with Morton.

Oh yes, she recalled the way the man had looked at her.

Rolfe was a Highlander. A man who lived his life by the code of facing his enemies. She didn't think him simple enough to discount the fact that some men didn't hold themselves to a code of honor, but he would still maintain his own, even at the risk of placing himself in Morton's power.

And for what?

Marcus was correct about Morton being very good at finding people's weaknesses. Duncan might try to protect her, even send her north again with Marcus, but that help would not come for free. No, she'd always know that her freedom cost something. Maybe they would keep the details from her, but she knew Morton would not be bested without extracting his vengeance.

It made her sick to think of the MacPhersons suffering for her. They had given her so much.

Damn her need to defy the world! If she had not been so childish and had minded Marcus, none of this ever would have happened.

You never would have met Rolfe…

Tears stung her eyes as she contemplated that. It tormented her, deep in her heart. Her feelings stirred, roiling as if they were about to boil over.

She would not let Rolfe lose his head.

No, the solution was simple, and Marcus had made certain she had the skills to see her decision made into reality. She pressed closer to the door, listening as the men planned.

Because she would be riding out with them.

❧

"Ye do nae have to remain wed."

Marcus spoke to her from beneath lowered brows. He was displeased with her as much as with the situation he was attempting to remedy.

"I apologize for riding out," she began. "It was childish of me not to think about who would come after me."

Marcus contemplated her for a long moment before he drew in a deep breath and let it out. "Rolfe has had a good effect on ye."

Katherine shrugged, feeling suddenly shy as heat teased her cheeks. She shifted, causing Marcus to narrow his eyes at her. His expression darkened slightly as he tightened his hold on his sleeves.

"Damn him." Marcus spoke at last in a tight voice. "Part of me wants to thrash him for putting that look on yer face."

"You must not." Once again her English accent was more pronounced as she became agitated.

"And the other part of me wants to shake his hand."

Katherine smiled, feeling as if everything was suddenly right with the world. There was a storm on the horizon, but for that moment, seeing Marcus nodding with approval, everything that mattered was in its place.

She ran toward him, jumping up to wrap her arms around his neck. He caught her and hugged her tight before setting her back on her feet.

"I mean it, though." His eyes were glittering with happiness now. "Just say the word, and I'll have ye on yer way back to MacPherson land. Being foolish does nae mean ye should have to live with a marriage ye do nae care for."

"More than one foolish action has resulted in dire consequences."

Marcus's lips curled a tiny amount. "Let others call ye hellion as an insult. For meself, I enjoy the frank way ye speak."

He beamed at her for a long moment before his expression went serious. "Ye'll tell me, Kat, if ye change yer heart? For all that I did nae want ye for me own wife, I would no' see ye unhappy."

"I was a child when Morton tried to force that match," she said, defending Marcus. "He's a monster, Morton is. You must convince Rolfe not to go to court."

Marcus stiffened.

"He's given his word to his father and laird," Marcus responded. "I agree with ye. Morton is black-hearted, but honor is no' something a man chooses when to uphold. I'd take ye home to MacPherson land, sheet or no soiled sheet, if Rolfe struck me as the sort of man who did nae keep his word."

He nodded, making it clear he considered the matter closed.

She knew he would not change his mind.

Why was it that all of the traits she loved about Scottish men were also the ones that threatened to take them away from her?

Fate was still intent on toying with her.

Marcus reached out and patted her on the shoulder. "I see ye care for him, lass. Go now, for he's leaving at first light."

It was a test of whether or not she'd left childhood behind. Women straightened their backs and bid their men farewell with dry eyes and confidence in their safe return, when they knew very well the risks.

Katherine sent Marcus a steady look before she lowered herself formally. It earned her a glint of approval in his eyes before he nodded.

"I'm off to find some sleep."

She watched him go and felt an urgency to seek out Rolfe.

Would he welcome her?

She discovered herself needled by the possibility that having had her once, he might be content. Was their marriage really a service to his honor? A means of righting the wrong he felt he'd done her by taking her to his father's land?

Both possibilities burned in her mind like coals in a fire. Of course, there was only one way to know, so she turned and set her shoulders before leaving the chamber.

❧

Rolfe was waiting for her.

She enjoyed the sight, but not because she found pleasure in knowing she somehow controlled him. No, she was simply happy to see him. He was pacing back and forth across the passageway while she finished talking with Marcus.

He turned and braced himself as she emerged, his jaw tight as he waited to see what she would say to him.

"I wish you would not go to see the earl."

Perhaps she was wasting her breath, yet she could not have stopped the words if she'd known he'd cut out her tongue.

"Morton will not deal justly with you."

"And what of ye?" Rolfe asked softly. "Will ye keep the vows ye made with me yesterday?"

He'd moved nearer to her, closing the distance and stealing her breath with the same motion. It was so abrupt, the way she responded to him, as though her will was not involved.

No, it had always been thus since she'd first encountered him. She responded with yearnings she'd never had for another.

"I told them to take the sheet."

Her answer earned her a softening of his lips. He nodded. "It's hanging in the hall."

Rolfe watched her to see her honest reaction.

Katherine stared straight back at him. "If I wanted to be free of you, Rolfe, would it not be best for me to send you off to see Morton? You forget that I know the man. You have only heard about him. I have faced him, and I ask you not to go."

Now he smiled. It was a tender expression that warmed her heart with the way it spread into his eyes. Those green eyes were as rare as he was.

"Come." He reached down and captured her wrist. His fingers closed all the way around it as he tugged her behind him.

He was taking her abovestairs to have her.

What would have scandalized her just two days ago was now permissible. She discovered herself delighted by the vows that made it so.

At last, Fate was delivering some treasures into her life.

Ones she was eager to touch.

❧

"Ye should thank me," Duncan Lindsey remarked before he took another bite off a chicken leg. He chewed it as he turned and looked at Marcus sitting next to him at the high table while supper was served.

He couldn't help but notice Rolfe and Katherine were not in attendance.

"A blind man wouldn't have failed to see the way they wanted to tumble each other," Duncan continued.

Marcus sent him a narrow-eyed look. "Ye are speaking of someone I consider to be under me protection."

"So I should act as though they are no' healthy and passionate?" Duncan replied. "See…" He shook the chicken leg at Marcus. "That is why I have no' wed. Where is the woman who can be frank with me? I have no understanding of the need to hold conversations about everything except what I crave from a lass."

Marcus slowly grinned. "I see exactly why ye have no wife, man, if yer idea of courting is to walk straight up to a lass and tell her ye'd like to see her tits."

Duncan stretched his arms out wide. "Is that no' honest?" He looked at his captains. "Is that no' what is on all of yer minds when ye encounter a comely lass for the first time?"

There was a round of chuckles in response. With no females at the head table, they indulged themselves in frank conversation.

Duncan wasn't finished yet. He leaned on his elbow toward Marcus. "Tell the truth, man. Would it no' be a lot simpler if yer wife told ye exactly where she likes ye to finger her?"

Marcus sent him an arrogant look. "When ye do it right, the moans tell a man so."

Two of the captains slapped the table as they laughed.

"Unless yer wife is coddling yer ego, as husbands like their wives to do."

They all frowned because it was the Head of House who had spoken. She delivered her words in a clear, unabashed tone while filling Duncan's goblet.

"Which brings me back to saying send me a female who will be blunt!"

Marcus grunted and took a swig of ale from his goblet. He wanted to drain it, that much was fact, but he set the goblet back on the tabletop. His brother had two daughters to look forward to seeing grow into women.

Marcus was going to enjoy telling Bhaic how much he wasn't going to like what men would say about his daughters.

And then he recalled that Helen had told him she would have a daughter.

His wife did tend to get her way.

Marcus reached for his goblet.

❧

"That was too fast."

Rolfe was still struggling to breathe.

Well, it was fair to say that they both were.

"I'm sorry, Kat," he rasped out.

"Do I sound…displeased?"

Her new husband rolled over with a soft groan and peered at her from where he braced his chin on his hand as he leaned his elbows into the bed. He looked at her, his green eyes shimmering with satisfaction as he searched her features.

"Women crave more than just the ride."

She felt her heart settling into a more normal rhythm, but her temper heated in response to his words. "And how many women have you enjoyed to know that?"

His lips parted in a smirk. She let out a snort and grabbed a pillow that she swung toward his head. Rolfe blocked it far too easily for her pride. She rolled over and right off the bed.

"I hope you enjoyed them," was her tart reply.

"Ye're lying." He sat up and contemplated her.

Katherine suddenly felt exposed. There was a certain knowledge in his expression as he looked at her bare frame that told her he knew exactly what a naked woman looked like.

And she didn't care for how jealous it made her feel.

So she found her chemise and put it on, earning a frown from her husband. He sat all the way up before standing and walking toward the small table in the outer chamber. He opened a bottle of honey mead supplied by Duncan and poured two glasses of it.

"Her name was Gret."

"I don't wish to hear about it."

Rolfe only offered her a glass. She glared at him, but he was unrepentant, so she took it and drew a sip of the sweet beverage.

Rolfe was still bare as the day he'd been born.

She really wished she didn't enjoy the sight so much. It was undermining her efforts to be cross with him.

"She was the widow of one of me father's captains," Rolfe continued. "A woman who had position, and therefore no reason to wed again and risk losing her freedom."

"Are you deaf?" Kat asked. "Or simply indifferent to my pride?"

Rolfe grinned at her. "I'm trying to tell ye I am no' the sort of man who keeps a mistress."

She hadn't expected that. In fact, Kat realized she knew very little about him. She felt a teasing of heat on her cheeks as she sat down on a chair and waited for him to continue. They did need to learn about each other.

"Gret caught me kissing a kitchen maid, when the girl had slapped me for following her."

"I hope she added a slap of her own."

He raised his glass to her in agreement before he emptied it.

"She hit me with a pastry roller, and it left a bruise that didn't fade for a month." He grinned at the memory. "Warned me that she'd crack me skull if I ever failed to respect a lass's wishes again."

"And still, she became your…lover?"

"In a manner of speaking." Rolfe held up his finger when she started to ask another question. "I learned from her that fucking and making love are two very different things. I was a very fortunate man to have a woman who took the time to instruct me."

He was moving toward her, plucking the glass from her distracted fingers and setting it aside before he gently raised her to her feet by cupping her elbows. It was such a tender touch, one he followed with a soft stroke of his fingers across her cheek.

"A woman is more sensual than a man," he leaned

down and whispered against her ear. She felt his warm breath teasing her neck a moment before he pressed a gentle kiss against her nape.

She shuddered.

Rolfe lifted his head, watching her response. What made her catch her breath was the way his eyes flickered with enjoyment, as though he found her delight pleasing.

"And if a man is wise"—he caught the soft fabric of her chemise between his fingertips and started to draw it up her body—"he learns to awaken her passion." The garment came between them, blocking him from sight as he pulled it up and over her head.

"Strength has its place, too." He caught her wrists while her arms were still raised high and held them prisoner in his large hands. "But tempered by an iron will."

He pulled her arms straight above her head as he came close enough for his body hair to touch her breasts. She shivered, gooseflesh rising on her skin as he held her gaze just as securely as her wrists. Her belly twisted with awareness. Of him, of his strength, of how much she wanted to feel it.

"Any man can claim a woman," he rasped in a voice edged with promise. "Only a lover can earn her passion."

He leaned down and scooped her up, cradling her against his chest as she settled into the embrace. It felt so very right.

Secure.

As though he was everything she might ever need.

He moved slowly toward the bed, his bare feet making soft sounds against the floor. When he laid her among the rumpled bedding, the ropes groaned as they took her weight and then his.

Her senses were heightened, feeding her all of the tiny details she had heard before when climbing into bed. Now, with Rolfe there, it all seemed much richer. As though she'd been swallowing her food without tasting it before.

Rolfe leaned down and kissed her, lingering over the press of his lips against hers. He didn't rush to part her lips, but took a long moment to taste her. It made her twist up toward him, slipping her hands along his wide shoulders and into his hair. The need to bind him to her was growing, like a newly lit fire. The flames began to lick at the wood before it popped and caught.

Her skin was heating, making being nude feel so very perfect.

"Do nae be jealous of Gret," he whispered against her ear. "She taught me to respect a woman's need to be aroused."

"That is…a puzzle…" Katherine rasped out as he stroked her sides.

He'd touched the parts of her she considered intimate, yet now he drew his fingers and hands along her sides in long strokes like he might with a horse. She stretched, the sensation a rush of delight that awakened her senses.

"It is," he agreed.

Her heart was speeding up again. But it was also thumping in hard, deep beats. She could hear the blood rushing in her ears as Rolfe drew his hands up to her shoulders and down to rest on her breasts.

She craved having him cup those tender globes long before he did so. She hungered for it, feeling as though every moment was a tiny torment she must endure before he would deliver satisfaction.

"Hmmm…" It was bliss when he finally put his hands to her.

"Such perfect handfuls." He leaned down, teasing one with a kiss.

It wasn't enough. She arched up, offering the puckered nipple. "Strength." She ground out the word as she tried to pull him toward her. "Let me feel yours."

He lay down on her, holding her wrists pressed against the bedding above her head and letting enough of his body weight rest on her to ensure she was pinned beneath him.

"I want to do that as well," he told her, watching her while she absorbed how much stronger he was than her. "Part of me longs to ride ye hard and hold ye so tight that there is no way for ye to break free."

Something deep inside her responded to his words. She felt a leap of excitement and a wave of heat washing through her. Her lips curled, just a bit, baring her teeth.

He grinned in response, but it wasn't a kind expression. No, it was menacing and bright with promise. Somehow driving home just how male he was while leaving her with certain knowledge that she was his counterpart, made to fit him.

Apart, they would always yearn for each other.

"Tonight, though"—he pulled away from her, stroking her once again—"I am going to prove I can be a man as well as beast in our bed."

He made good on his words, stroking her and then

following his large hands with a hundred tiny kisses that felt like butterflies. She'd never realized her skin might be so sensitive. With only his delicate touches, she seemed to be focused more on waiting for the next kiss to land and, therefore, more aware of it when it did.

She writhed against the sheet, unable to remain still, reaching for him, needing to share the bliss between them. She heard his breathing deepen, roughen, as he fought for control. She was already wet and aching for his possession, but he resisted the invitation she tried to make by parting her thighs beneath him.

Instead, he slipped down her length, rubbing her as he went and driving her nearly insane with need.

At least, she thought she was that far gone until he settled over her spread sex.

"Rolfe William Brian McTavish."

He sent her a satisfied smirk in response, but flattened his hands on her inner thighs to keep them spread. "Did ye know the older women say a woman will nae conceive sons if she is no' satisfied?"

Katherine felt her cheeks burning with what must have been the hottest blush of her entire life. He was hovering right over her open slit, teasing the mound of her curls with his fingertips.

Why had she never noticed how it felt to have those hairs touched?

"That's…preposterous."

He grinned at her and drove a little deeper into her curls, so that he was touching skin.

"I like the way ye sound more English when ye are agitated."

She scoffed at him. "You don't care for anything English."

One of his eyebrows rose. "No' true, lass." He drew his fingers lower until he was touching the little bud at the top of her sex. "I find I enjoy ye…quite a bit."

She wanted to take issue with him, but her thoughts scattered like a broken strand of pearls as he teased her clitoris. The pleasure was so intense that she cried out, and then didn't stop because there was no way to keep it all contained inside herself.

Rolfe wasn't content with merely fingering her. He leaned down and licked the same spot, pushing her into a new realm of twisting need. She was poised on the pinnacle, suspended there between a hunger so intense she thought it might drive her insane and the pleasure that would break her in two. She was straining toward him, desperate for release, one he denied her.

"Damn you…" she hissed when he held her in place for more torment.

"A damnation we will share, Kat."

He was suddenly rising up, giving her a glance of his hard body, his member stiff and jutting out from it. She shuddered at the sight, reminded of how much she craved his strength. He came over her, granting her that wish at last, settling between her thighs as he thrust into her body.

It was a smooth motion but a hard one. One of them grunted, or perhaps it was both. In that moment, they seemed to unite in a common goal. She craved him; he hungered for her. The bed rocked as he thrust into her, riding her as hard as she'd demanded.

But it wasn't enough. She sank her nails into his shoulders and then drew them down his arms. He growled and caught her wrists, pinning them once more to the surface of the bed. They were both rushing toward completion, the hunger building, growing hotter, and driving them past thinking. There were only the cravings left when pleasure tore through her. She arched up, grinding herself against him as he came down in a thrust that buried his member to the hilt.

That moment seemed to last forever. She couldn't draw breath, couldn't do anything but feel the pleasure blossoming inside her body. His seed was pumping into her, adding to the moment, until it flung them both back into reality as though those brief moments were all the paradise mortals deserved.

It was enough.

And yet she found herself realizing that it might have to be exactly that—enough. The uncertain future ahead of them tormented her, but she was too spent to stay awake and think of ways to fend it off. Sleep dragged her into its embrace, as Rolfe's breathing near her ear eased her concerns.

☙

He meant to leave her before dawn.

Katherine watched Rolfe pleating his kilt while the sun was just breaking night's hold. She stayed still, wanting to soak up those moments, dreading the coming parting.

He smoothed the wool with sure motions, confident ones. There was no valet to dress him, such as she recalled her father needing.

Of course not. He was a Scot, and a Highlander at that. In her father's house, they would have labeled him a savage.

She loved everything about him.

"The sooner I go, the sooner I shall return."

Rolfe proved he was aware of her, even when she thought she'd managed to remain still. He looked up at her, sending her that arrogant grin before he lay down on the pleats and pulled his belt around his trim waist to buckle it.

She sat up, bundling the bedding around herself as he stood and the wool fell down to cover his legs. The pleats in the back were longer, so he might raise them up to cover his head if it rained because the belt was across the center of the fabric. He reached for a second belt and secured it over the folded wool and then looked toward her.

Satisfaction lit his eyes and curved his lips. "Do nae move, Kat. I want to remember ye exactly as ye are, warm and tousled, and in me bed."

She reached up to smooth her hair back, earning a chuckle from him. He came close, leaning over into the bed to kiss her. Determination flickered in his eyes when he withdrew. She knew the expression, and there was no arguing with it.

"I will return to ye."

He believed it, or at least he would not allow himself to show her doubt.

It didn't matter if he maintained his confidence. Her belly was still knotting with dread because she knew firsthand the sort of monster he was riding out to meet.

Rolfe paused at the door, looking back at her a final

time before he slipped into the passageway like the night shadows dissipating in the light of day.

He might have been no more than a figment of her imagination.

Except for the tears that stung her eyes and the ache that twisted her heart.

She loved him.

In that moment, there was only that feeling and the knowledge that she was fortunate beyond words to have encountered a man who filled her with such emotion.

But it also filled her with determination to ensure he did not suffer a dire fate due to having met her.

She crawled from the bedding and moved with solid purpose toward the vanity, where she plucked a comb from its surface.

A hellion she might be, but today, that would serve her very well indeed.

~

Marcus let out a foul curse. Duncan looked up from the bed in Katherine's chamber. "Well, ye're the one who raised her."

"I know it." Marcus rubbed a hand down his face. When he was finished, he looked at the maid who had been sleeping in the chamber. "Ye should have refused her."

The maid was not young. She looked back at him with the steady confidence of a woman. "I did it willingly and do nae regret it."

"I can remedy that, mistress," Duncan informed her with thick promise in his tone.

The maid merely lowered herself before her laird

and rose again to face them. "If she had stayed and let him shelter her at the expense of his own suffering, there would never have been any acceptance for her in the Highlands. When she told me that, I agreed, because everyone must earn their place. English or not, I respect her for it."

Duncan drew in a stiff breath. "Go on with ye." His tone was soft when he spoke because he realized that he could not argue with her.

"I'm riding up to fetch Symon Grant."

Duncan looked at Marcus. "And then what? Morton likely has a good memory of the way ye and Symon's sister duped him."

"True," Marcus replied. "But the man also wants the Highland lairds to support him. Since we can nae be obedient to him, I suggest we gather enough of us together to make him think our opinion is worth something."

"He might just hang ye all and have yer sons raised at court."

"In that case," Marcus reached out and slapped Duncan on the shoulder, "be thankful ye do nae have a son."

"Aye," Duncan grumbled as they left the chamber and made their way down to the hall. Marcus wasted no time in gathering the MacPhersons and heading into the yard. They were racing against time now, and every man among them knew it.

Duncan might have refused to go, but part of him was impressed with the way Katherine had managed to earn the respect and love of the MacPhersons. It was evident in the way they followed Marcus. Men might be ordered to ride, but a wise leader learned to read their body language. These retainers didn't hesitate or drag their feet. They were off to help one of their own.

So he'd be going along, too.

Morton was about to learn that he'd been successful in ending the feuding in the Highlands, and that meant the man would be facing them all as a united force.

Duncan was going to enjoy seeing the look on the man's face.

❧

"Finished at last?"

Katherine didn't take offense. She was too tired to care what the men around her said. They enjoyed teasing her, thinking her a young lad. It served her purpose well, because they gave her more chores, since they felt their age granted them the authority.

She took the duties without complaint because it took her away from them. Hiding her face, she let the dirt build up on her skin, forbidding herself to wash it away. Rolfe had keen eyes. Staying out of his sight was the only way she would succeed.

So she did all of the work her companions heaped upon her and collapsed into an exhausted sleep well after dark every night. The days were longer with summer upon them, and they rode at a pace that covered ground quickly.

As they came into the Lowlands, there were more people on the road. More towns as well, and ones that were larger, with two-story buildings and paved roads. The horses' hooves made a *clip-clop* sound on those streets while they rode past curious Scots who wore pants instead of kilts and peered at them suspiciously.

The barbarians of the north.

There were times when the Lowlanders were pleased to see Highlanders on their streets, such as when the English were roaming on Scottish land. Now, mothers hustled their children off the streets and peeked out of windows while they rode by.

At least the feeling was mutual.

None of the McTavishes or Lindseys cared to be there. Rolfe was riding for the stronghold where young King James was. Few ever saw the king because he was still being tutored and raised to adulthood. The Earl of Morton ran the country, and many whispered that he would continue to do so until he was forced to give power back to the king.

Of course, with the way it was at court, there would be men willing to help the young king wrest control from Morton's hands. Such help would come at a price, though. As they rode through the gates, Kat looked around and wondered who was there to position themselves for the coming power struggle.

It would be soon. James was fourteen and approaching an age when he would no longer accept being treated like a child.

In fact, she would have sworn she felt the tension in the air. There were men watching everything and everyone, looking like wolves contemplating their next meal.

A chill was taking root inside her as she found herself back in the courtyard and dismounted. Years before, she'd dressed in Helen Grant's worn clothing and escaped while Brenda Grant took her place. The gamble had landed Brenda in dire circumstances because she had been the one left to face the Earl of Morton's fury.

Katherine risked a glance toward Rolfe. Determination was etched into his face, along with a sternness that she recognized as the way men held themselves when they were about to do something for all of the right reasons.

Such as duty.

Honor.

And noble intentions.

She loved him more for it, even though he might never forgive her for disobeying him. She looked back at the horse, working on the saddle as she accepted the fact that Rolfe was pure Highlander. He might jest about enjoying her being a hellion, but the reality was, he wouldn't take help from his wife.

Not when it came to business matters.

Which was why she was there. She pulled her bundle from the saddle and pushed her bonnet low on her forehead. Her choice had been made, and there was no way she was going to allow Rolfe to suffer for her.

The only thing left to do was pray that God might decide to grant them both freedom. The only problem was that she doubted Morton answered to God.

❧

"Marcus MacPherson," Symon Grant bellowed. "It's good to see ye, man."

Marcus made a brisk path toward his friend. Symon's grin faded as Marcus closed the gap.

"Ye look half dead."

Marcus raised an eyebrow in response. "I've more strength in me than that."

"Glad to hear it," Symon responded. "But the look in yer eyes tells me I am no' going to like the reason ye seem to be riding yer horse into an early grave."

"Ye aren't, and that's a fact," Marcus confirmed. "We need yer help to deal with Morton."

Symon's expression darkened as he listened.

✑

The Earl of Morton had a great number of people waiting to see him.

Rolfe discovered himself among other lairds and ambassadors outside two large doors that were only opened when the Douglas retainers allowed them to be. Inside, the earl sat in a throne on a raised platform, with tapestries draped behind him.

In the main court, men clustered together in their clans, while women looked on. Tension filled the air, as each man waited for his name to be called.

"Just what we need." Adwin spat on the floor. "Gordons."

Rolfe turned and watched a new group enter. Diocail Gordon came to a stop as their gazes met. The man slowly grinned and turned his head, giving Rolfe a view of the side of his bonnet. Three feathers were raised high and held in place by a brooch.

"So Colum finally left the rest of us in peace," Adwin remarked. "About time."

Rolfe stepped toward Diocail. The men waiting in the other room moved back. The bad blood between the Gordons and the McTavishes was well known. Rolfe offered Diocail his hand, stunning their audience.

"I've come down to swear my allegiance to the regent." Diocail spoke loud enough to be heard by those listening. "Colum Gordon is dead."

"I'm glad to see the Gordon clan being led by a good man."

Whispers rose behind them in response.

The doors opened, drawing everyone's attention.

"McTavish," a Douglas retainer called. "Ye are summoned."

Katherine watched him go, hiding near the wall as the men resumed their whispered conversations.

⤜⤏

"Are ye simple?"

The Earl of Morton was gripping the arms of his throne with hands that showed how agitated he was.

"Nae."

The earl sat forward and glared at him. "Yer father promised me Katherine Carew."

"Aye, he did," Rolfe answered. "Before I wed her. Now that she is me wife, I expect ye to understand why I did nae bring her."

"Ye…what?" The earl leaned back. "I gave no permission for that."

Rolfe stood his ground. "Ye wanted her wed to Marcus MacPherson for the alliance it would gain. I am a better alliance."

The earl looked at him through narrowed eyes. "That was years ago."

"Are ye saying ye are done trying to settle the feuding in the Highlands?"

The earl slowly smiled, and there was nothing kind about the expression. The man was hard and cold at his center. Rolfe decided Morton looked very much like Colum Gordon in that moment. The only thought in the earl's mind was how to gain the most from the situation. His desires were the only ones with merit.

"The matter at hand is one of a promise made and not upheld," Morton said very clearly. "I want Katherine Carew, and yer father promised her to me."

"She is me wife now," Rolfe responded. "So ye'll have to understand I will nae be handing her over."

The earl drew in a deep breath and leaned forward. "Nay, McTavish. Ye and yer kind will be understanding that I am Scotland, and ye will no' cling to yer clans before me!"

"I am here." The response gained him a flicker of respect from the earl, but that was all.

"Because yer father ordered ye here."

Rolfe nodded. "Honor does nae bend to personal preferences. I gave me word I would face ye, and I willingly decided to take Katherine to wife to keep her from ye. She was me prize, no' me father's, and I intend to keep her. If that means there will be no title, I will tell me laird so without shirking."

"Aye," Morton agreed. "I believe ye, son of the McTavish."

The earl held up a thick finger. "But the difficulty remains with ye Highlanders thinking ye can decide when to obey me. Katherine Carew is the natural-born daughter of the Earl of Bedford. The man is one of Elizabeth Tudor's closest advisors."

"Katherine has nae seen the man in over a decade."

"Blood is blood," Morton shot back. "Is nae that the code ye Highlanders live by?"

He chuckled when Rolfe was forced to nod. "Ye craved an alliance with a Highland clan. It is done with me," Rolfe said.

The earl smiled again. "I'm tempted to take that offer, just because I suspect yer father will no' be so pleased with the bargain ye are trying to strike with me."

Rolfe grinned. "He'll be furious. Me sire has no liking for the English, even one with blue blood flowing through her veins."

"But if I did, there would be no respect for me in the Highlands."

Morton truly had a great deal in common with Colum Gordon. Rolfe watched the way the man coddled his pride above everything else.

"Obedience…" The earl spoke loudly so his guards could hear him clearly. "That is what I will have of every Highland clan." His eyes glittered with his temper. "Ye have defied me and will learn the error of yer ways."

⤜⥟

"What are ye doing here?"

Diocail kept his voice low, but Katherine heard the reprimand in it nonetheless. She kept her chin tucked, but the quick glance she chanced at the man told her he'd recognized her.

"Aye," he confirmed as he looked out across the

room. "I wondered who might be looking after Rolfe McTavish like a starving kitten."

"And yet you do not unmask me."

He made a low sound under his breath. "I was there to set ye free."

She knew instantly what he spoke of. That moment when he'd stepped from the shadows and let them escape from the Gordon stronghold.

"And since I was willing to take the risk of going against me laird..." Diocail was still talking in a low voice and looking away from her, as though he were merely passing the time with someone he considered beneath him. "I will know why ye are risking yerself once again."

"I won't let Rolfe be harmed because of me."

Diocail looked straight at her.

"He has a plan to deny the earl what his father promised him in exchange for a noble title," she explained.

Anger flashed in Diocail's eyes. "You?"

Katherine nodded. Diocail made a low sound under his breath. "Ye have a unique fate, one I do nae envy." He swept his eyes over her, from head to toe. "Ye seem to rise to the challenge of it well enough. But if what ye say is true, ye need to leave."

"I will not," she assured him. "I will never leave my husband to answer for my cursed lot in life."

Diocail offered her a slight curving of his lips before the large doors opened again. There was the pounding of a staff against the stone floor before the herald cried out.

"Diocail Gordon."

"Wait." She reached for his arm. "Where is Rolfe?"

Diocail sent her a hard look. "If he did nae come back through those doors, lass, he's likely on his way to the dungeon."

She stiffened and felt Diocail grasp her forearm. "Do nae rush in. Let us see what Morton is planning first."

The herald was looking at Diocail, and Adwin was trying to decide why he was hesitating. She didn't duck her chin fast enough, and Rolfe's captain recognized her. There was a flash of fury before Diocail pulled her along with him and left her in the captain's care.

"I'll see what news there is of yer master."

Adwin gave Diocail a brief nod before he clamped his hand around Katherine's wrist and pulled her into a passageway.

"Are ye daft?"

He bit back the word *woman*.

"Determined," she answered in a whisper. "I will not let Rolfe suffer for me."

"He'll no' like hearing that ye are here."

"Of course not," she agreed, causing Adwin to lower his brows in vexation. "You both know I am not submissive or obedient."

Adwin snorted in response.

"So it should not shock you to find I am here," she said. "And I will give myself up to save Rolfe. It's my cursed lot."

Adwin looked around to see the other McTavish retainers had followed them. They were glaring at her in disapproval until she finished. She wouldn't say they gave her their full approval, but their expressions eased as her words hit them.

"There might be another way," Adwin said as he

held tight to her arm. "I can nae in good faith allow ye to step into harm's way."

"It wouldn't be the first time," she reminded him.

Adwin merely grunted and cast her a stubborn look.

Katherine reached out and grabbed his jerkin. "I am a hellion, and I will not allow Rolfe to shield me from my fate."

Adwin's eyes twinkled with admiration for just a moment. But they were distracted by the huge doors opening again. Diocail and his two senior captains came striding out as the herald called another name.

Diocail strode past them without stopping. He sent a swift look toward Adwin that had the man following a few moments later.

"Release me," Katherine hissed at the captain, who was still holding her arm. "Or it will be whispered that you prefer boys in your bed."

Adwin responded instantly, but he glared at her. "Stay right beside me, gilly."

He stressed the word *gilly*, making sure she understood she'd better act the part of his apprentice servant or he'd suffer the rumors. It was enough of a reprieve. She fell into step behind him, tucking her chin as she became just another of the McTavish retainers. It was a skill she'd been perfecting for years on MacPherson land.

Of course, she'd never thought she'd have so much to lose if she failed to dupe those around her.

"He's in chains." Diocail was waiting behind a huge stone pillar in the outer entryway. "Morton took a great deal of delight in telling me all about what happens to Highland lairds who do nae give obedience to him."

"His fate?" Katherine asked.

"Undecided," was the hushed response. "I'm forbidden to leave until the matter is settled." He sent her a hard look. "I believe the earl wants to make an impression on me to carry home to the Highlands."

Her belly knotted in response. Diocail reached past Adwin and grasped her arm because the blood was draining from her face. She drew in a deep breath and ordered herself to remain strong.

She was a hellion, not some damned weak-kneed girl.

"Go…" She had to roll her lips in because they were suddenly dry. "Go and tell Morton…Rolfe was just attempting to best him. That I am here."

Adwin had crossed his arms over his chest. "Maybe it will come to that. Maybe no'. For the moment, we need to strengthen our position."

"Which means we're no' giving up our one advantage," Diocail added.

The men around her grinned. She knew the look, had seen it plenty of times when they were raiding one another and trying to best each other.

"This is not about a few cows," she argued.

"The earl sees ye as little more than a fine one," Diocail corrected her. "We'd be fools to hand ye over, trusting in his mercy."

"He doesn't have any," she was forced to admit.

"Exactly, lass," Adwin said. "So we'll have to see who is here to aid us, since Marcus dares not show his face."

"Gordon and McTavish working together," Adwin said. "The earl might approve, if we were nae intent on defeating him."

There was a soft round of chuckles in response. Katherine would have liked to join in, but she was too busy fending off the dread trying to smother her hope.

She had to keep it alive, had to find the way to free Rolfe.

Without a doubt, she knew it would be worth even her life.

∾

"Bridget Hussy would be satisfied."

The Earl of Morton shifted his attention to his adviser, William Ruthven, the Earl of Gowrie.

"I crave an alliance with the Earl of Bedford, not his wife."

"Both have advantages," Ruthven continued without cringing over the tone Morton used. "The countess controls a vast wealth. Since Rolfe wed the girl without a contract, ye could keep the dowry."

Morton nodded reluctantly. "And yet that is no' an alliance with England."

"Francis Russell has not left Elizabeth's side in eight years," Ruthven argued. "The girl is just a bastard."

"An acknowledged one."

Ruthven nodded. "Yet she has been in Scotland for seven years now. Too long for the man to want her back. Better to press the countess for a dowry and leave Katherine Carew wed to McTavish."

"Which will not satisfy the question of disobedience," Morton said.

The Earl of Gowrie sent Morton a long look. "That need to satisfy yer pride is becoming very costly. The Bedfords have more money than the Queen of

England. More gold than a single by-blow is worth. Considering that ye stole the girl, getting anything for her is gain enough."

"Scotland needs unity," Morton growled. "If ye can nae put that foremost in yer mind, ye are no good to me. Get out."

Beyond the private chambers of the Regent of Scotland, William Ruthven, Earl of Gowrie, encountered the Earl of Angus. Morton had dismissed Angus the week before.

"That man thinks he's king," Ruthven remarked in a hushed tone.

"Aye," Angus agreed. "And James is getting old enough to do something about it."

William looked around, making sure they were not being overheard. "Only if we get that lad away from Esmé Stuart."

Angus grunted at the mention of the king's new, very French friend. "This is a dangerous topic of conversation."

"I am more concerned about how dangerous it might be if we leave it unspoken," Gowrie said. "It's one thing to insist on a few weddings in the Highlands to bring feuds to an end, but another to throw a man into chains for no' being willing to hand over his own wife."

"Morton should be pleased to have the English bastard out of his hands and no longer looking to him for her keep," Angus agreed.

"He's talking about hanging the McTavish."

Angus snarled. "Bloody Douglas. What does he think that is going to accomplish?"

Gowrie looked around again. "From what I can see, Diocail Gordon is staying to see the outcome."

"Morton just might succeed in uniting those clans after all," Angus said. "But against us Lowlanders."

"Aye," Gowrie answered. "It's growing past time for Morton to be removed from that throne he likes to sit in."

"Maybe we can use this to our advantage."

Angus lifted an eyebrow in question. Gowrie sent him a grin. "I'm going to find Diocail Gordon and see how deep his ties with the McTavish run."

❧

He didn't regret anything.

Rolfe shifted and tried to find a spot on his knee to lean his head without pain. The chain connected to the collar around his neck was too short to allow him to lie down on the floor of the cell. Looking at the built-up muck, he decided that was likely a good thing. The stench told him exactly what the dark filth was composed of. If the smell didn't clue him in, the lack of a toilet bucket in the cell did.

He didn't regret it.

None of it.

A man only had his honor to call his own.

His father would argue that he'd been a darned fool, and perhaps it was a fitting label. All that admission did was make Rolfe smile. Being a fool for Katherine, well, he'd happily live with that.

The first time he'd seen her, he'd known she was unique.

He'd had to have her.

And it had been worth it.

No matter what.

Was that bewitchment? Love? He had no idea, except for the fact that even there, in that stinking cell, he was sure he could smell the delicate scent of her hair. When he closed his eyes, she was there, looking at him with midnight eyes, the very opposite of his own green ones.

Hellion…

Oh yes, she was that.

But she was his hellion.

⌁

"Morton doesn't have any mercy," Katherine said.

Adwin had a mug in front of him, but he wasn't drinking the contents. Rolfe's captain eyed her with a look that twisted her heart.

"I care for him." She came closer, sitting beside Adwin on the bench. The fire in the hearth had died down, and the men had made their way abovestairs to sleep. She'd sat in her tiny room, waiting for the noise in the small town-house to die down. "You must allow me to free him."

Adwin shook his head. "I could no' fail to protect ye, lass. I've watched over that lad for nearly a decade now. He is me life."

She slowly smiled. "I know. It's clear on your face when you look at him."

Adwin offered her a grin. The captain kept a full beard that made him appear gruff most of the time because it was so thick and dark.

"What makes ye think Morton will let Rolfe go,

even if I tie ye up in a bow and deliver ye like a trained dog?"

She sighed. "I don't know for certain."

Adwin made a grunting sound.

"However," she continued, "I know Morton likes to have his way. So if his desire is to trade for me, we should convince him that Rolfe was simply testing his nerve."

"Needling him?"

She nodded. "He might see the humor in it. Convince him a Highlander like Rolfe means such as a compliment. After all, there would be no point in trying the nerve of, say…an Englishman."

Adwin snorted and reached for his mug. "That might well get me thrown in chains alongside Rolfe."

Katherine smiled at him. "Find me a dress, and the earl will think me as helpless as I was when he knew me before. As such, I doubt he will place me in chains. Such circumstances will be far easier to escape than the ones Rolfe finds himself in now."

Adwin went still. She watched him contemplate her with a critical eye. It was a compliment to be looked at in that manner, because he was seeing beyond her gender now and weighing it against what he knew she'd done.

"I did nae think of it that way." He slowly started to chuckle, a sound that was very menacing.

"Nor did I." Diocail emerged from the shadows. "But she snuck down here to tempt ye with it when she hoped ye were alone. That tells me she thinks there will be those among us who do nae agree with her. She's playing on yer soft feelings for the lad."

"Why do you always emerge from the shadows?"

Diocail sent her an arrogant smirk. "Because it's harder for people to kill me when I see them first."

A tiny tingle went down her spine in response. There was more than just arrogance in his tone; there was hard, firsthand knowledge that was sobering.

Adwin set the mug down with a firm sound, recalling them to the conversation she'd begun. "The idea has merit."

"She is a woman."

"Aye," Adwin answered. "And yet, no' so very like others. Marcus trained her."

"He did," Diocail replied. "Better remember that fact, because if ye return to the Highlands without her, Marcus will have yer balls."

"Marcus taught me how to smash a man's balls." She leaned forward and sent Diocail a hard look. "I assure you, I was a very accomplished student who will not be content to sit abovestairs while you attempt to rescue my husband."

Diocail was hard to read. His expression remained tight for long moments while she refused to bend. A corner of his lips twitched at last.

"In that case, we'll get ye a dress."

Seven

"THE EARL WILL HEAR NO PLEAS FOR MERCY."

Adwin tightened his hold on his belt and resisted the urge to curse the herald. "I'm no' looking to go in there and babble like some English ambassador."

The herald's eyes flickered with amusement, even though his expression remained smooth.

Adwin leaned closer. "Tell the man I have what he wants."

The herald locked gazes with him. Adwin stared him straight in the eye.

"Go on, man," Adwin urged him.

The herald gave a reluctant nod before he disappeared. Adwin rocked back on his heels as he waited, being careful not to look where Katherine was. There was a tap on the floor when the herald returned.

"The Earl of Morton will see you."

Adwin tugged on the corner of his bonnet when he entered the room. "As far as courtly manners, that's about as much as I know."

Morton was angry, but Adwin caught a flicker of amusement in his eyes in response. "Truth be told, I have little patience for French fashion—and even less for the games the McTavishes seem intent on playing."

Adwin faced off with the man, gripping his belt and tightening his resolve. Telling tales by the hearthside was one thing; this was another. Today, whether his audience was convinced would have serious consequences.

"The lad is young," Adwin began. "Sense... Well, that takes a wee bit more time to grow."

"Rolfe McTavish lacks it, sure enough."

"That's why the laird has me watching out for the lad."

Morton leaned back in his chair and made a motion with his hand. "Get on with it. I am a busy man."

"I have the girl," Adwin said.

Morton sat up again. "Here?"

Adwin nodded. "Of course. Rolfe was just attempting to swipe the cheese out from under yer nose."

Morton bared his teeth.

"Lads do such things," Adwin was quick to add. "I pulled a few stunts of that nature in me own day that are still bringing me grief. And there are a few stories about ye making the rounds in the Highlands."

Morton grunted but relaxed. "Why did ye nae bring her in yesterday?"

"Had to fetch her up from where Rolfe left her in the country," Adwin answered. "And I do nae mind saying plainly that it likely did the lad a bit of good to spend the night in chains. Maybe it will teach him some sense."

"Bring her in."

Morton snapped his fingers, and his men opened the doors. Adwin watched the man's eyes narrow when he saw Diocail Gordon bringing Katherine forward. He had a disgusted look on his face as he half tossed her toward Morton.

"English chit," Diocail declared. "I pity the man ye wed her to."

"You swine." Katherine drew in a deep breath and looked at Morton. "How much longer must I endure this country?"

"As long as I tell ye to, madam." Morton sent her a stern warning look.

Katherine played her part, folding under the power of the earl's gaze and lowering herself before him. When she straightened, she began to pluck at the front of her skirt as though she was nervous.

"So, is it an agreement?" Adwin pressed the earl.

"A poor one, if ye ask me," Diocail added. "One day in her company, and ye'll be begging her father to take her back."

"You cannot expect me to enjoy being taken to your barbaric Highlands," Katherine informed Diocail. "Savages. The lot of them."

"Hold yer tongue, woman." Morton pointed at her. "Or I'll have ye locked in a bridle."

Katherine shut her mouth, inwardly cringing at the thought of such a device being used on her. It was a cage of sorts that went over the head, with a plate inserted into the mouth that often included hooks or barbs to cut into the tongue. It would be locked at the back and was often used on women for gossiping.

Adwin let out a bark of laughter. "No' so happy to be here now… Are ye, mistress?" He reached up and tugged on his bonnet again. "Sorry, my lord, but I can nae hide the fact that I will be well rid of her. Still do nae understand what Rolfe was thinking to try to keep her."

"He claimed to have wed her."

Adwin grinned, and Diocail made a show of smothering his amusement. "His father would have his balls first."

Even though it was part of the charade, Katherine still cringed. Rolfe's father wouldn't receive the news of their wedding well. Of course, at the moment it hardly mattered. Morton was much the same. She shied away from thinking that he looked even more arrogant, because circumstances were dire enough without adding to them.

The dress they'd found for her was a sturdy wool one. It was a fine, soft weave that was dyed a dark blue. As she'd come through the court, she'd passed ladies in full court fashion, with farthingales, face paint, and even wigs. Some of them wore a fortune in pearls and gold.

Morton himself was turned out in a fine doublet made of brocade. His buttons were solid gold and his fingernails buffed from being attended. He looked down at her from his throne and contemplated her in exactly the way she'd remembered. As if he was gauging her value.

"Ye can have yer master back," Morton declared. "And he can go home and tell his father why he is no' gaining the title I promised. That will be the price for his son's disobedience."

Adwin started to argue, but the earl slapped the arm

of the chair. "That is the only offer I will make. Take him and go, before I decide to keep them both."

Adwin made a show of wrestling with the earl's warning. He reached up and tugged on the corner of his bonnet at last, earning a grunt from Morton.

"And tell yer fellow Highlanders what happens to ye when ye try to dupe me."

Relief moved through her. Katherine looked at the floor to hide the feeling. She didn't dare allow it to be seen. She heard the outer doors opening, and there was a moment when Adwin and Diocail hesitated to leave her. It endeared them to her, but she couldn't allow it, so she lifted her face and wrinkled her nose at them.

"At last, I am free of you."

She made sure to enunciate her words. Beyond the doors, her English accent was clearly noted, earning her as many scowls as curious looks. It was nothing new; neither was being in the Earl of Morton's power. The doors closed, leaving her facing the man.

"Well, now, mistress, ye are no' too young any longer." His gaze lingered on her breasts. "No' a bit."

❧

"Are ye daft, Adwin?" Rolfe was seething. They'd barely made it off the street and into the boarding-house before he let loose. "How could ye give Kat to that man?"

"Truth was, it was her idea."

Rolfe growled, his temper darkening his complexion.

"The best idea we had at hand," Diocail Gordon added as he placed a bowl on the table. "Ye could no' have done better."

"I would never take me freedom at the cost of me wife's," Rolfe sneered.

"Thing is," Adwin replied, "she was right about one thing. The earl will no' be putting her in chains."

"And there was no other way, short of divine intervention, that we were going to get ye out of that dungeon," Diocail added. "So we listened to the lass. It was sound thinking."

Rolfe wanted to argue more, but his belly was knotted with hunger. While his will was raging, his flesh was needy. Two days without food, and the scent of the stew being served to him was making his mouth water, reducing him to little better than a hound.

He mopped up the last of the bowl's contents with a hunk of bread. Diocail and Adwin had settled down beside him, the rest of the tables in the boardinghouse empty after they had tossed some silver on the tables to encourage the occupants to leave.

"The lass will be abovestairs somewhere." Adwin spoke softly. "The earl does nae suspect she is anything except a biddable female."

"It was the reasonable choice," Diocail said.

"Perhaps for ye it was," Rolfe growled at him. "She is me wife. I am duty bound to protect her, no' cower behind her. Morton tried to wed her when she was but fourteen. Do ye have any idea what he might plot now that she is woman enough to no' cause a commotion with his actions?"

"He'll want to get a good amount for her," Diocail said. "So it will take him some time."

"And she played the part well, wrinkling up her

nose as if she hated us," Adwin said. "Morton has no reason to suspect she is no' happier here."

"Unless one of his spies has told him of the MacPherson hellion," Rolfe countered. "He has spies all over the Highlands." He snorted. "Morton would put her in chains in an instant if he suspected he had need of them to keep his prize."

All three men went silent with the gravity of the situation.

"In that case"—Diocail stood—"we'd best get on with rescuing the lass."

❧

"She's tight."

Katherine felt her cheeks burning as she glared at the physician. The man paid her no mind as he continued to speak with Morton. She knotted the tie around her dressing robe and pulled it tight, but that didn't remove the feeling of having the man's hands on her intimate person.

"Perhaps not a virgin; it's very hard to tell for sure." He looked over at her. "The mortification proves a certain level of innocence."

"The prospective groom is only interested in a maiden," Morton said.

"Give her a knife to cut herself and bloody the sheet," the physician remarked as though it was far from the first time he'd been called upon to offer such advice. "And impress upon her how dire her circumstances will be if she fails to make the union binding."

Morton slowly smiled before he nodded and waved

the man out of the chamber. That left her alone with him, which made her belly knot with apprehension. Two of his retainers stood nearby, the same two men who had been instructed to hold her down while she was inspected.

The shame was theirs.

She repeated that a few more times, trying to force herself to believe it.

"Ye think I am a monster."

Katherine turned to look behind her and discovered she was alone with the Earl of Morton. He was a huge man, one who hadn't allowed himself to run to fat. It was a telling fact that should be noted, because he wasn't the sort who sat around talking about things he never did with his own hands.

"Scotland was in the grip of a civil war when I took the regency," he continued. "The Church was split, and the Highlanders, well, they were doing their best to kill each other. If Mary had her way, she'd have taken this country into a holy war, first with our own people and then on to England."

Still caught in the grip of mortification, Katherine wanted to loathe him, but the truth sliced through her temper. The earl nodded slowly.

"It's good to see that ye have a bit of sense, madam." He considered her. There was a way he looked at people that reminded her of Rolfe, so very intense, as though he approached life more seriously than some people. "Ye were a child the last time we met."

"And yet you considered me ready for marriage."

"An alliance with England would end two hundred

years of wars," Morton cut back. "Alliances made through marriage. Fate decided that ye would be born with blue blood."

"So what now?" she asked. "Now that you have had me prodded by your physician, which I suspect was merely to impress upon me how much power you have over me."

His lips curled up into a grin. "The groom's family insisted on the physician. I am the one who paid him enough to ensure he will never let it be known he isn't sure if ye are a virgin."

"So now," she said softly, "you are here to impress my circumstances upon me?"

The earl's grin grew wider. "As a child, ye would have bent to whatever situation I put ye in. Now, though, ye are grown."

And the earl was attempting to gauge what manner of will she had. It surprised her because it meant the man was not simply dismissing her as an object to be bartered at his whim. No, he was more calculating than that, and she was impressed with his dedication to ending wars. She would be the monster if she failed to recognize the value of that.

"Yes, grown." She tempered her tone. "Old enough to understand that a good marriage is important."

It was the sort of thing little girls were taught to say. Even little boys earned such lectures from the Church when they came back from the playhouses with fanciful ideas about wedding the woman of their heart's delight. Such was fine and good for an afternoon's entertainment, but not very practical.

"Are ye wed to Rolfe McTavish?"

"I'd be a fool to admit it," she countered. "You can make a much finer match for me."

The earl's grin became menacing. "The Bedfords are rumored to have more money than the queen. It appears ye are yer father's daughter."

"I could be." It was a risk, being so bold.

The earl drew in a stiff breath. "If I made it worthwhile to ye?"

"Nothing quite so...lacking in feminine grace," Katherine answered.

"Explain yerself, woman."

"I am simply suggesting that I might be so...much more than a prisoner." She flipped her hand in the air. "Consider this. If I were to apply myself to my union, with grace and...happiness."

"Ye'd be a fool to do otherwise," the earl said. "No man suffers a shrew."

There was a thick warning in his tone. He followed it with a stern look before he quit the room. She gained a quick glance at the men beyond the outer door. They tugged on the corner of their bonnets as the earl passed them and firmly closed the door behind him.

She'd heard their boots on the stone floor the night before. Not so very unlike the sound of the stake being readied in the Gordons' yard.

Well, you escaped that fate. So you will not abandon hope now.

She'd escaped with Rolfe's help.

And once more, she was in dire straits because she had helped him.

Star-crossed lovers.

Truly, the phrase described them well. She just hoped

they didn't end up as a tragedy, as so many lovers did in theatrical plays.

However, she couldn't seem to stop herself from acknowledging it was very, very possible.

⌀

"Ye're playing a dangerous game."

Rolfe cut Diocail a side glance. "As are ye."

He nodded and continued to watch who was arriving and exiting from the court. "A pair of Highlanders willingly staying at court. That will raise a few eyebrows."

"Why do ye think I'm wearing breeks?"

Diocail shifted in his own set of breeches. "I do nae fancy them meself."

Diocail snorted and slapped Rolfe on the shoulder. "Men have done worse in the interest of claiming the lady they desire."

"She is me wife," Rolfe growled back.

Diocail wasn't impressed. "Are ye saying ye do nae desire her?" He slowly shook his head. "Now that is a shame. One I think I may have to remedy by stealing her from ye."

Rolfe sent him a grin that made it clear he'd enjoy the attempt. "Careful, Diocail, I'm in need of a good fight, and a Gordon and a McTavish going at it... Well now, that will no' be anything to take notice of."

Rolfe turned back to watching the main entrance to the court.

"What are ye waiting to see?"

"The Earl of Bedford's secretary arrived this morning." Rolfe sent Diocail a satisfied smirk. "If Morton has a mind to wed Katherine to someone for an alliance, well, he'll be needing her father's agreement or—"

"It would be worthless because the union was made in Scotland." Diocail slowly laughed. "Ye've a fine head on yer shoulders, Rolfe. Of course, ye'll be needing all of yer wits when ye get the lass back home. I hear yer father is nae too fond of the English."

"An English heiress would be a bit more welcome."

Diocail didn't answer right away. Rolfe knew the man was thinking the facts through. It didn't take him long to fit the pieces of the puzzle together. "And ye'll likely be asking for less than the Earl of Morton."

"Almost certainly."

Diocail nodded slowly. "Unless the Earl of Bedford wants an alliance. I hear the Bedfords support the troops in the Netherlands. Morton has been raising the king as a Protestant. Bedford would approve."

"There he is." Rolfe caught sight of the man wearing the pin of the Earl of Bedford. The man looked enraged as he came out of the gate with his attendants hurrying to keep pace. Rolfe moved along the street, following the man until he ducked into a town house.

Rolfe stayed out of sight. Morton wouldn't forget to have the entrance of the place watched, and there were too many people on the street during the day.

⁂

"The earl has sent a bath for ye, mistress."

A young maid came through the door and happily informed Katherine of what Morton had sent to her. The girl smiled as two men carried a fine copper tub into the room. They were followed by a line of boys, all laden with yokes and buckets of fresh water.

But what Katherine was focused on was the way the guards at her door kept their eyes on her, their expressions tight. They might have no liking for their duty, but they were devoted to it nonetheless.

There was a splash as the maid poured hot water into the tub. Another maid had arrived, carrying a silver tray with a cloth over its contents.

"Fine French soap, mistress," the maid exclaimed with a happy smile. "And lavender oil. The earl has been most generous in providing all of the things a lady might wish for."

"I believe you mean to say, all the things my groom might expect me to make use of before a wedding."

The maids both lowered themselves and clapped their hands together gleefully. "Yes, yes, it is all here. We will have you...perfect in no time at all."

There was a distinctly French manner about the maids. French women were considered the most beautiful in the world, but Katherine soon discovered that they had some very odd preferences about their bodies. Once she'd risen from the tub and dried off, the maids refused to give her a dressing robe, but instead came toward her intending to bare her mons.

"Come, come, mistress..." One of the maids cajoled her like a frightened child. "You do not need all of that hair."

"Barbaric," the other insisted. "You want your lover to kiss you there? Yes? So, the hair must go."

Their words sparked a memory that heated her

cheeks. The maids laughed and pulled her back toward the chair they had been using.

By the time they left her, there wasn't a single hair left anywhere except on her head. Katherine wandered over to the mirror and untied the tie of her dressing gown. She let it slip from her shoulders, refusing to cower away from the sight of her own body.

Was she pretty?

She didn't know.

Now, though, every bit of her was on display, the little bush of hair that had hidden her cleft gone.

She missed Rolfe.

Alone with her thoughts, she realized she was a wanton indeed. Her clitoris was throbbing gently as she recalled their time together. As she looked at her reflection, her nipples drew tight.

"Good." The Earl of Morton announced his presence with a snicker. "Ye are ready to be wed."

Katherine hissed and sank to where her robe was puddled around her ankles. Morton didn't look away as she struggled to pull it up and over her shoulders to cover herself.

"The French do know a thing or two about preparing a bride," he offered in a tone that made her temper flare. He tossed a small knife on the table near the hearth and sent her a warning look. "Ye'll be the one to suffer if ye displease yer husband. Think on that before ye defy me."

"I am wed to Rolfe McTavish." The words burst out of her. Desperation was clawing at her insides as she looked at how confident Morton was of his plans for her.

The earl moved closer to her. There was a flicker of something in his eyes that reminded her of Colum Gordon. A moment later, she was reeling from a vicious slap.

"Do nae ever say such again."

The earl was standing still, watching her absorb how easily he struck her. She knew what that flicker was now. It was confidence, absolute confidence in his plans.

"James will inherit England because Elizabeth Tudor is unwed," the earl explained. "She's also wise enough to know that the only way she will keep her crown is to never choose a groom, because the moment she does, the rest of the countries of the world will send their armies to try to take her kingdom from her. As long as she keeps them dancing to the tune of courting her, they will not risk the cost of a war."

The earl paused for a moment and offered her a satisfied grin. "Ye will wed tonight to secure yer father's devotion to making certain James remains Elizabeth's heir by keeping Catherine Grey's sons illegitimate."

He was so very different from Rolfe.

Perhaps the thought was misplaced just then, but Katherine really didn't care. She found herself absorbed by how straightforward Rolfe was, while Morton was as twisted as the plots he devised.

Of course, that opened the gates she had been using to hold back hopelessness. It flooded her now, dragging her down as the earl sent her a satisfied look before leaving her to a new group of maids who brought her wedding dress with them.

"What?" the Earl of Bedford's man exclaimed. "What is this?"

The shadows shifted, and Rolfe emerged from them. Adwin still clung to them but made sure the man caught a glimpse of him to drive home that Rolfe wasn't alone.

"I've come on business," Rolfe said.

"These are my private chambers, sir!"

"Aye." Rolfe moved farther into the room and sat down. "I believe ye'll understand why I do nae care to have any of Morton's spies reporting our meeting back to the man."

The Earl of Bedford's man clamped his teeth together as his expression became one of disgruntlement. "I should enjoy never pleasing that man myself, so who are you?"

"Rolfe McTavish."

The man perked up. "Now I have heard that name."

"The question is, what would ye like us to do about the lass?" Adwin asked.

The Earl of Bedford's man cleared his throat. "Well now, my master has bid me to make an amicable agreement with the Earl of Morton."

The man held up a finger when Rolfe started to speak.

"However, Bridget Hussy, the Countess of Bedford, has made it plain that she has no desire for her step-daughter to ever be heard from again. In England, that is. She wishes no harm toward the bastard."

Rolfe slowly smiled. The Earl of Bedford's man did the same. He leaned toward Rolfe. "So, my good… Highlander…if you were to take your bride home… is it north?"

"Very much so," Rolfe confirmed.

The secretary nodded. He moved to a small table and struck a flint. Little sparks of light fell into a tinder pile before catching. The man used it to light a candle before he reached into the collar of his nightshirt and pulled out a key that was hanging around his neck. He fit it into a writing desk and opened the lid.

"Here," he said at last. "An official offer of dowry for the girl." He handed it over to Rolfe. "Rather generous."

Rolfe read it over, astonished to have in his hands the means of placating his father's objections.

"Of course, you will have to steal her away from her wedding."

Rolfe looked up, all interest in the offer gone.

"Yes, Morton has promised her to one of Lord Campbell's nephews." The secretary's tone made it clear that he disapproved of the match. "You will have to hurry if you plan to steal her away before the vows are consummated."

Rolfe was already heading toward the door, but Adwin stepped into his path. "Sign the offer and seal it."

The secretary nodded and fumbled in his desk for a wax stick. He melted it with the candle and pressed the seal of the Earl of Bedford into the wax. Adwin pushed Rolfe back toward the table.

Rolfe snorted at his captain, but took the quill offered to him and affixed his name to the document.

Adwin took it and nodded. "Do nae be thinking no' to transfer these funds."

"As long as you are successful in making certain there is no marriage with the Campbells. There must be witnesses."

"I wed her in front of witnesses," Rolfe declared.

"A Catholic wedding?"

"It is nae illegal in Scotland," Adwin advised the man.

"Yet her dowry resides in England, where a Catholic wedding is not recognized," the secretary stated in a firm business tone. "If Lord Campbell's nephew consummates his union with her, the marriage will be considered valid."

"She'll be a widow if he does," Rolfe snarled before he left the house.

"Ye will no longer need that dress."

The Earl of Morton had followed her right into the bridal chamber. Katherine turned to consider the man who was quite determined to see her consummate her wedding. "There seems little reason to remove it."

Robert Campbell was lying in the middle of the bed, flat on his back, where his father's men had tossed him after carrying him away from the wedding feast. He was snoring loudly, the stench of French wine rising off him.

Morton cursed. He moved over to the bedside and shook Robert's shoulder. He earned a snort and sputter from the man before the snoring resumed.

Katherine turned back toward the door as a giggle alerted her to more company. Two couples were coming into the chamber with excited looks on their faces.

"We are not too late," one of them exclaimed. "The bride is still dressed."

They came right in and stood by the bed, intent on watching everything as though it were a new play.

Katherine felt like retching.

Depravity had merely been a word until that moment.

"I will return," Morton announced. He stormed through the chamber and sent the others scurrying with a flick of his hand. He paused for a moment and grabbed the pitcher of wine set out on the table with a selection of cheese and fruit.

There were sounds of disappointment from those waiting to watch while they went toward the chamber door. A moment later, Katherine was sealed in with nothing but the sound of Robert's snoring.

A reprieve.

Honestly, she was not sure if it were a blessing, because it allotted her more time to dwell on her circumstances.

She looked toward the bed and felt disgust well up in her.

A reprieve was a reprieve.

The dress was the most formal thing she had ever worn, with a tightly laced corset, a hip roll, and a farthingale. There were long, hanging sleeves, and tight inner ones, all decorated with pearls. The silk swished when she moved, and the entire thing required a great deal of concentration on her hips and posture to keep it from swinging like a large church bell. She wanted nothing more than to be rid of it, but couldn't reach the laces.

It was also dreadfully heavy.

She plucked a few slices of cheese from the plate as she made her way to a chair and sat down.

Life was so much more practical in the Highlands.

Tears stung her eyes. She was never going to see those places again.

Fate had reclaimed her.

❧

"That is no' how ye wear it," Adwin chastised one of his fellow McTavishes in a rough whisper.

"As if ye know any better," the man argued. "It's too tight."

"I dragged that one in here because he's the same size as ye." Adwin pointed at the man lying unconscious on the floor of the small storage chamber. He reached out and tugged on the doublet until it came up and over the retainer's arms.

"No muscle on him."

"Aye," Adwin agreed. He looked over at Rolfe, who was struggling to button a doublet. "They'll draw and quarter us for this if they catch us."

"One fine thing about Morton refusing to ennoble those around him for the past few years..." Rolfe pulled the hat down on his head. "We're all commoners."

"That won't make a bit of difference," Adwin argued. "And the Campbells will slit yer throat for wearing their colors."

Rolfe merely grinned. "They'll have to catch me first."

He leaned down and stripped a young boy of his outer garments and boots. He stuffed the clothing under the front of a doublet one of his retainers was wearing that had come off a man with a large, round belly.

"Let's go get me wife."

There was no pleasure in his tone, simply pure determination. The consequences didn't concern him.

Only the very real threat of being unsuccessful.

❧

Katherine indulged her need to think of the Highlands and drifted off into sleep. Her dreams were light and filled with memories of the place she'd called home for the last few years. Marcus and finally Rolfe.

God, he was a handsome brute.

Perhaps it was a sin, but she adored looking at him. Her wedding had been attended by men in silk and brocade, with servants aplenty to groom them. Their clothing sparkled with precious gems, and yet she preferred the way Rolfe's green eyes shimmered when he was about to kiss her.

"Kat…"

She let out a little hum of enjoyment. Her dreams were so full of details tonight. She heard the rich timbre of his voice keenly.

Someone shook her shoulder, and she let out a huff because she didn't want to let the dream go.

"We've got to go, lass."

Katherine blinked, having trouble absorbing what she was seeing. Rolfe pulled her up and onto her feet while she tried to clear slumber's hold on her brain.

"Lad is out cold."

Adwin's voice was the slap across the face that she needed. The brassy Highlander's humor made her smile as she looked into Rolfe's eyes.

"How…?"

"I'll tell ye how." Adwin was walking back toward them. "Through assault—what those court fops will likely call attempted murder—and deception."

"And ye enjoyed every moment of it," Rolfe informed his captain with a smirk.

Adwin tilted his head to the side. "So long as we do nae get caught."

"Aye." Rolfe had spun her around to get at the laces

on the dress. Katherine turned to face him, needing to confirm he was not a dream. He frowned at her, turning her again and resuming his task.

"We've precious little time, Kat. Explanation will have to wait until we've gotten ye free of this place."

That was all the encouragement she needed to stand still while he tried to open the dress. There was a flash as Adwin pulled out a small dagger and simply slit the laces. She let out a sigh as the bodice sagged, and they both dug their hands into it to raise it above her head. She bent her knees to help, coming up on the other side of the skirt in her underpinnings.

"Never seen so many layers of clothing in me life," Rolfe muttered as he pulled at the farthingale and tried to free her from the hip roll.

"Are ye in there, lass?"

"I wish I wasn't," she answered as she tried to help. "I believe they put this on me to keep me from running away."

"Oh, in that case, please continue."

They all froze as Robert Campbell spoke from the bed. He was sitting up, his legs slightly apart, which afforded them all a fine view of the bottom of his shoes. "Please don't think me a beast, dear, but I really do no' want a wife or to go to the English court. Getting stinking drunk was the only thing I could think of. But I am no' quite as drunk as I put on."

"Thank you," Katherine said sincerely as Rolfe tossed a pair of pants at her. Down to her smock and corset, she pulled the clothing on as she began to shake with anticipation.

Maybe…

Just...*maybe*...

"Morton came to witness the consummation, along with some others," she told Robert. "They will be back."

Robert shrugged.

"There will likely be repercussions," Rolfe added as he looked at Robert.

Her groom slowly grinned. "You Highlanders are not the only ones who enjoy having a bit of fun at the earl's expense." He shot an arrogant look at them. "We'll cross paths again."

"I'll call ye friend when we do," Rolfe assured him.

"We need to be gone." Adwin pushed a hat onto Katherine's head.

Rolfe was stern, grasping her wrist and pulling her behind him. She cast a last glance back toward Robert, who sent her a grateful little smile before he collapsed back onto the bed.

❧

The passageways were lit by candles.

Katherine had never seen such a waste of candles, not even in her father's home. They were left burning every ten feet or so. That left plenty of shadows, but afforded far more light than she was used to having at night.

"Let go of my wrist."

Rolfe's fingers tightened in response.

"I am your servant," she stressed in a whisper. "My duty is to follow you."

There was a shuffle and a smothered cry, confirming they were far from alone. Huge tapestries hung over the walls, making plenty of hidden alcoves for couples interested in darkness to hide their actions.

Rolfe released her, but Adwin was behind her. Every footstep seemed to take forever as her heart pounded. She strained to see through the murky light, hoping she wouldn't see Morton coming around one of the turns in the passageways.

Their footsteps seemed to echo as loud as thunder while they made their way. She caught the scent of the kitchens before Rolfe headed through them. The servants looked away when they entered, clearly not wanting to recognize them. It spoke of a harsh life, but with Morton ruling, Katherine had firsthand knowledge of how much easier it must be to remain obscure.

Diocail Gordon was waiting for them with horses. "Marcus and Symon are a half day's ride out since neither of them dares to be seen here."

Rolfe nodded. He made sure she was on her horse, a satisfied look entering his eyes before he swung up and into the saddle himself.

They rode out, uncaring of the darkness or the way the rain was starting to fall.

After all, they were Highlanders, and there was nowhere else she'd rather be.

❧

Morton stared at the scattered pieces of the dress. Robert snored away while the earl slowly laughed. It was a rare indulgence. One he didn't allow himself lightly.

Being bested by Rolfe McTavish? Well, that was unexpected. He might be a man, but he was a young one who had yet to fully taste life. Wisdom came with that desire, or perhaps it was more correct to say that one gained knowledge after being tossed aside by life.

It was always a humbling experience to discover that while the flesh was strong, circumstances might still defy brawn.

Katherine and Robert's preferences were insignificant next to what their marriage would have accomplished. Besides, Morton knew they were both young and would have learned to make the best of their arrangement, be that through learning to like each other or taking lovers. If it prevented war, he didn't care a bit.

Because he couldn't.

No, a man had to choose what to fight for.

Tonight, Rolfe had won the day. Morton awarded the victory silently before he turned and moved his thoughts to the next order of business.

❧

They rode hard, only stopping near the afternoon for the sake of the horses. Adwin and the other retainer happily went off into the bushes to change out of their court clothing.

Katherine waited long enough for Rolfe to have some privacy to relieve himself before she followed him. He turned as she came around the bushes, and she rushed into his arms.

She was breathless and giddy, but Rolfe didn't return the embrace. He was stiff and unyielding, making her draw away.

"Ye need to be taken in hand," he said tersely.

Katherine felt her eyes widening. Rolfe nodded at her response. He wore only a shirt, his kilt lying on the ground, but he left it there while he stared at her.

"Aye, ye heard me correctly." He'd stopped with

his hands on his hips, as though he was deciding on her punishment. "Ye will never allow yerself to get into danger such as that again."

"It was the only way to free you," she countered. "Even Adwin saw the correctness of it."

Rolfe snorted. "I'll be dealing with Adwin soon enough for allowing ye to do it."

"What are you saying?" She was reeling. Her happiness was being shattered by his wounded pride.

"Is it no' clear enough, woman?" Rolfe exclaimed. "Ye are me wife."

Her temper got the better of her. "You have that correct, and if you think I will stand by while you rot in chains, think again."

"Ye will *never* place yerself in danger like that again, and I'll strap yer arse if that is what it takes to teach ye to mind me."

She recoiled from him. "You will do no such thing."

Rolfe's expression changed, becoming one of reluctance. "I would no' enjoy it, but ye will never put yerself in such danger again or I swear I will."

It horrified her, and drove home how little they really knew each other. She was reeling as reality drew its claws down her, reminding her that a husband did have the right to beat his wife, and that she had willingly signed the contract to place herself in his keeping. No one would interfere.

Rolfe frowned, not caring for the way she shrank from him. "Kat, ye must know I mean only the best with such a promise."

"And you should know well what sort of woman I am," she countered. Tears stung her eyes, and she fought to keep him from seeing such weakness. "I thought you accepted me as I am."

"I did." His tone was edged with passion now. "Did I no' wed ye knowing me father forbade me?"

It was an unexpected blow. "He forbade you?"

Rolfe drew himself up, shutting her out, but she stepped toward him. "Answer me."

A curt nod was her response.

And now Rolfe would be bringing her home—without the noble title his father had sent him to court to gain. She turned and walked away before the tears gathering in her eyes betrayed her.

She'd never known a pain so deep before. It was centered inside her, the agony nearly enough to buckle her knees. Never once had it crossed her mind that there would be anything to worry about once they were both free.

It seemed she had greatly miscalculated. Somehow, she had convinced herself Rolfe was unlike other men. That he was somehow accepting of her nature and will.

The truth was, now that he'd claimed her, he expected her to submit to his will in all things.

At least that idea warmed her temper. Men made so little sense. They claimed to enjoy spirit in women and then expected their wives to bend to their dictates. They treated a woman like a hawk that would be kept in line by starvation. Yet when one looked into the creature's eyes, its wildness was still there. And that enhanced its value.

She couldn't live like that.

Wouldn't.

Even if it killed her.

They met up with Symon and Marcus just before sunset. The welcome she'd been looking forward to from Rolfe was finally hers when Marcus pulled her feet right off the ground while he nearly crushed her ribs in a hug.

Once he set her down, he reached past her and lightly punched Rolfe in the shoulder. "Well done, lad! I'll admit, I had me reservations about this marriage, but ye've proved me wrong."

Katherine bit her lip and drifted away. Symon Grant, Diocail Gordon, Marcus, and Rolfe all clustered around the fire. Their expressions turned serious as they listened to the tale of what had happened.

Morton's words rose from her memory.

Scotland was in the grip of a civil war when I took the regency. The Church was split, and the Highlanders, well, they were doing their best to kill each other...

Now, MacPherson stood next to Gordon, and McTavish broke bread with Grant. It was a fine sight. She would be the monster if she ignored it. Living with the MacPhersons, she'd heard the tales of raids and feuds. Seen the children growing up without fathers and watched as Ailis Robertson sat beside her husband, Bhaic MacPherson, when Morton had forced them to wed. Ailis had done so with grace, when she had been anything but welcome in the stronghold of her enemies.

So Morton had his uses, it would seem.

As did she.

Perhaps Rolfe didn't care for her taking risks, but he was standing there, and she soaked up the sight of him before she turned and contemplated the setting sun. Day surrendered to darkness as she felt herself accepting the harsh reality of Rolfe's nature. It had always been his devotion to his honor that had attracted her to him. Yet she'd been foolish not to realize that the trait that enamored her would trap her if she stayed with him.

He'd not accept a hellion as his wife.

No, she'd be expected to be as graceful as Ailis and Helen. Taking her place and learning to obey her husband.

She couldn't do it.

Honestly, it wasn't a matter of wanting to or not; she simply didn't know how. For the first time, she realized her education was lacking. Severely so. No one had taught her to run a house, to keep the books, to ensure there was enough food stored to last through the winter. There were memories of such lessons back in her childhood. That only served to shame her. She had always thought of her stepmother in harsh terms, yet Bridget Hussy had made sure her stepdaughter had tutors.

It all left Katherine feeling as if she were standing in a puddle and the rain was pouring down on her, threatening to make the puddle much deeper. The question was, how long would she be able to stay there before it became unbearable? Would it be long enough for the rain to stop? The uncertainty ate at her.

"He'll come to terms with it, lass."

She jumped, so absorbed in her thoughts that she hadn't realized Adwin had ventured after her. The captain gripped his wide belt, clearly not accustomed to soothing a female's melancholy. He offered her a bundle, and she saw it was a dress, rolled in a length of McTavish plaid.

Katherine took it, feeling as though it were as heavy as chains.

"Rolfe has more devotion to honor than most," the captain continued, searching for words he thought a woman would like to hear. It was a strange pairing to say the least, with the bushy, dark beard that went from his face to his neck, the scars that decorated his cheeks, and the two breaks in his nose. He was a hardened Highlander, suited to his environment and thriving on the challenge of living in the northern country.

"It's to be expected that he'd be less than…gracious about accepting help. Seeing as how he did vow to protect ye at yer wedding."

And she had promised to be obedient, submissive, and meek.

"Perhaps it was a mistake," she muttered. "For us to wed."

Adwin tilted his head to one side, clearly perplexed by her words.

"Since his father detests me," she continued. "And now Rolfe is vexed."

There was no arguing with the two points she had made. Katherine watched Adwin try to think of something to say. "It was kind of you to try to soothe me, Adwin."

She started to turn away, realizing the best she could do was to release the man from any feelings of obligation to her unhappiness. No, it was hardly his fault she was unsuited to the task of being Rolfe's wife, or that she was English.

Adwin reached out and caught her upper arm. It surprised her, drawing her attention back to his face.

"I will no' forget." His tone was deep and hard. She watched a look of respect cross his eyes. "Ye might have left him in chains, and no one would have blamed ye because ye are a woman." He released her and nodded firmly. "I will no' ever forget ye kept him from that fate. No McTavish will curse yer name in me hearing."

A man such as Adwin only gave respect to those who earned it. At least she seemed to have done something right. In his eyes, she witnessed the belief that she had.

"Well, except for your laird." She'd meant it as a way to lighten the mood. A mild jest, something to take her mind from the turmoil her emotions were in.

Adwin nodded again. "Well, as ye say, except for Laird McTavish. I can nae be smashing him in the jaw."

"Do not smash anyone on my account," she implored him. "I did what was correct."

Adwin snorted. "Ye did it because ye love that lad. Do nae deny it. I see it in yer eyes." He looked back toward Rolfe. "The lad is young, and blind. He'll come 'round."

She tried to let the confidence in his tone soak into her. Adwin took it as a sign she'd accepted his reasoning on the matter. He tugged on the corner of his bonnet before he turned and returned to the camp.

The fire illuminated the faces of the men as they talked. It wasn't that she felt they would send her away if she ventured toward them, but they would change their demeanor. Right then, they were relaxed, teasing one another as they shared stories of a nature they'd deem unfit for her ears.

And yet she'd heard them.

Still, time had caught her firmly in its grasp, making it so she was no longer in their world. At least not as one of them. As a woman, yes, and along with that came the expectation for proper behavior.

Hellion...

Truly, it was what she was.

She'd been naive to believe Rolfe would accept her as such. She was far from the first bride who'd discovered the courting finished once the soiled sheet had been flown. She belonged to him now, and a man who could not control his wife would never be followed by men.

That hopelessness returned. She settled down and pulled the skirt of the dress around herself. She was being perverse in refusing to use the plaid, but she wasn't in the frame of mind to be objective. The dress was made of wool and warmed her, luring her off to sleep as she floundered in a sea of unruly emotions.

❧

She heard someone venture near her just before first light. A soft step on the ground, just a shifting of gravel beneath a boot heel. It brought her awake in an instant, because Marcus had bedded his training troops down in the yard more than once to sharpen their skills.

Waking up blurry-eyed and slow-witted was an

invitation to get kicked in the backside by one of the captains.

Rolfe bent his knees and hunched down near her. The sky was just starting to lighten. It wasn't day yet, just that hazy time when it was no longer night and the first birds had yet to sing in welcome to the dawn.

"Ye do nae care to wear me colors?"

The length of McTavish wool was lying a couple of feet from where she'd slept. She'd used the hip roll as a pillow and slept in the skirt of the dress. Rolfe didn't care for what he saw, but there was only one way to appease him, and that was with submission.

"You do not care for my ways." She'd sat all the way up and was perched on her feet, crouching low, as secure in the lunge as he was. Surprise flickered in his eyes for a moment.

"I never deceived you as to what I am," she stated clearly.

"Nor did I hide from ye what I felt ye needed to learn," Rolfe answered her, his expression becoming stern. "Ye still wed me, Katherine, of yer own free will. Get dressed. We can come to agreement once we're out of Morton's reach."

"You mean to say that I can accept my lot."

He'd pushed to his feet but looked back at her. She watched him grip his belt and set his jaw. He left it unsaid between them, turning his wide shoulders on her and walking back toward where the horses were starting to stir.

Refusing to put the dress on would have been childish and foolish, considering she started to shiver now that she was clothed only in the thin court clothing. Silk might be very pretty, but it was completely ill-suited to nights spent outdoors in Scotland.

The cold was cutting through the fabric, making her clench her teeth to keep them from chattering.

She gave a little huff and gathered up the parts of the dress before moving behind some bushes to dress. Stubbornness wouldn't keep her warm. When she emerged, one of the younger retainers was standing there. He'd turned his back on her position, nodding when he heard her come around. He offered her the length of McTavish plaid, having plucked it from the ground where she'd left it.

Confusion flickered in his eyes when she didn't reach for it. He didn't seem to think it worthy of a question, but followed her down to where the horses were waiting and tossed the wool across the back of a mare.

Her will meant nothing.

And the knowledge of that was like salt water flowing into a garden. Her happiness strangled on it, poisoned by harsh facts and blunt reality.

❦

"Still being stubborn?"

Rolfe looked up and found Adwin contemplating him.

"She did ye a service."

Rolf finished his business and dropped his kilt. "Ye should never have allowed her to show herself. Christ, Adwin, Morton might have wed her to a bastard who would have been happy to have her."

Adwin looked straight back at him. "Life is no' fair. I taught ye that lesson a long time ago, and do nae

forget it was me. For all that yer father is laird, he was
no' the one riding beside ye, taking the same risks ye
were, willing to stand in front of ye to shield ye from
harm. I've had plenty of experience protecting ye, so
do nae start suggesting I will be changing me ways.
I'd have done anything to get ye out of that dungeon.
If that makes me a bastard, so be it, but I'm one who
watched yer back."

Rolfe rocked back on his heels. "I'd do the same for
ye, Adwin, but hiding behind a woman?"

"Morton was nae going to hang her," Adwin
responded. "I'd no' have allowed her near the man
if I'd thought her life was in danger. And before ye
argue with me further, yer bloody life was in jeopardy.
Morton is a mad bastard. He'd have chopped off yer
head as an example, and ye're a fool if ye do nae
believe so. He'd been bested already by Marcus over
Katherine, so he had a great deal to lose if he was
duped again."

"So I am to just accept that me wife might have
been called upon to prostitute herself on me behalf?"

Adwin stepped toward him and lowered his voice
so it didn't carry. "Ye recognize she does nae put herself above ye. That's a rare thing, lad. I've lived more
years than ye have, and I'm warning ye, do nae let her
affection be strangled by yer pride."

"It's more than me pride to want to keep her from
being bedded by another. A man she did no' choose.
That's rape, Adwin. Something I'm sworn to shield
her from."

Adwin closed his eyes, and when he lifted his eyelids, there was a hard glint in the dark depths. "Better

some fucking than yer head rotting on a pike. Hate me for saying it, but at least ye're alive to do it."

Adwin turned and left. Rolfe watched him go, feeling as though he'd been smashed in the jaw.

"I can kick ye in the balls if ye do nae see the wisdom in what yer man said."

Rolfe turned to discover Marcus MacPherson standing behind him. The war chief had stopped in his favorite pose, feet braced shoulder-width apart as he crossed his arms over his chest.

"Yer turn to have a go at me?"

Marcus only curled his lips back and gave Rolfe a flash of his teeth.

"I'd think ye would disagree with Adwin on the matter of being raped as something to be dismissed."

Marcus's grin faded. "Aye, I do."

"So ye understand why I took her back to McTavish land."

"That's a matter that has been laid to rest," Marcus responded.

"No, it has nae," Rolfe responded. "Do ye think I enjoy reprimanding her? Would ye have me allow her to place herself at risk? What manner of husband would that make me?"

"A dead one," Marcus informed him. "By my hand. I promise ye so."

Rolfe snorted. "Then ye understand why I can nae find peace with her trading herself for me."

Marcus slowly shook his head. "Nae, ye've got it wrong, lad. It was yer father who put ye both in the position of having to deal with Morton."

"It was me duty to see the man. A son's duty."

"Aye, and yet ye chose to shield Katherine from him," Marcus continued. "Ye forget, I know something about that meself. I could have wed her as a child, when Morton tried to press her on me, but I reasoned with meself about the fact that she was too young to take to me bed. Aye, I might have placed the good name of me father and me clan before me own decency, telling meself I'd bed her once and she could simply come to terms with it as more than one bride has been forced to do. Brenda Grant might have refused to help her, too. Lord knows, Brenda has taken her fair share of abuse in this life and did nae need to be the one to face Morton when the man discovered both meself and Katherine gone."

"Another reason Katherine must learn to mind me."

"Everyone has a choice in life," Marcus explained slowly. "Katherine made the decision no' to live in fear. I let her train to build her confidence. So, ye'll have to understand that I will no' allow ye to crush her. If ye can nae come to terms with the fact that she stood by yer side and it is her nature to do so, I'll take her home to MacPherson land."

Rolfe stiffened, feeling every muscle he had tightening. "Ye will nae."

Each of the three words came out in a clear warning. Marcus wasn't a naive man when it came to such things. He stared straight at Rolfe, taking his measure.

"Do ye recall how ye felt when I took Helen from ye?"

Rolfe's question caught Marcus off guard. The man growled, and Rolfe grinned at him.

"I can see that ye do."

"What point are ye trying to make?" Marcus asked.

"Was yer union any more settled than mine is?"

Understanding dawned on Marcus. He shook his head reluctantly.

"So do nae threaten to take Katherine from me," Rolfe warned him softly. "We've no' had the time to learn to trust each other, and here on the road is no' the place for us to be settling things between us."

"So ye're thinking I am going to allow ye to take her into yer stronghold while she is miserable?" Marcus asked. "I can nae do that, lad. She's dear to me, make no mistake about that."

"Be careful about letting me father hear ye say that," Rolfe replied. "He'll be pressing ye for a dowry."

"If Katherine were content in the union, I would gladly provide it." Marcus drew in a deep breath and let it out. "I'd no' have Helen without Katherine. Many might say Katherine was simply a pawn caught in the scheme, but I do nae care about the details. I believe in gifts from God."

"Katherine is as much mine," Rolfe stated clearly. "I will nae allow ye to take her, and before ye argue further, know I am staying away from her because all I want to do is kiss the hell out of her." Rolfe shot Marcus a knowing look. "No' exactly a fitting thing under our current circumstances."

Marcus growled at him, low and deep.

Rolfe didn't take it from him.

"I recall the way ye had Helen cornered on a riverbank." Marcus stuck a finger out at him in warning, but Rolfe only smirked. "So taken by her that I snuck up on ye." He snickered at the memory. "I'm no' going to lie. That tale has done me name well."

Marcus popped his knuckles and made a fist that he sent smashing into his opposite palm.

Rolfe stopped toying with the man and sent him a hard, serious look. "Do I strike ye as any less taken by Katherine? I defied me father to wed her. Only once before have I ever willingly committed such defiance against him."

There was a long silence between them. Marcus contemplated Rolfe, searching his gaze for long moments before he nodded.

"I believe ye, lad."

"So, ye'll be telling her no," Rolfe clarified, "when she comes to ye looking to go home with ye?"

Marcus closed his eyes. "Aye." He opened them, granting Rolfe an unguarded glimpse into his thoughts. "It will tear something inside me to do it, and I'm warning ye"—Marcus pointed at him—"I will be checking back to make sure she's settled to her satisfaction."

"I expect no less."

Marcus shook his finger at Rolfe before he left. Rolfe stood for another few moments, realizing just how uncertain he'd been of the outcome of his conversation with Marcus. Satisfaction moved through him in a slow wave that left him with a growing sense of urgency to reach McTavish land.

Katherine was withdrawing from him.

It was like a raw wound that wasn't healing. One he needed to tend to in private.

She'd be his. He refused to accept anything less.

He just wished he didn't know firsthand how often life made him take what he didn't want.

Eight

She needed to ask Marcus to take her home.

Katherine put it off for several more days, coming up with excuses of not wanting to spoil the camaraderie of the trip. People watched them as they passed, the news of four clans riding together making its way ahead of them.

Yes, that was it. She didn't want to sour everyone's disposition.

You don't want to shame Rolfe...

That was also true. Which just made her sigh because she cared for him.

Love, you mean...

Her inner voice was being perverse.

And annoying.

Yet true...

Fine, yes, yes, and yes again. It wasn't really fair to shame Rolfe by deserting him when he was only expecting what every man wanted from a wife.

"Marcus and Symon will be splitting off tomorrow."

Rolfe had followed her for a change, placing himself between her and the fire. He offered her a plate with part of a roasted rabbit on it.

"Ye're to be commended, Kat," he said after she'd taken it. "I do nae think I've ever heard of a woman keeping pace with Highlanders. Yet ye have nae asked for a single break along the road."

"You know full well that I am trained." She offered her comment in a soft tone, realizing the time was at hand to broach the topic of leaving him. Her appetite died as she looked at him and searched for words that were not too sharp.

"I do," he answered before he leaned down and stopped her from setting the plate aside.

She realized he hadn't touched her in days. She felt it keenly, as if they completed each other in some strange, magical way.

He felt it too. She watched passion flicker in his eyes. "Just as ye know that no one makes ye feel like I do."

He released her, letting her experience the parting of their flesh. It was acute, sending a little ripple of lament through her.

"I've had words with Marcus," Rolfe informed her softly, but that didn't keep her from catching the warning in his tone. "Ye will be coming home with me, Kat."

"No." She stood up, the plate tumbling out of her lap. "I will not."

Rolfe stayed exactly where he was. That meant she was only a step from him once she straightened. He took instant advantage of it, hooking his arm around her body and binding her against him.

"Yes." He captured her nape with his other hand and held her still as his breath hit her lips. "Ye will, *Wife*."

She both hated and loved the sound of the word *wife*. He meant it as more than a legal term. Oh yes, there was a flare of possession in his eyes, right before he pressed his mouth down onto hers.

It had been too long since he'd touched her.

That realization burst on her as he kissed her hard. It was a mark of possession, a declaration of intention, and a warning to her that he wasn't planning on being defied.

She tried to push him away in response. Oh, it wasn't that she really thought about it. No, this was impulse, the need to prove her strength to him just as much as he needed to claim her.

His kiss was hard, yet not brutal. She twisted and he followed her, pressing her lips apart as sweet sensation went surging through her, awakening a hundred points on her body that longed for his touch. Yearnings rose up from inside her, demanding satisfaction now that she knew he could wring pleasure from her flesh. Her doubts about their compatibility dissolved as he held her still and kissed her until she ripped her mouth from his to draw in ragged breaths.

She was pressed to him from knees to chest, so aware of his hardness, wanting it inside her.

It frightened her.

She recoiled from him, struggling against him. He let out a snort before releasing her, only to have to grab her by the upper arm when she stepped on the hem of the dress and would have landed on her backside if he hadn't caught her.

She shook off his hold the moment she had her balance. "I cannot be the wife you desire."

"And yet desire is drawing us to each other," he countered.

"We can find it with others, too." She didn't care for how hollow that made her feel, as if she were shredding her own heart.

"Ye are mine, Katherine," he warned her. "Ye wed me of yer own will, and I will nae allow ye to take that back. Ye gave me yer promise, yer solemn vow."

"Because I thought you accepted me as I was." She felt as though she was floundering in a pool of water, just trying to stay afloat.

"Ye knew very well me reasons for taking ye back to McTavish land," he said. "Ye take risks that are selfish, woman, and I will teach ye that lesson. Never will ye place yerself between me and danger."

"So you would have had me stand idle while Morton held you?"

He nodded firmly.

"You are arrogant beyond compare," she hissed. "I recall the vows we took as well. Among them was 'I plight thee my troth.'"

Rolfe made a low sound of warning under his breath. He was fighting to keep his hands off her. She recognized the flash in his eyes and the way his nostrils flared.

"We'll be talking more…once we make it to a chamber with a solid door."

"And why is that?" She really should have left well enough alone, but Rolfe always had unleashed a daring inside her.

Now it was flaring up, gaining strength as her heart started to pound and she caught the scent of his skin. Passion was heating her; the chill of the night was perfect coupled with the heat warming her. Their clothing was suddenly so unnecessary.

And she truly wanted to rip his open.

She wasn't alone in the grip of that need. It flashed through his eyes a moment before he was leaning over. He put his shoulder right against her belly and pushed toward her, taking her off her feet with a little whoosh of air.

He carried her as though she weighed nothing, taking her farther into the forest until the sounds from the camp were faint.

"Now, we are going to come to an agreement." He let her down, but didn't allow her to step away from him.

"You think a tumble is all that is needed to sway my mind about the rest of my life?"

He cupped the sides of her face. "I think it's a fine place to start."

Her body agreed with him, feeling as if it were glowing when he sealed her mouth beneath his again. It was a hungry kiss this time, drawing her to him with just how much he craved her. She couldn't seem to deny it, not when he needed her.

Her thoughts became muddled as his tongue swept across her lower lip. She let out a little sound more breathless and feminine than she'd thought she might ever produce. He answered it with a male sound of approval.

"I like that," he whispered against her ear, his fingers threaded through her hair as he kissed the side of her neck. "Knowing that I make ye cry out with passion. I enjoy it, lass…"

He turned her around, putting his chest to her back. "I intended to wait…until we were home…to save yer blushing to know every man behind us knows what we've gone off to do."

She shuddered. It wasn't shock. No, it was anticipation. Blunt. Hard. And it hit her like a solid blow. Her passage had never felt so empty, so much in need of being filled. Rolfe was tugging on the lace that held her bodice closed, freeing her breasts. Her chemise was a thin barrier, yet one that irritated her because she wanted to be bare.

Like some pagan rite.

He found the thin tie that held the neckline closed and gave it a tug. The knot popped, allowing him to reach in and cup her breast.

"But seeing the moonlight on these… Well, now I do nae much care if ye spend all of tomorrow with rosy cheeks." He was whispering in her ear as he teased her breast, cupping it, stroking it, and teasing the nipple until it rose into a hard point beneath his touch.

"Perhaps I should confess that I will enjoy knowing yer blushing confirms to every man here that ye belong to me."

"I do not." She stepped forward but only heard him chuckle behind her.

Rolfe made good use of the moment, unbuckling his kilt and flinging it across the ground while she turned to face him for her argument.

"Ye do." He scooped her off her feet and lowered her onto the wool. It was still warm from his body, and he was hotter still as he came down with her, reaching back into her open bodice to lift her breast into the open. "And I am going to enjoy proving it to ye."

She ended up flat on her back. Rolfe controlled her expertly, coming down beside her, one of his thighs trapping her legs as he leaned over her and captured her nipple between his lips.

"Oh…"

She meant to say something, but Rolfe sucked on her nipple and the thought refused to form into anything solid. Instead, she was arching back, astonished by how good it felt to have his lips wrapped around her flesh. Never once had she realized how sensitive it might be.

She needed to be closer to him. Reaching for his shoulders, she pulled him toward her. He seemed just as impatient to be in contact with her flesh. There was the cooling touch of the night air against her legs as he tugged her skirt up and she knew the joy of feeling him stroking her upper thigh.

Gooseflesh rippled across her skin in response as he stroked her again, this time moving closer to her mons.

"What have ye done?"

He'd lifted his head as he teased the recently bared folds of her sex. It was still as smooth as a newborn's.

"French maids," she rasped out. "Morton sent a couple of them to…ah…help me prepare for my wedding night."

"Ye were already wed to me."

He'd meant it as a warning, but he was still teasing her cleft, clearly distracted by the lack of curls to guard it. Rolfe was twisting and shifting until he was hovering over her sex and pressing her thighs wide.

"You turn me into a wanton…" The words crossed her lips in a husky tone that earned her an arrogant look from Rolfe. He was teasing her slit with his thumb, his eyes narrowing as he caught the first drops of welcome from her passage.

"And I will gladly feed yer cravings, lass, for it is the only way to satisfy me own."

His words held as much impact as the first touch of his mouth against her sex. She writhed, unable to remain still. The pleasure was white-hot, feeling like it was twisting up into her belly as he licked her slit from top to bottom, along both sides, and then he spread her folds, baring her clitoris so that he could treat it to the same attention.

She cried out, her eyes shutting as he sucked on that point. There was no way to control anything. No, at that moment, there was only reaction, impulsive response to the need he was building beneath his tongue. He had slid his hands under her skirt to hold her hips, sending a strange feeling of intensity through her, as though she enjoyed knowing he was holding her in place for his pleasure.

He kept her on the edge, easing off when she thought she was going to peak. Over and over again, until she was certain her sanity was about to burst instead.

"*Rolfe…*"

He lifted his head, satisfaction on his face as he looked up her spread body. "Do ye want me?"

"Yes."

He rose, pushing back onto his haunches. He reached down and gripped the hem of his shirt, pulling it over his head. The moonlight cast him in silver and shadow as his member stuck up, hard and promising.

"Ye want yer husband?"

She realized he was going to extract his punishment from her. He'd left the hunger blazing inside her as retribution for rejecting him. But he needed her as much as she did him. She curled up, surprising him as she kept going until she had her thighs wrapped around his waist and her arms around his shoulders.

His member was between them. Trapped against her wet folds. She squeezed her thighs tightly and gently rocked her hips so she was stroking his length with her slit.

"Christ…" he ground out, locking his hands around her hips.

"Do you want me to be your wife?" she whispered back to him. It was an agony of sorts, moving against his member. It felt delicious and yet increased her craving to have him inside her. She gripped his hair, pulling his head away from where it was buried against her shoulder so their eyes might meet. "As I am?"

"Katherine…"

His tone was strained as he fought the same battle against the tide of need for each other. It pulled them into its grip, refusing to allow either of them to maintain their personal identities. They both resisted, needing each other, craving it, and still too stubborn to submit.

He lifted her, his member straightening so he could plunge her down onto it. Their cries mixed together as they became one. It wasn't gentle; they strained against each other, riding hard, forcing each other up to a crest that, when it peaked, ripped them both in two. Pleasure cracked through her like a whip, and she felt it tear a cry from his lips as his seed began to flood her. At the last moment, he clamped her down onto him, so he was as deep as he might go, and pumped his offering inside her.

He was shaking when he eased her off his lap where she crumpled, completely spent. He curled around her, the night cooling her as she struggled to breathe. Somehow, the sight of the moon and the stars fit the moment.

They were wild.

And she had no defense left against admitting how much she needed him.

Wanton...

Yes...

And more.

She was craven. Feeling as though her very soul cried out for his touch.

Whatever she was, there wasn't any strength left in her to debate the rightness of her feelings. Sleep tugged her away, and she felt his breath on her head as he smoothed the hair from her face.

❧

"Do nae ask, Katherine."

Marcus spoke before she got the chance. He turned to face her, looking older than she recalled.

"I know what ye seek, and I must tell ye no."

She shook her head in shock. "You deny me a place? Now?"

Marcus drew in a stiff breath. "I trained ye, lass."

She nodded. "Something I am grateful for, and it has surely served its purpose."

"That might be debated and justly so, for if I had no' allowed ye into the training yard, ye'd no' have fallen into Tyree Gordon's hands to begin with."

She wanted to argue, but this was Marcus. Between master and student, there was no room for dishonesty. "That is true. Yet there is no turning back time."

"No," he agreed. "Ye are a woman now, one who is wed by her own choice."

"I did not know his father forbade the match."

Marcus's eyebrows rose. "Well, that's a difficulty, to be sure."

"I should think so."

"Still…" He took a moment to weigh his words before speaking.

Her shoulders tightened because she knew the expression on his face. It was the same one that she'd witnessed before he pronounced judgment. This was the MacPherson war chief, about to make a decision.

There would be no arguing with it once it was cast.

"I do nae accept cowards in me yard."

She stiffened.

"So, ye will no' run away from yer new father-in-law. William McTavish is an arrogant goat, one I expect ye to face with yer back straight. Ye have naught to be ashamed of."

"He will not change his thinking about English blood."

She knew better than to argue, and yet she couldn't seem to hold the words in. It felt like the ground was crumbling around where she stood, getting closer and closer to her feet. If Marcus denied her a hand to cling to, she'd fall into an unknown abyss.

"Ye are no' running away from William." Marcus sent her a stern look. "I was guilty once of thinking women are more suited to being taken away from their homes. Helen taught me the error of me ways. It is a difficult thing, leaving yer home to wed, yet I expect ye to do so with courage."

"Rolfe does not accept me as I am." She opened her hands. "I wish it were otherwise, but I do not know how to be anything else."

Marcus smiled at her, but it was the way a father would look at a child being sent to do a duty expected of her.

"It's me fault ye are more fearful of this day than need be," he said. "For that, I am sorry."

"Yet you will leave me with a man who wishes to crush my spirit?"

Marcus inhaled sharply. "Helen charged me with the same thing more than once."

That brought Katherine up short. "You and Helen are so very happy."

"Aye." Marcus nodded. "We had to learn how to be, Katherine. To many, it might seem Helen settled in, but I will tell ye bluntly, it took both of us to make our union what it is. Think on that, lass, for ye can be certain I'd no' leave ye here if I had not already said as much and more to yer husband."

A little tingle of warmth filled her. Marcus was more of a father to her than any other.

"I am not the one who is digging his heels in," she groused, feeling the point well and truly lost.

Marcus slowly smiled, flashing his teeth at her. "Well, now, Helen had to get through to me, through me stubborn pride, and it was no' a simple matter. There were times she needed things to help her bring me around to sensible thinking."

"Such as what things?"

Marcus chuckled, the sound dark and ominous. "Such as pitchers."

He looked past her, and she turned to see Rolfe coming toward them. The expression on his face drew her attention. At first, it seemed to be anger, but at second glance, she realized he was determined. Deeply so. He'd heard the last part and raised an eyebrow.

"Pitchers?" he asked. "What do ye need a pitcher for, Kat?"

Marcus snorted, nearly choking on his amusement. He slapped Rolfe on the shoulder. "Pray she does nae ever answer that, lad. It leaves a hell of a ringing in a man's ears when he gets walloped with one because he is behaving like a fool."

∽

Laird William McTavish was happy to see his son return. So much so that he made his way onto the steps as the McTavishes flooded out of the hall to greet the returning men. His joy faded when he caught sight of Katherine.

She tried not to let it bother her, sliding from the back of her mare and keeping her chin level.

The McTavish laird was not the only one glaring at her. Rolfe reached up and tugged on his bonnet before he turned and gestured her forward.

I do nae accept cowards in me yard.

Marcus's words rose from her memory but she would have moved forward anyway, because there was no way she would be ashamed of who she was.

"Best we go inside, Father."

William McTavish frowned, clearly not caring for his son's words. His captains sent Katherine looks that made it clear they thought her the cause of trouble. What surprised them was the way Adwin came up beside her, taking a stance a half pace back and off to her right.

Laird McTavish stared for a long moment at Adwin and the retainers who had joined him. Those on the steps quieted, sensing the tension in the air.

"Aye," William replied. He turned and began to make his way back into the hall. His wooden leg made a pounding noise on the stone floor as he went.

He suddenly stopped and turned to look at Rolfe. "I should introduce ye to Anne Grahan." There was a movement off to the side as a woman stood up. "Yer bride."

The girl came forward and lowered herself. She didn't look up, not even when she straightened.

"It's time ye were wed, and I have taken care of the contracts while ye were away." He waved away Anne, who went happily.

"Father."

William was settling himself in his seat at the high table. "Ye may express yer gratitude."

"I am already wed," Rolfe spoke clearly. "To Katherine."

She expected outrage, but instead William McTavish

merely cast her a rather uninterested look before returning his attention to Rolfe. "I agreed to no such match."

"It is done," Rolfe insisted. The hall was so quiet that she heard the wind whistling in the open windows.

"I am yer laird." William's tone became harder. "And I say I have contracted ye to Anne Grahan."

"The vows were consummated and witnessed," Rolfe told his father. "By Duncan Lindsey."

William leaned forward, his pallor increasing. "I sent ye down to give this English chit to Morton."

"Katherine was me prize," Rolfe informed his father. "So mine to keep."

William shook his head. "Nae if yer laird disagrees." He shifted his attention to her. "Perhaps the rumors of ye being a witch are true. It seems ye have somehow turned me son against me."

There was more than one gasp. Katherine felt her insides knotting. Just the mention of the word *witch* drew her back to the moment when she had watched the stake being raised and readied for her.

But it was Anne's horrified face that Katherine ended up staring at. The girl was terrified of William now.

"Hate me for being English." Katherine spoke up.

"Oh, I assure ye I do," Laird McTavish answered her loudly. "And ye will no' speak to me unless spoken to."

It would have been wiser to keep her mouth shut, but the look on Anne's face wouldn't let her. Katherine refused to be so fearful of life. If that meant she died as a witch for it, so be it.

"I find it very difficult to believe that a spineless woman gave you a son as fierce as Rolfe."

William opened his mouth the moment she started to speak, clearly intending to cut her off, but her words distracted him.

"Me wife was a strong woman. Strength begets strength," he declared, to the approval of his clan members.

"And yet," Katherine pointed at Anne, who was watching them with red-rimmed eyes as she wept in fear, "you have brought him a woman who cringes over another woman being insulted."

Attention turned toward Anne, who stiffened and held her breath.

"Get out of me sight, witch!" William insisted.

"She is me wife," Rolfe stated firmly.

"I want her out of me sight," William declared. "This is a discussion for men. All of ye, be gone!"

It was Ceit who came forward and grasped Katherine's wrist. The Head of House offered her a kindly warning look before she tugged on the wrist.

Leaving the room was the last thing Katherine wanted to do, but Rolfe stood there, firmly facing his father, and she knew it was the only way the matter could be resolved.

But do you want it resolved?

Katherine admitted that she was torn. Marcus had been her mentor for a long time, and she trusted him. His advice had always been sage, and it had filled her with hope the day before. That confidence was struggling to stand steady in the face of William McTavish's hate.

Strangely enough, Anne's stricken form was what restored Katherine's balance. Ceit made it clear that she was of the same mind the moment they made it into the kitchens.

"Thank Christ we'll no' be having that spineless creature as mistress," the Head of House said. The activity in the kitchens slowed in response. Ceit propped her hands on her ample hips and stared at her staff. "Aye, ye all heard me right. And I'll call ye lazy if any of ye try to convince me ye'd prefer that little simpering miss. The only reason would be because ye know ye can spend half yer day napping because she does nae have the spine to reprimand ye."

There was a round of laughter before work resumed. Ceit smiled at Katherine. "Welcome, mistress."

They heard William shouting in the hall and Rolfe answering him almost as loudly.

"A welcome that will be spoken of for years to come," Katherine replied, to the delight of the Head of House.

Ceit offered her a merry smile, while her eyes sparkled with mischief. "It will, at that."

There was comfort in Ceit's welcome. Katherine didn't want to admit just how desperately she needed a friendly face.

Or how much she feared William McTavish would have his way.

Hers would be far from the first marriage annulled in spite of a soiled sheet being flown. William would hardly spare any compassion for her loss of virtue over it. Marcus might raise an objection, but Marcus was not laird of the MacPhersons. Shamus MacPherson was a master at preserving peace at all costs.

She wouldn't expect Shamus to threaten to go to

war over her reputation being shredded. It would be considered her due for riding out and away from the protection of the clan.

No, the best she might hope for was a place with the MacPhersons. It was a fine place, too, one many would be content with.

Frustration claimed her at last as she recalled that Rolfe was displeased with her, too. It was likely he was seeing the error of his ways now, realizing she was simply more trouble than she was worth.

✦

"'Tis a fine way ye repay me," William growled. "Wedding an English girl—and no' just that, but she has nae a single piece of silver to her name."

"She is me choice, Father."

William snorted. "Yer choice? Well, I say change yer bloody mind. Ye've had her now, so set yer thinking to wedding for the right reasons."

"It is done."

"And I say it is nae." William slapped the tabletop. "No Englishwoman is ever going to be lady of this keep."

There was a round of agreement from some of the retainers.

William was nodding in agreement with them when there was a sound of flesh meeting flesh. A man went sprawling, and another one had risen to come to his friend's aid. William looked past his son to where Adwin was making it clear he'd take on more men if they dared speak up.

"What in the devil has gotten into ye, Adwin?"

The captain turned and tugged on his cap. "The lass did more than her share to make sure yer son came back from the dungeon Morton put him in." The captain turned to look at the other retainers. "So I will no' be hearing any cursing of her name."

William opened and closed his mouth a few times, clearly struggling to absorb what Adwin had said. He wasn't alone, either. All of the men who had ridden in with Rolfe stood there, lending themselves to the stand Adwin was taking.

William pointed at Adwin. "Ye will no' be telling me what to say."

"Since you are me laird"—Adwin reached up and tugged on his bonnet—"I will no'." He turned and glanced behind him. "But the rest of ye will know the lass has earned me respect."

Men who had risen to join the fight suddenly sat down, unsure of what was happening.

"I am dissolving this union," William stated.

"No, Father," Rolfe replied respectfully. "I owe ye many duties, but I have given me word, in the presence of God. If ye insist, I will leave with me wife."

William was silent for a long moment. "Clearly, ye need time to think the matter through. Properly. I will see ye at supper."

Rolfe tugged on the corner of his bonnet as his father stood and retired to his private study. Adwin came up beside him.

"That went rather as I expected it might," the captain muttered.

"Aye," Rolfe agreed, not caring for how easily his father had named Katherine a witch. For himself, he didn't care at all, but he'd be a fool to dismiss how many did take such things to heart.

"What are ye thinking, lad?" Adwin knew him well—too well—because the captain recognized the look in Rolfe's eyes.

"I'm thinking MacPherson land might be the only safe place for Katherine if me own father is going to go so far as to name her a witch."

"Anything else we can weather," Adwin responded.

"But no' witchery," Rolfe admitted.

And that tore him nearly in two, because he knew he'd do what he had to in order to protect her.

⌇

"Ye are going to lose this argument."

Niul waited for his brother to finish snorting before he came farther into the room. William's study was draped in tapestries, most of them having come with brides who quickly learned that their finery was now the property of the laird.

Just as they were.

"Rolfe is me son," William stated. "The only one who lived long enough to become a man."

"It is a fact that he is a man grown, which means ye can nae tell him who to wed," Niul continued.

William scoffed and took a long drink from his mug. "I am laird. The day has not yet arrived when I will no' be telling him what to do."

"Think on how well that worked when ye sent him to see Morton."

There was a long silence. If they had been in the open hall, William would have argued. It was a matter of saving face. Now, in the privacy of his study, he took a moment to stop his posturing and contemplated what Niul was saying.

"Rolfe will have her," Niul said. "Forbid him, and ye will lose yer son."

"Well, then," William said, "I will just have to make sure the wench is the one who leaves."

Niul wanted to argue but knew he'd only be encouraging William. The man made the word *stubborn* seem too weak for just how unbendable he was about having his way. Niul hoped Katherine was every bit the hellion she was fabled to be.

Because supper was going to be a true test of her mettle.

&

"Ye'll sit beside me," Laird McTavish told Katherine.

She cast Rolfe an uncertain look, but couldn't really decide on a valid argument against it. Not unless she simply wanted to be perverse. She might not be willing to bend to William's will, but dropping the subject… Well, that wasn't too much to do.

So she nodded, earning a pleased look from Rolfe.

Her husband.

She hadn't really thought about him in those terms before. The idea was a strange one, and it intoxicated her, making her slightly giddy. Ceit was happily making sure the head table was set with enough places. Anne had taken up a position between William and Niul.

To his credit, Niul didn't seem vexed by being moved down in position. He grinned and raised his glass toward Katherine as she sat down.

The bread was brought to the tables. William took a round as everyone bowed their heads. He spoke a prayer before ripping a portion off and handing it to Rolfe, and then next to Anne.

Katherine felt her appetite dying. His actions were a public declaration of her standing, or lack thereof, in the eyes of the McTavish laird. He dropped the bread onto the plate without offering any to her. Rolfe tore his and gave half to her, earning a narrowing of his father's eyes.

And so it begins…

She'd be a fool to think that all Rolfe had to do was tell his father they were wed and William McTavish would welcome her with open arms. No, there were going to be more objections from the man.

Supper began as maids carried in platters of food. Conversation started up, but it was hushed as everyone waited to see what might happen at the head table, while trying not to look as though they were anticipating the entertainment of another fight between the laird and his son.

"I have something to say," William declared as he hit the tabletop with his fist. Those sitting in the hall quieted, giving their laird their attention.

"Me son was right about Katherine Carew."

There was a ripple of surprise from those watching. Rolfe appeared taken unaware as he glanced back and forth between her and his father.

William looked at Rolfe with a smile on his lips. "She is yer prize and ye have the right, as any Highlander does, to keep what ye steal. I was wrong to try to claim her from ye."

A hush had fallen over the hall, one Katherine felt down to her toes. There was a look in William's eyes that promise Rolfe a reckoning.

"And I was wrong to call ye a witch." Laird McTavish looked straight at her. "I hope ye'll forgive me. Ye're English, true, but that is no' the same as being a cocksucker of Satan."

There was more than one gasp in response. Katherine had never been more grateful for her time in the training yard because it allowed her to not react to the blunt words. She'd heard such before and only offered William a mild expression.

"Now." William looked over at Anne, as he patted the girl's hand. "A prize is meant to be enjoyed, and I must admit, I would certainly enjoy fucking the fabled MacPherson hellion."

There was a round of coarse snickers from some of the men even as Ceit started to gesture some of her younger maids toward the doors.

"So keep her, me son, and enjoy her," William stated firmly. "Anne will be yer wife, and her dowry will fatten our coffers, while her father will pledge his friendship toward us. The hellion will be yer slut, to do all the things a wife has no business knowing men crave."

William slapped his hand down on the table. "Done. Mistress is a fine position for a hellion. No doubt the MacPhersons never made her a match because they couldn't find a man willing to risk bedding her. Ye should be grateful."

William ended his speech by looking straight at her. "And I am a bit jealous of me son. Perhaps when he tires of ye, I will let ye suckle me cock."

Katherine pushed her chair back. William flashed her a pleased look, but she denied him any outpouring of words. She looked at Rolfe and lowered herself, making it clear whom she deemed worthy of respect before she left the hall.

Conversation started immediately, voices debating their laird's correctness.

She didn't care a bit for their opinions.

Only for the fact that Rolfe had said nothing.

That hurt her deeper than anything ever had.

❧

Rolfe came into their chamber earlier than she expected.

Much earlier. Only an hour later, he was there.

Katherine eyed him uncertainly. Her husband offered her a grin before he pulled a hand around in front of him. He set a pitcher on the table between them.

"Is that meant as some sort of apology for sitting there silently?"

She really hadn't wanted to ask the question. Her pride seemed to think she should leave it all up to him to explain, and yet she couldn't seem to stop herself.

"It is," he answered. "I know I should have said something."

"Indeed." Her English accent was back again.

Rolfe held up a finger. "But I needed to see what he was getting at. Me father enjoys planning things. It's always best to let him bluster a bit before charging into the trap he's laid for ye. Besides, I was looking at Anne and wanted to see what she was going to make of it all."

Katherine ended up thinking about what he'd said for a long moment. Rolfe cracked a grin, which annoyed her, and she sent him a glare.

"She likely thought you found it all to your liking." She shook her head at how it must seem.

Rolfe merely shrugged.

"Well, in this case, me father miscalculated how strong ye are, lass."

"Is that a fact?"

Rolfe nodded. "As for Anne, she was begging Adwin for an escort home before me father finished his supper. Claimed she would not marry into a family with such an unchristian nature."

Relief touched her like a welcome breeze on a July afternoon. "I suppose talking about sucking Satan's cock might be considered unchristian."

"Coupled with me sitting there saying nothing against the idea of keeping ye both."

"That was unkind of you." Katherine twisted her knuckle against his breastbone in reprimand. He flinched, but didn't back up.

"Why do ye think I brought the pitcher with me?"

"It would serve you right if I did hit you with that." She meant every word, and yet her tone betrayed how touched she was by the offer. "And Helen hit Marcus in the great hall, so this is hardly an even exchange." She gestured around the chamber.

"Aye," he countered. "However, I am no' trying to force ye to wed one of me men."

"Only expecting me to stay where I am not wanted."

"Ye are wanted here, Kat." His tone went hard.

"By me. Ye are hardly the first bride to encounter a cantankerous father-in-law."

He'd moved toward her. She felt her belly flutter in response and let out a little sigh. "How can it be so very…perfect when you are near, and yet so horrible when you are not?"

"Ye are no' the only bride who faces such."

He came close enough that she felt his presence looming over her, sheltering her. His scent teased her senses as he stroked the side of her cheek. Pleasure rippled across her skin, raising a smile on her lips.

"Feuds have been settled for years in the Highlands by weddings," Rolfe explained.

"That does not make it easier."

He stroked her cheek again. "Nae." He slid his hand into her hair and cupped her nape. It made her very aware of his strength, of the fact that he could crush her throat if he cared to. The fact that he held her like an egg made her feel cherished.

So unexpectedly tender.

He leaned down and kissed her, and she stretched up onto her toes to press herself against him. Desire began to pulse through her. Inside the chamber, she could give it free rein. It took him longer to disrobe, since all she had on was her dressing robe.

"Ye are so beautiful…" His voice was full of awe. He stood back for a moment, sweeping his eyes over her from head to toe. Words paled next to the way his eyes narrowed and his lips thinned. It was the sort of compliment no words could truly express. It was there in his expression, and Katherine felt her insides tightening in response.

She liked the way he looked, too. All hard, with his member rising as need built between them. It was strange the way her senses became keener when he was near. Now, she could feel her heart accelerating and hear the way his breathing began to rasp between his teeth.

That was another compliment that might be savage, but it suited her well.

"Touch me," he said. "Come to me because ye want to be here."

She'd never heard him sound so needy before. It hit her in the heart as she struggled to accept that beneath his hardened exterior was a person with doubts, just like her.

"We are more alike than ye think, lass," he explained. "For all that I appreciate ye seeing me as a man who is capable, the truth is I wonder if I will ever please me father, me clan, or anyone else in this life. And I wonder why I can nae seem to do so."

She ended up smiling at him, moving toward him and feeling as if she was approaching the only safe haven in a storm. He cupped her shoulders, smoothing his hands down her arms. She reached down and handled his member, teasing it with soft strokes of her fingers. For a moment, they stood there, petting each other and fanning the flames of desire.

"We should make a habit of retiring early."

He grinned at her through gritted teeth. "Aye…" he groaned.

A sense of victory went through her, for drawing that tone from him. So many times, she had writhed beneath his touch; now she wanted to prove that she was every bit as much his match.

So she slid to her knees.

"Kat."

He didn't get another word out before she'd opened her mouth and licked the top of his member.

He jerked, but he'd caught a handful of her hair and kept her in place as she licked him again and again before opening her mouth to seal her lips around the head of his cock.

"Christ almighty…"

He was hissing as he strained and arched, pushing his member farther into her mouth. She took it, using her tongue to stroke it as he did when he lapped her slit. It seemed to reduce him to the same state of mindless pleasure, so she continued sucking, licking, and using her hands to stroke him. His breathing became rougher, his member hardening even more. She tasted the first drop of his seed and licked it away from the slit on the top of his cock.

"Nae…" He pulled her away, tightening his grip when she tried to resume. "Ye'll unman me."

"You do so to me often," she argued.

Rolfe bent down and scooped her off her knees. That quickly, control shifted between them once more. He cradled her, proving how much stronger he was, but the look in his eyes when he came down on top of her—she'd put that glitter there.

"But I'll no' leave ye unsatisfied, lass."

He sank into her body. She arched and purred with pleasure, reaching up to lock her hands on his shoulders. He pulled free and thrust into her with a slow, unhurried motion that left her eager for more friction.

"Nae, never unsatisfied…" he muttered in a tight voice.

She realized he was fighting back the urge to pound her hard, taking the time to build the urgency until she was bucking beneath him, every bit as eager for a hard ride as he was.

Pleasure shook them both, like trees in a summer thunderstorm. They had no choice except to dance under the power of the wind as they shuddered and collapsed in a breathless heap.

Rolfe rolled back toward her sometime later, after they had both cooled enough to touch. Now, he folded her against him as he lay behind her, his hand cupping her breast like it was a treasure.

"When you touch me, I forget why this cannot work."

He rose up and looked down at her. "Does that mean ye are nae going to swing that pitcher at me?"

She snorted and sent a jab at his lower belly. He curled up, faking fear.

"It would serve you right if I did."

Rolfe left the bed, stopping to put on his shirt before he went across the bedchamber and into the outer one. He looked back at her. "I want to show ye something."

There was a serious note in his voice. She left the bed, plucking her chemise from the floor as she went. He'd pulled something from a leather case hanging near one of the wardrobes. It was a rolled parchment that crinkled when he opened it. He kept it flat on the table by setting the pitcher on top of it.

Katherine read it through twice before she looked up at him. "My stepmother offered a dowry for me?"

"Marcus as well," Rolfe confirmed. "Ye are quite the heiress, lass, and interestingly enough, worth more in the Highlands than in England. Yer stepmother made it a condition of this dowry that I take ye north and keep ye here."

"But…" She walked a bit away from him, unable to stand still. "Why haven't you told your father? It would quiet him."

"I know." Rolfe answered her swiftly and in a tone that made it clear he had no liking for the fact. "Yet if I did so, ye would always doubt I wanted ye for my wife no matter what ye brought me."

She stood there stunned, feeling as though he had plunged a dagger straight through her heart. Tears trickled from the corners of her eyes, falling down her cheeks in hot drops.

"Oh Christ." He looked toward the ceiling but then back at her, jumping forward to wrap her in his arms. "That was meant to please ye. I swear it."

She wiggled against him, pushing until he released her with a frustrated snort.

"You did."

Rolfe stared at her, trying to decide if he believed her. "Ye are weeping."

"With joy."

He drew in a deep breath and let it out in that way men often did when they were completely confounded by a woman's logic.

Katherine smiled at him. "I didn't think there was any possible way for you to prove such a thing."

He nodded firmly. "I'll tear the parchment up if ye like, Katherine."

"No," she responded with a wicked grin. "I cannot wait to see your father's face when you present it to him."

Rolfe slowly curled his lips back, offering her a menacing grin that promised William McTavish hell.

"I love you."

His grin faded in response, his expression becoming serious. He moved toward her, folding her back into his embrace. "As I love ye, lass."

"I am still not going to become the model of a good wife."

He stroked the side of her cheek and locked gazes with her. "I suppose that all depends on what a man thinks a perfect wife should be. For meself, I fancy hellions."

∽

"And the Earl of Morton will retire from the office of regency."

Morton glared at the man reading the list of demands from the Earls of Gowrie and Angus. But they had the king. Part of him was relieved to know the young James was locked away from the newly arrived Lennox.

Lennox clearly intended to draw the king into a carnal relationship. Morton curled his lips in disgust at the idea. Men coupling with men—it turned his stomach.

He nodded. "Long live the King!"

Everyone seemed to expect more resistance from him. Morton gladly disappointed them. It was never wise to allow anyone to know too much about himself. He walked past the counselors who had answered to him for almost a decade, and didn't care for the way they only half lowered themselves now that it was clear he was leaving.

It wasn't until he was a day's ride from the city that he drew his horse up and realized something.

The damned castle stank.

He drew in a second breath and let it out slowly. When he reached his estate, he was going to lay out new gardens. Anything to get outside. He'd spent too much time indoors. Scotland would have to be content with his efforts.

Of course, not everyone viewed him as a champion of Scotland. No, many saw him as a monster. They sought vengeance, now that they believed him in a position they might strike at.

Morton grinned. Let them try. For he might not be regent any longer, but he was still a Douglas.

❧

Gordon land

Diocail pulled his horse up, raising his hand to let his retainers know he was stopping. Ahead of him was the Gordon stronghold. Half of it was dark stone, giving the place a sinister look. His horse seemed to sense it, dancing from side to side. Diocail reached down and patted the stallion's neck soothingly.

"Wondering if they are going to welcome ye back?"

Diocail flashed a grin at his captain. Muir was a few years older than he was and had a calm demeanor that Diocail liked. The man also had a keen wit that was helpful.

The wind had whipped up, promising cooler days as summer neared its end. The breeze also carried the sound of a bell ringing. It was joined by another and then more.

"It seems they are ringing a fine welcome for ye, Laird."

Diocail closed his eyes, drawing in a deep breath as he let the sound seep into his soul.

"Let's go home, lads!"

And he had every intention of making it a home. One that had everything he had never known but heard good men craved.

Home, hearth, and family.

He'd spent most of his life living for the moment when such treasures might be his. Today, he would begin building those dreams and forging them into reality. It would not be easy, especially not for a man who had only heard of a loving family. His mother had taught him of love, but she'd died a long time ago, leaving it a distant memory.

He was going to brighten that recollection and polish it, so he'd know the woman who would help him create a family when he met her. A good woman, strong like Katherine, willing to look at him with love in her eyes.

He'd find her.

Somewhere.

⤜⤛

"I made this tart for you, dearest Father."

Katherine made sure her accent was very English as she delivered the misshapen pastry to Laird McTavish.

William snorted before pushing it onto the floor. His hounds jumped up and immediately began to lap up the mess.

"Oh dear," Katherine exclaimed. "Are your hands trembling? Age is such a burden. Shall I fetch you a tonic?"

"I do nae need it. Me hands are as steady as a young lad's," William exclaimed. "I can assure ye, me daughter Joan did nae go to her betrothed with the lack of skill that ye have."

"Yes, I am English, after all."

Katherine shot him a pleased smile before she left the great hall. Adwin was nearly purple with holding in his mirth. Most of the retainers had taken to making sure they were in the hall when supper was served, because Katherine would never fail to try to please her father by marriage.

"Ye're devious, woman." Niul spoke from where he'd been watching her from the doorway of the kitchen. "If me brother comes over that table and locks his hands around yer neck..."

"We will make quite the spectacle sprawled upon the floor," Katherine finished.

Niul raised his mug to her. "I thought ye could nae run a house."

Katherine shrugged. "I am learning."

"Did ye make that tart?"

She winked at him. "I did. So I shall apologize to the hounds later."

He grinned at her, but his attention lowered to her belly. She wasn't very far along, but the news that she'd conceived spread fast. Even William had looked pleased by the announcement that she was breeding.

If a toad could appear in any way pleasant, that was.

"Why have you never wed?"

It really wasn't her concern, and yet she'd decided that she liked Niul. At that moment, he offered her the most serious expression she had ever seen on his face, and it dawned on her that his smile was a shield.

"Ye may have noticed how me brother feels about being in control," Niul said. "I am bastard born, and William plans to keep the legitimate line of this family for himself."

She heard the lament in his voice and found herself drawn to him. "His grip has been loosened."

Niul contemplated her for a long moment.

"I do believe my husband would welcome the news of your wedding."

"Ye've convinced a woman to take ye to husband?" Rolfe asked as he came through the doorway behind her.

Niul stiffened. Rolfe didn't miss it. For a long moment, they looked at each other.

"I would toast to yer happiness, Uncle."

It took a moment before Niul's lips parted in a grin. "And I will gladly pledge me sword to ye and yer father for all of me days."

There were smiles all around the kitchen, even as the staff tried to appear as though they were not listening. Rolfe caught Katherine around her waist, settling his hands over her belly.

"There is nothing to feel yet," she advised him softly. Her husband was obsessed with her condition, petting her belly and speaking to their unborn babe every night before he slept.

"I disagree, Kat," her husband whispered against her ear. "I feel the love ye bring to this hall."

"Your father seems to be moved by it."

Rolfe snorted against her ear. "Aye. Do I want to know why his hounds are vomiting in front of the hearth?"

"I am improving," she offered. "Last month they wouldn't eat it at all. The maid had to scoop it up."

"I see." Her husband was choking on his amusement. "Planning to wear him down?"

"Precisely."

Rolfe laughed out loud before kissing the side of her neck and releasing her. He winked before disappearing around the doorframe, his kilt pleats swaying as he went. The breeze was brisk now, fall fully upon them. All around her, the last of the harvest was waiting to be sorted and stored for winter. The kitchen was full of activity, and even with her limited skills, there was plenty of work for her to do. Ceit seemed to possess a great deal of patience when it came to tutoring her.

Katherine went to pluck an apron off a hook and tie it around her waist to return to work.

She thought she felt something flutter inside her. It was soft and yet persistent. She stood for a long moment, trying to make sense of it, and then it came again.

Tap-tap-tap.

Soft and yet undeniably there. Like a little jab on the inside of her womb.

"Are ye feeling the babe?" Ceit asked excitedly.

The Head of House wiped her hands on her apron and hurried over to lay her hand against Katherine's belly.

"I think…perhaps I did." And her voice was filled with the wonder of it. She'd known she was with child, had known the moment she began being sick every morning within moments of opening her eyes. Yet now, it was suddenly so much more real as she felt the little poking motion once again, laughing with joy.

"If ye feel it already, it's a strong babe for certain," Ceit exclaimed with her eyes sparkling. "Like his mother."

Katherine realized that at last, her need for strength had somehow merged with her gender. It was true she could not turn a loaf of bread very well or seem to get the proportions correct on a tart, but as the months passed, she swelled round and large, and when her labor came, pushing her babe into the world was just another challenge she was ready to face. Fear was not something she allowed to spoil the experience.

Her son came into the world howling, his body pink and all of his limbs waving in fury at being forced from her womb. Katherine laughed through the pain, happily cradling her son as he gulped air for the first time. The pain was more a welcome for her child than a misery to be endured. Every contraction brought her closer to meeting her child, so she smiled when they began and gritted her teeth as they intensified. She sweated and groaned when at last she felt the baby leaving her womb, bearing down as the midwife ordered her to.

And then, there was only the excitement of meeting her son. They wiped him clean, soothing him as he opened his eyes and looked for her. There was a small army of women in the chamber who swaddled the baby and cleaned away the evidence of birth, wiping her down with damp cloths before they gave her a clean smock to wear.

She was sitting on the edge of their bed when Rolfe was let into the chamber at last.

He rushed toward her, his face lit with excitement. William was right on his heels. The old goat even appeared to be grinning.

"No' a single scream," her father-in-law commended her. "Ye are fearless, lass, and as strong as a Valkyrie."

"What do ye expect from a hellion?" Rolfe asked his father in a hushed tone. He was cradling his son, looking awkward as he tried to make certain he wasn't hurting the infant. Ceit corrected his arms, a happy smile on her lips.

"A grandson," William answered. "And so ye have delivered one to the McTavish."

Happiness shimmered in his eyes. Rolfe allowed him to hold the baby.

It seemed she'd found her place after all, for it certainly took a hellion to bring together the McTavish laird and his son.

KEEP READING FOR A LOOK AT THE NEXT BOOK
IN THE HIGHLAND WEDDINGS SERIES

HIGHLAND FLAME

Gordon land

THEY WERE WAITING FOR HIM TO BLESS THE MEAL.

He was laird, and it was his place to begin the evening supper with a prayer. Somehow, in all the times his mother had spoken of that moment with longing in her eyes, she had never mentioned to him just how much it would remind him of facing down his enemies.

More than one man was giving him a glare that made it plain they felt they were as entitled to the position at the high table as Diocail was.

Diocail Gordon eyed the bread his staff delivered and hesitated. It was misshapen, and when he did grasp it, his fingers sank in because it was wet, the top part of it soaked with water as though it had been sitting out in the rain. He cleared his throat and said the prayer before ripping the bread to indicate everyone might eat.

The hall was only half full, which surprised him. The laird provided supper for his retainers, yet it appeared a good number of them were choosing to find their meals elsewhere. The clumps of wet bread glued to his fingertips might be one reason—if a man had a wife to turn him better bread—but that didn't account for the number of retainers missing.

Diocail sat down and watched, seeking out more clues. Maids were entering the hall now, and they carried several large trays toward his table. While the bread might have been lacking, these platters were full of roasted meats that looked very good to his eyes. It was a bounty to be sure, and his predecessor's captains began to help themselves.

Along the table that sat on the high ground were men who had served Colum, the last laird of the Gordons. Diocail had given them all a chance to challenge him, and none had. Instead, they maintained their high positions. At the moment, that entitled them to a good supper, served to them in front of the rest of the clan to make their position clear. There wasn't an empty chair, and each man had a gilly behind him to take care of his needs. Some of the older captains had two young men standing at the ready, which made Diocail narrow his eyes. When a man was young, he often became a gilly to learn focus, but there was a gleam in these young men's eyes that didn't make sense.

Diocail didn't suffer in ignorance for long.

Supper began to make its way into the hall, but it was far from sufficient. Men fought over what was brought, elbowing each other as they grabbed it from maids, who tossed their trays down because of the fray, afraid to get too close to the tables. There were

clear pockets of friends who clustered together to
defend whatever they had managed to grab from the
frightened kitchen staff. Any man who tried to break
into their ranks was tossed aside like a runt.

Diocail never started eating. He watched the
squabbling and then realized exactly why his men
were fighting when no more food came from the
kitchens. Whatever a man had managed to grab was
all there was, and the lucky ones devoured their fare
quickly before someone else managed to rip it from
their grasp.

"Colum was a miser," Muir told him. Diocail's
newly appointed captain was making a face as he tried
to chew the bread. "Dismissed the Head of House in
favor of one who would be willing to serve less food
without complaint. There is nary a rabbit within a
mile of this keep because so many take to hunting to
fill their bellies."

Muir was disgusted too, looking at the piece of meat
in his hands as though the taste had gone sour. Diocail
realized it was because a young boy was looking at it
as well, his young eyes glistening with hunger. Muir
lifted the food toward the boy, and the lad scampered
up the three steps to the high ground to snatch it.

"Even though I am no' in the habit of questioning
the Lord's will," Muir growled out between them, "I
confess, I wonder why that man was graced with such
a long life when he sat at this table feasting away while
his own men starved."

"It makes me see why no one else was willing to
defend him," Diocail answered. "Seems it was justice
that saw him stabbed in his own bedchamber."

"A justice ye did yer best to shield him from." Muir sent him a hard look.

"He was me laird," Diocail answered. "A man I had sworn to protect. His lack of character did no' release me from the bonds of honor. Yet I confess, I am grateful I lost that battle, and I am no' sorry to say so. The bastard needed to die for what he's allowed the Gordons to become."

"Aye," Muir agreed, looking out at the hall once more. There was now a cluster of children in front of them, all of them silently begging for scraps. All of them were thin, telling him that they weren't just intent on being gluttons.

No, they were starving.

And that was a shame.

A shame on the Gordon name and Diocail's duty to rectify. He waved them forward. They came in a stumbling stampede, muttering words of gratitude as they reached for the platter sitting in front of him and Muir.

The platter was picked clean in moments.

Diocail stood up. The hall quieted as his men turned to listen to him. "I will address the shortage of food."

A cheer went up as Diocail made his way down the steps from the high ground and into the kitchen. Muir fell into step beside him. The kitchen was down a passageway and built alongside the hall. Inside, the kitchen was a smoke-filled hell that made Diocail's eyes smart and the back of his throat itch. He fought the urge to cough and hack. It was hardly the way to begin a conversation with his staff.

"The weather is fine and warm," he declared. "Open the shutters."

Instead of acting, all the women working at the long tables stood frozen, staring at him. Their faces were covered in soot from the conditions of the kitchen. Many of them had fabric wrapped around their heads, covering every last hair in an effort to keep the smoke from it. Muir opened a set of doors, allowing a cloud of smoke to roll out. Diocail looked at the hearths and realized the smoke wasn't rising up the chimneys. No, it was pouring into the kitchen, and the closed shutters kept it there.

The staff suddenly scurried into a line to face him. They lined up shoulder to shoulder, looking at the ground, their hands worrying the folds of their stained skirts.

"Where is the Head of House?" he asked softly. It was God's truth that he'd rather face twenty men alone than the line of quivering females who clearly thought he was there to chastise them.

Colum had truly been a bastard of a laird. He'd made his people suffer when the true duty of the laird was to serve the clan.

One of the women lifted her hand and pointed. Diocail peered through the clearing gloom and spotted the Head of House. She was seventy years old if she was a day. Whoever she was, she was deep in her cups and sitting in a chair on the far side of the kitchen as she sang and swayed.

"Sweet Christ, little wonder the supper is a poor one," Muir remarked next to Diocail's ear.

"Who is her second in charge?"

The women continued to look at the floor. Two of them were beginning to whimper. Muir took a step back, but Diocail reached out and grabbed the man's kilt. "Do nae ye dare leave me here alone," he muttered under his breath.

"Someone must be making decisions," Diocail said as gently as he could in an effort to coax one of the women forward. What did he know of speaking to frightened females? Two more started crying, proving his knowledge was extremely lacking. Their tears left smears down their cheeks.

"Mercy, Laird," a younger woman wailed. "I need me position. I swear, I will serve less, *please* do nae dismiss me."

The entire group suddenly dissolved into desperate pleading. They came toward him, backing him and Muir up against the wall as they begged him not to send them away.

Diocail had never been so terrified in his life.

"No one is being dismissed." Diocail raised his voice above the wailing.

It quieted them for the most part, which allowed him to see that a good number of his retainers had made their way into the kitchen after him. Those men were now glaring at him, making it plain that these were their wives or women and they didn't take kindly to him upsetting them.

Diocail looked at the woman who had spoken. "Mistress?"

"Eachna." She lowered herself but looked up at him, proving she had a solid spine, and while there was a worried glitter in her eyes, there was also a flash of temper that made it clear she thought his visit was long overdue.

Christ, he'd only been back at the castle for two days.

But he'd known that taking the lairdship meant his shoulders were going to feel the weight of the burden that went along with the position. He intended to rise to meet it.

He gestured for her to rise, and the rest of the women suddenly lowered themselves.

"Enough of that." Diocail felt Muir hit him in the middle of his back because his voice had gained a frustrated edge. Diocail drew in a deep breath and regretted it as his lungs burned.

"I am here to resolve the issue of supper, no' have ye all quivering. So…" He resisted the urge to run his hand down his face in exasperation. "If ye might explain the lack of food? There was no' enough served, and I would see the men satisfied."

He looked to Eachna, and her companions seemed quite willing to allow her to be the target of his inquiry. They shifted away from her, proving Colum had dealt harshly with his staff.

Not that such was a surprise. The old laird had been a bitter man who'd died with hatred in his eyes while his blood drained out of his body from stab wounds inflicted by a man hungry to take the lairdship.

About the Author

Mary Wine is a multi-published author in romantic suspense, fantasy, and Western romance. Her interest in historical reenactment and costuming also inspired her to turn her pen to historical romance with her popular Highlander series. She lives with her husband and sons in Southern California, where the whole family enjoys participating in historical reenactments.